COLD-BREWED MURDER

Coffee Cup Mysteries: Book 2

Neila Young

Cold-Brewed Murder
Coffee Cup Mysteries™
Red Adept Publishing, LLC
104 Bugenfield Court
Garner, NC 27529
http://RedAdeptPublishing.com/

This is a work of fiction. Names, characters, places, and incidents either are the product of the author's imagination or are used fictitiously, and any resemblance to locales, events, business establishments, or actual persons—living or dead—is entirely coincidental.

For my children, Eli and Georgia, who inspire me every day.
I love you more than you will ever know.

Chapter One

Excitement filled Blake Harper as she spun in a slow circle on the rooftop patio of Mystery Cup Café. October was her favorite time of year. The fall breeze carried the crisp scent of autumn, and the reddish leaves of the Bradford pear tree across the street almost sparkled in the twilight.

Her smile faded as she spotted the red sticker on the large coffee carafe in the center of the orange-and-black-decorated table. "Decaf? Why, in the name of all that is holy, are we serving decaf?" She crinkled her nose as she adjusted the fluffy white scarf wrapped around her neck. Her café was going to be the happening place that night in Wilton, Missouri, but if people saw a pot of decaf, they might run in the opposite direction.

Blake's sister-in-law, Rachel, tossed her a smirk as she centered the heavy chrome carafe in between a crepe-paper ghost and a bedazzled jack-o'-lantern. Her big brown eyes rolled heavenward. "*Dios mio,* some of us don't want to be up all night."

Blake arched a brow. "We live in a haunted town, it's two weeks before Halloween, and you have six-year-old twins who are scared of Scooby-Doo. I would hazard a guess that you're not getting much sleep as it is." Warmth filled her as she thought of her niece and nephew. Her brother's two children had captured her heart from the moment they were born. She couldn't wait to take Aiden and Emma trick-or-treating.

Rachel straightened, stretching her back and covering a yawn. "Tell me about it. The problem is, Aiden thinks he can handle anything. I found him in front of the TV at two o'clock this morning, watching *Monster House*. I swear, that boy will be the end of me." Even as she said it, her mouth turned up into a smile.

Rachel had more get-up-and-go than the Energizer Bunny, and Blake couldn't think of anyone else with the vitality to handle the spirited duo that was Aiden and Emma. She also couldn't think of any other woman who was such a perfect match for her big brother. Rachel's boisterous spontaneity complemented Ryan's quiet charm and seriousness. She made his life more fun, and he grounded her in a way no one else could.

Blake's coffee-bean bracelet jingled as she adjusted the jeweled crown atop her wavy dark-blond hair. "Well, tonight, the kids are at your mom's, and Ryan is off work. You *should* be up all night. It's a partay!" She grinned and gave her hips a little swing against Rachel's. "Hey, thanks again for picking up this glorious addition to my costume after you dropped the kids off."

She fiddled with the bobby pins holding her crown in place. It had taken her until that afternoon to decide what she was going to be for Halloween. Unfortunately, when she'd finally decided, the pop-up Halloween store in the strip mall on Jefferson had been fresh out of crowns. Since Rachel had made the hour drive to Kansas City to drop off the twins at her mom's, she was able to swing by a Halloween store and grab a crown for Blake before she made the drive back.

A twinkle lit Rachel's big brown eyes, and she winked. "You're lucky I'm in a good mood. Tonight is the perfect opportunity to jump my husband's bones."

As much as Blake loved her brother and sister-in-law, the thought of them doing the horizontal baby dance sent her gag reflex into high gear. "*Huk*... Rach! Not. A. Visual. I. Need! *Huk*."

Her sister-in-law smacked Blake's arm with the back of her hand, not bothering to stifle a laugh. "Ten years of marriage. One of these days, I'll be able to talk about my hot mambo time with your brother, and you won't—"

"Stop!" Blake's hand went up as if she could physically push the words back at Rachel. Oh lord, the queasiness was starting again. "You've made my stomach churn enough with the decaf. Don't start in with talk of... wait a second. Hot mambo? *Huk... huk...*"

"I hear the gagging. Rachel must be talking about jumping your brother again." Giselle stepped onto the roof, carrying a big basket of pastries. "Thanks for stringing lights on the stairs. It drives me nuts that it's not even six o'clock, and it's dark already."

Blake was pretty impressed that the girl could carry a full load of goodies up the wooden staircase on the side of the building without breaking a sweat. She would be gasping for air if she made the trip with her arms loaded. Giselle deserved a raise, no doubt. Blake had hired her as a barista, but in the past few months, the young woman had helped with baking, management duties, scheduling, and event planning. She'd impressively performed the numerous roles seamlessly, and Blake didn't know what she'd do without her.

Giselle blew a wisp of blue hair out of her face as she set the basket down on the main serving table next to the coffeepots. When she looked up, her gaze darted around the patio. "Wow, the rooftop has really shaped up to be the perfect spot for this year's Halloween bash." A crooked grin lit her angular face as she clapped her hands.

The place did look pretty darned awesome, and it hadn't even taken that much work. Blake marveled at the patio's transformation. Strands of purple lighting were draped around the perimeter, lending an eerie glow to the tables that dotted the space. Ghost and pumpkin centerpieces topped each table, and spiderweb confetti and spider rings were strewn across each one. Strategically placed bowls of Chex mix, popcorn, and pretzels completed it. They just needed to put a plate of pastries on each table, and everything except for the caramel-pumpkin lattes would be ready.

Giselle removed a loaf of chocolate-chip-pumpkin bread from the basket along with a serrated knife. "I can't believe how much business has increased with all this extra seating."

"Right?" Rachel stood next to Blake and crossed her arms over chest as she surveyed the rooftop. "I wasn't sure how it was going to go once the city refurbished all these old buildings downtown, but it really worked out great for you. An outdoor patio on the roof of Mystery Cup? You can't beat that."

A smile tugged at the corner of Blake's lips. When she'd first opened Mystery Cup, she had never imagined it would be one of Wilton, Missouri's downtown anchors. Tourists streamed in from all over for her coffee and pastries, especially each month's Mystery Cup creation. Since it was October in their haunted little Midwestern town, that month's secret ingredient had been an easy one to pick.

"Mmmm." Rachel stepped over to grab a slice of pumpkin bread then ripped off a corner and popped it in her mouth. "Pumpkin, pumpkin, and more pumpkin. Best Mystery Cup ingredient ever," she said with a mouthful of the sweet bread.

Blake couldn't agree more. Pumpkin-spice lattes, pumpkin-caramel lattes, pumpkin scones, pumpkin bread, pumpkin seeds. She couldn't get enough. She picked up a loaf of the bread and reached in the basket for another knife. "We can slice them and put them out on the tables so people will have something sweet to munch on." Blake pointed to the corner of the stone patio. "The big table with a Crock-Pot of caramel-pumpkin lattes can go over there. That way, we can just ladle it up rather than making each one individually."

"I am not lugging the big Crock-Pot up these stairs." Giselle shook her blue hair back and forth. "Seriously, can't we discuss putting in an elevator?"

"If I could get the city to approve that idea, I would be all over it. And I don't think the Crock-Pot is *that* heavy."

Giselle's eyebrow quirked up as she perched one hand on her slender hip. "We're expecting about a hundred and fifty people, and I swear you made enough drinks and food for twice that many." She jetted a finger in the air, looking as though an idea had just popped into her head. "Never mind. I'll have Eli bring it up. That'll get him out of my hair for a few minutes."

Eli had defected from Café Muerte a few months ago, not that Blake blamed the kid. She couldn't have worked for Sabrina Lang, no matter how much the pay was. After Blake had hired him, she'd been pleasantly surprised to learn that although he was a little scatterbrained, he was quite a latte artist. Word of his latte-foam art was really spreading around town, and Mystery Cup was getting new repeat customers because of it.

Blake poked through the basket, looking at the different pastries. "Oh, give the kid a break. He's a hard worker."

Giselle narrowed her eyes. "Well, I don't care if he can draw a monkey in the latte foam. If he calls me Janelle one more time, I'm going smack that mop top right off his head."

Rachel let out a belly laugh. "You know, I'm pretty sure he does that because he knows it gets a rise out of you." She wiggled her eyebrows. "Maybe he has a crush on you."

"Oh gawd." Giselle clapped a hand to her chest. "He's, like, seventeen. Ew."

The corners of Blake's lips twitched. "He's nineteen, and you're twenty-two. It's not that much of an age difference. But don't worry. We're all well aware that you're too busy ogling Orlando Merryfield."

Giselle's eyes widened in mock innocence. "I don't know what you're talking about." The pink in her cheeks gave her away.

Blake tried to suppress her laugh. "Uh-huh. I know you're not running up and down to the rooftop a few times a day just to check on coffee refills."

Giselle's face grew redder. "What? A rooftop patio has its advantages. I've actually taken off a few pounds over the last couple of months of running up and down the stairs. I mean, the chamber of commerce pretty much gave us free rein up here. I don't know what me coming up and refilling coffeepots has to do with Orlando."

Orlando Merryfield, the new owner of Buttkick Training and Fitness, had all the women in town drooling. Rumor around Wilton was that he used to be a model for Calvin Klein.

Rachel pointed in the direction of Buttkick. "Come on. The man is super hot."

When Blake and Giselle both raised their eyebrows, Rachel looked innocently from one of them to the other. "What? I didn't say he was my type. I may be married, but I can still appreciate all those muscles."

Blake smiled and shook her head. He was hot, but he didn't make her stomach flutter like Sean or Adam did when they walked into a room. Her heart and her brain were so busy trying to decide which of those two she was more romantically interested in that no other man was really on her radar. Giselle, on the other hand, did a poor job of concealing her interest in Orlando. Blake wasn't quite sure why the girl bothered hiding it. Well, on second thought, they did tend to tease her like a little sister.

Giselle started listing the reasons they were way off base with their theories about her and Orlando. "Too old for me. Flirts with what's-her-freak that works for Sean." A finger popped up as she listed off each reason. "He's a vegetarian, and I love my pulled-pork burritos."

As Giselle prattled on, Blake reached for a container of espresso brownies in the basket. When she did, her hand bumped something hard and plastic. She pulled out a small pair of binoculars and sighed, her eyes darting to her assistant. "Ahem."

The younger woman held up her hands in mock innocence. "What?"

Blake held the binoculars up. "What do you mean, 'what'? Buttkick is a block and a half down the street. You think I don't know who you're spying on with these?"

"Ooh, can you really see into Buttkick from here?" Rachel snatched the binoculars out of Blake's hand and pressed them to her eyes. After she moved them around and adjusted the focus, she gasped. "Oh, hot damn, you sure can. Wow, he works out shirtless!"

Giselle reached for the binoculars, but Blake grabbed them first. "You guys! You can't spy on the neighbors. That has to be illegal. It's, like, an invasion of privacy or something."

"Oh, please." Giselle propped her hands on her thin hips. "Rachel's married to a hot doctor, and you have two gorgeous men chasing you down. It's not going to hurt anyone if I watch Orlando Merryfield doing pull-ups in his new loft." Her eyes shifted to Rachel. "Is he doing the pull-ups yet?"

Blake pressed her fingertips to her eyelids in exasperation as Rachel nodded vigorously.

"What ever happened to Micah?" Blake put the binoculars back in the basket and pulled out a serrated knife to cut pumpkin bread. "I thought your googly eyes were still all over that boy." She didn't miss the way Giselle's whole body seemed to sag when she asked about Micah, and she immediately regretted bringing him up.

Rachel and Blake exchanged glances as Giselle continued to lay out pastries. For a moment, Blake didn't think the younger woman was going to respond, but finally, Giselle looked up.

"It was just a crush. I don't think he ever really returned my feelings. Besides, he just hasn't been the same since his sister went to jail. It's like he's drawn into himself. So different than the fun-loving guy he was before."

A stab of pain went through Blake's chest at the mention of Micah's twin sister, Molly. "Smuggling cocaine in bags of coffee is never something I thought I would see around here."

Blake shivered at the memory. She'd barely escaped with her life. She heavily owed her thanks to her younger sister, Detective Kyle Harper. If Kyle hadn't shown up when she had... "I don't want to think about Molly right now. Once I get sucked into thinking about everything that happened last spring, I start into a downward spiral. I just want to move on."

"Good plan." Rachel bounced up and down on the balls of her feet, sending her wavy black ponytail bobbing. "Let's talk about something more fun—which of your hot men is coming to the party tonight? Sean or Adam?"

"Come on, Rach." Giselle moved her hand up and down, gesturing at Blake's outfit. "Look at her costume. It's easy to figure out which man she's dressed for."

A deep V formed in Rachel's brow as she took in Blake's gold crown, coffee-colored dress, coffee-bean jewelry, and fluffy white scarf that mimicked whipped cream. After a moment, Rachel grinned broadly. "Omigod. I can't believe I didn't figure it out before. You're a coffee goddess."

Blake smiled, thinking of Sean Larsen's nickname for her. "*A coffee goddess? No, no, no. I'm *the* coffee goddess." She would never forget the way his green eyes had sparkled when he walked into Mystery Cup for the first time a few months ago. "*I'll just call you Coffee Goddess.*" And she had swooned. Big time. She just hoped her costume caught Sean's interest. Low-cut wasn't her thing, but the dress hit just above the knee, which made it shorter than pretty much anything else she owned. She would still classify it as modest, but it was snug enough to show off her curves.

A giggle caught Blake's attention, and she looked up to see Rachel grinning at her. "From the look on your face, I'd say you're thinking about Mr. Book Hottie right now."

Giselle brushed her hands on her apron. "What's the scoop on him, anyway? Any smoochies? Any jumping of his bones? Maybe you can make Rachel gag for a change."

Blake's smile faded as she thought about her date with Sean last week. At least she thought it had been a date. After he'd closed up Macabre Reads next door, they'd gone and played pinball at the new retro arcade out on Highway 71. The camaraderie between them was easygoing, and they'd laughed and talked as he'd driven her home. Everything had been peachy until he'd walked her to the door. "Let's just say I'm pretty certain I've been friend-zoned where Sean's concerned."

"Friend-zoned?" Giselle shook her head. "You're crazy. I've seen the way that boy looks at you. Trust me, none of my *friends* look at me like that."

Blake scrunched her face. "Yeah, well, when he brought me home the other night, I thought he was finally going to kiss me. I mean, he was standing so close, and he was staring right at my lips. And then you know what he did?" She crossed her arms and let out a long sigh, internally cringing at the memory. "He gave me a light punch in the arm." She mimicked the motion then recrossed her arms. "You know, like 'way to go, slugger.'"

Giselle's jaw dropped. "No way. You totally should have jumped his bones."

She shook her head. "I think I was in so much shock, I couldn't move. I seriously stood there with my mouth hanging open for a good five minutes after he left."

Rachel started giggling, totally oblivious to Blake's plight, so Blake scowled in her direction. "What's so dang funny?"

"Sorry." Her sister-in-law dabbed pretend tears of amusement from the corner of her dark eyes. "I'm just happy because now you can focus on Adam."

Giselle narrowed her eyes at Rachel. "Oh please, Adam's a Boy Scout. She needs Sean."

Rachel frowned at Giselle as she reached up to tighten her ponytail. "She does not need tall, dark, and brooding. Adam is a nice guy. And he's hot. Come on, blond hair, blue eyes. How can she not love that?"

"Omigod, would you two please stop talking about me and my love life like I'm not standing right here?" Blake jabbed a finger in Rachel's direction. "And Adam's no better. He's given me a couple of light pecks, like I'm his sister or something. I'm beginning to think there's no passion going on from him, either. Besides, he's been so busy at the hospital, I've barely seen him in weeks."

But her friends' descriptions of the two men really rang true. Sean was the literal definition of tall, dark, and handsome, complete with those mouthwatering tattoos that curled up his arms. Adam, on the other hand, was a golden boy. He actually looked like a Nordic god with that light-blond hair and eyes the color of a summer sky. The men were very different, but they were equally as tempting, which did not make her decision any easier.

A *boing* sounded from Rachel's phone, and she tugged it out of the front pocket of her apron. "Oh crap. I didn't realize it was so late. Ryan's at home, getting ready. I gotta go." She looked up at Blake. "I'll be back in an hour and a half in my full-on Pink Lady costume." She wiggled her eyebrows. "And with my very own T-Bird." Any costume would look good on Rachel. She had curves that didn't quit, no matter how much pumpkin bread she indulged in.

Blake grinned as she began taking more pastries out of the basket. "Don't get too crazy just because the twins are at your mom's for the night." She could see Ryan and Rachel getting so wrapped up in each other that they forgot about the party.

"Oh, it's going to be crazy, all right. *Noche romantica.*" Even though Rachel didn't have the strong Mexican accent that her mom did, she could roll her r's with the best of them.

"Out!" Blake made a shooing motion. "Before I start gagging again."

With a finger wave and a laugh, Rachel headed to the stairs.

Giselle pushed her hair out of her eyes. "Hey, I'd better go turn the caramel-pumpkin-latte crock to simmer, then I have to change."

"Go. It takes a while to transform into a steampunk vampire. I'll finish getting things set up here."

Giselle hustled down the stairs, and Blake found herself humming "Monster Mash" as she continued to lay out trays of cookies, pumpkin bread, and scones on the tables. She tried to get her mind off of the men in her life. But she kind of hoped something might happen at the party. Sean would be there early, and Adam would be there after his shift in the ER. It was her shot to make a move with at least one of them. She just had to gather her nerve and decide which one she actually wanted to make a move with.

As she reached into the basket, her hand knocked against Giselle's binoculars. She gave a wry grin and pulled them out. "Or maybe I could just do what Giselle does and ogle Orlando Merry-field." She walked to the edge of the roof, where she leaned her elbows on the stone ledge. The binoculars had a dial on the top, and Blake turned it to adjust the focus.

The lights of the downtown lofts dotted the landscape, and a few neon signs from some of the businesses shined their beacons in the dark night. She aimed the binoculars at Buttkick. "I suppose it doesn't hurt to look, right?" she mumbled.

Of course, all she saw was the side of a brick building. Peering over the binoculars, she realized that was because she was aiming them at Sliced Bakery and Café, which was catty-corner from Mystery Cup. She panned the binoculars up a bit until she saw through the window of the loft above Sliced. She was surprised to see the lights on, as she didn't think the place had been rented out yet. Her curiosity would give her a good reason to talk to Micah. Even though he owned Sliced, he didn't have anything to do with the loft, but still, he might know who was moving in. Poor guy had been keeping to himself the last few months and only just seemed to be acting a little more like his old self. Blake would take any excuse she could to bring him out of his shell.

As her thoughts drifted, she lazily moved the binoculars, looking around the sparsely furnished apartment, which included a red futon, a big wooden desk, and a small industrial-looking kitchen with a little dinette. A bouquet of fresh daisies wrapped in green paper lay in the center of the table. And they made Blake frown.

Why would there be fresh flowers in an apartment that doesn't look lived in? She twisted the ends of the binoculars, sharpening the focus, and her eyes widened as she saw an ornate arrow lying next to the flowers. "What the crap?" That was a weird-looking arrow. She bent forward and adjusted the focus of the binoculars. Wait a second. It wasn't an arrow. It was a dagger of some sort. But it was a weird-looking dagger. The pointy end looked like it almost had a 3-D blade that looked like an arrow. And the handle seemed odd too. From what she could tell, it had intricate carvings that she couldn't quite make out, but the turquoise and ruby jewels in it really got her attention.

"Well, that doesn't look like the best choice of knife to cut flowers." She found herself leaning over the edge of the roof, trying to get a closer look, until it hit her that she was peeping into someone's apartment, and it was none of her business. Just as she started to move the binoculars away from the building, a burst of color obscured her vision, making her jump.

She lowered them and backed up a step. "What the heck was that?" Squinting, she looked through the window down the street and she saw a person dressed in colorful clothes. She lifted the binoculars again. "Wait, that's a clown! What is he doing?"

The person stood so Blake could see their profile. Even though "he" was the term that popped into her head, she wouldn't make the mistake of assuming anyone was a man or a woman after last spring.

The clown wore a red polka-dotted clown suit with a flared collar. A rubber mask covered the person's face, and it looked super creepy even though it had an eerie smile painted across the mouth. A shiver went through her. "I really freaking hate clowns." She assumed the person was talking with the way he waved his hands around, but she couldn't tell if his mouth was moving under the mask.

The clown backed up a few steps, and another person stepped into her line of vision. This new guy was dressed in all black except for a white mask, which obscured most of his face. A black cape, a black hat, and a white mask. Wait a second. Was he dressed as Phantom of the Opera? She moved the binoculars from the clown to the Phantom and back again before letting out a chuckle. "Well, that is one interesting party."

Feeling bad for looking in on someone, she moved on. She wondered if any of the other lofts had been rented out yet, so she panned the binoculars farther to the left to see if any other lights were on. They crossed over to the loft in the next building, where she saw a couple kissing and— "Oh, holy crap." She rapidly moved the binoculars away. "People really need to learn how to shut their blinds."

Shifting the binoculars farther down the block, she came across the next building and the loft above Buttkick. She knew Orlando had just moved into the loft, and there he was. Some sort of contraption filled up the big open space, and Orlando stood in front of it, yanking a pulley of weights up and down. He was shirtless, and his olive skin shone under a sheen of sweat. His black hair appeared slightly damp, curling where it fell at the nape of his neck, and his muscles rippled as he pulled the weights. "Oh lord, what am I doing?" Blake set the binoculars down next to her and pressed her palms to her eyes. *I just need a date with someone who looks at me as more than a buddy.* She thought of Sean's punch in the arm and winced.

She started to pick up the basket so she could finish setting the pastries out, when movement across the street caught her eye. The clown and the Phantom were moving rapidly. It looked as though they were dancing.

I really shouldn't pry. But she found herself lifting the binoculars to her eyes once again. She spanned the building again until she landed on the window and gasped. They weren't dancing. They were struggling. The Phantom threw a punch, and the clown stumbled back into the dinette table. "What on earth?"

Who are these people? Blake squinted through the binoculars, but she couldn't make out the Phantom's facial features since the mask covered his eyes and half his face, and the clown was a lost cause because he was still wearing that ugly rubber clown mask. But she could tell the clown was angry by the way one of his fists was clenched. He put his hand on the table to steady himself, and when he stood up straight, he was holding something. He'd picked something up off the table, but she couldn't tell what it was until he turned.

Blake's breath came out in a rush. The dagger. The weird-looking, ornate, arrow-like dagger. The man's knuckles were white as he gripped it in front of him, pointing it outward. The Phantom backed away from the clown and shook his head. But the clown moved forward, slowly and deliberately. The Phantom was blocked in. He couldn't move to the left because the desk was in his way, and to the right, he would only corner himself in the kitchen.

But the clown was still advancing, lifting the knife.

No, he wouldn't. Surely, he wouldn't.

But he did. He brought the knife down in a hard, stabbing motion into the Phantom's chest. A grimace twisted the Phantom's mouth as he slid down the wall.

Blake stood in shock, the binoculars pressed to her face. *No. They have to be pretending.* Maybe they were rehearsing for a play. It wasn't real.

But when the clown turned, the dagger was clenched in his fist, red blood dripping from the point.

Blake dropped the binoculars and screamed.

Chapter Two

"Your fingers are going to start bleeding if you don't stop." Ryan Harper yanked Blake's hand away from her mouth and eyed her nails. "You've chewed them down to nubs."

Her brother's pursed lips and disapproving stare had her lowering her hands before she looked back up to the window above Sliced. A memory from last spring flashed through her head, and she recalled a similar night, during which she was standing on that very sidewalk outside of Sliced, waiting for her sister to investigate a murder. She shivered in the cool night air. With a shake of her head, Blake looked back at her brother. "Your nervous energy would be out of control, too, if you'd seen what I did."

After dropping the binoculars, she had run downstairs. By the time she managed to spill what she'd seen to Giselle and Eli and they'd all run to the window, the blinds on the windows above Sliced had been drawn. Blake had called the police, while Giselle and Eli had kept eyes on the loft. No one had gone in or out.

The stiff leather of Ryan's T-Bird jacket made a creaking noise as he lifted an arm and put it around her shoulders. Blake leaned into her brother gratefully as she looked up at him. His dark-blond hair that normally matched hers was slicked back with way too much gel, making it appear brown. And his wire-rimmed glasses framed blue eyes that mirrored her own. Blue and red lights from the police cruiser swirled across his face.

"How did you know to come down here, anyway?" she asked him.

"I called him." Her sister, Kyle, took the last two steps down the wooden staircase on the side of Sliced Bakery with a scowl on her face. Her chestnut ponytail bobbed as she walked over to her police car and reached in to shut off the lights. Then she turned to the two men who had gathered on the sidewalk nearby. "Show's over, gentlemen." Thank goodness only looky-loos had gathered—the nearby business owners, Mr. Bishop and Mr. Jeffries.

Wilton was quiet on a Sunday night, with the majority of downtown businesses closed. Plus everyone was home getting ready for the big Halloween party, which started in—Blake looked at her watch—less than two hours.

Crap! The party! She still had to get the table set up for the DJ... Wait a second—she didn't know what the heck was she thinking. She couldn't have a party when someone had just been murdered.

Blake stepped away from Ryan and closer to her sister. "At least there aren't many people around to watch you take out the body." She craned her neck to look down the street. "When's the coroner going to be here?" Last time, the coroner had arrived moments after the police. So had the crime scene guys. "Shouldn't what's-his-name be here, swirling black powder over everything?" She looked the other direction down the street, expecting to see another police car swing around the corner at any moment.

Kyle gave her a look that was somewhere between pity and annoyance. "The coroner's not coming."

Blake could feel her brows drawing together. "No coroner? But you can't just leave the dead body up there. What if"—Blake gasped—"Wait! Is he not dead? Omigod, Kyle! Where's the ambulance, then?" The fire department wasn't that far away. Ambulance sirens should have been wailing in the distance.

Kyle said nothing but looked at their older brother. Her expression seemed to communicate something to him that Blake didn't quite understand.

As far as she was concerned, her siblings had gone mad. "What is wrong with you? People are going to be downtown soon for the party, which I have to figure out how to cancel. You don't want everyone just hanging out in gaggles to watch you—"

"Blake! You're not canceling the party. Neither the coroner nor ambulance will be here because there's no body, dead or alive."

"No..." Her brows knitted together. She must have heard wrong. "No body?"

The creak of the stairs signaled Jason Hart's descent from the apartment above. "No, Micah. No need to come down." Jason, Kyle's partner and semi-serious boyfriend, sauntered down the steps, talking on his cell phone. "No, it's fine. We got in, and we didn't find anything." He paused, listening to the person on the other end of the phone. "I looked through Sliced too. Nothing's out of place. There's no need to worry." Catching Blake's eye, he nodded in greeting as he finished his conversation. "You, too, man. Sorry to bother you."

Blake could feel her jaw drop as Jason pocketed his phone. It took a full ten seconds before she could gather her thoughts enough to respond. She looked from her sister's unreadable expression to Jason's and back again. "Kyle, if you're screwing with me, this isn't funny."

Her sister's face softened as she reached up to adjust the crown Blake still wore. "Sweetie, I'm not screwing with you. There's no body. There's no anything. No one's up there."

"Well then, you missed it. You didn't look everywhere." Her mind searched for some sort of rational explanation. "It took you twenty minutes to get here. The killer obviously had time to clean things up."

Kyle's concerned blue eyes flicked to their brother again. "Blake, it's a small apartment. And you said yourself that other than the time it took you to run downstairs from the roof, either you or Giselle had your eyes on the apartment the whole time. There's one exit. If no one came out of it, and no one's in the apartment, what are we supposed to think?"

Blake opened her mouth to respond then stopped. Her sister had a point.

Ryan pressed his hand to Blake's back. "Let's go across the street and talk about this at Mystery Cup, okay? Too many prying ears out here."

With a deep breath, she glanced around and realized that Mr. Bishop, the middle-aged owner of Fatal Shot Gifts, had taken a step closer to them, while Mr. Jeffries was straining to hear. The sixtysomething man had recently purchased the Crime Time Museum and renamed it Dead Sleep Living History Museum and Ghost Tours. The two businesses sandwiched Sliced, which was one reason the men were probably so interested in what was going on.

In a daze of confusion, Blake allowed her brother to lead her across the street as Kyle slid behind the driver's seat of her patrol car and flipped a U-turn so she was parked in front of Mystery Cup.

Giselle waited at the front of the café with the door open. "What's going on? Why aren't they still over there? Where's the body?"

Blake shook her head. "I don't know."

Giselle's eyes widened under the brim of her steampunk top hat as something across the street caught her attention.

With a glance behind her, Blake saw Orlando Merryfield rushing toward the café, a frown on his handsome face. Great, the last thing she needed was another looky-loo, even if it was a hunky one. At least he'd put on a shirt. Ugh, she never should have spied on him in the first place.

"Don't worry. I'll take care of Orlando." Giselle's flushed cheeks belied her firm tone as she rushed to meet Orlando before he could make it to the door of the café.

Ryan led Blake past the solid-oak tables to the fluffy couch in the corner of the café as she replayed the events of the evening in her head.

Kyle and Jason came in a minute later then sat in heavy oak chairs across from her as Ryan sank down next to her on the couch.

"Okay, let's start from the beginning." Kyle leaned forward as Jason got out a small tablet and began to tap away on it.

Blake took a deep breath. "I was on the roof, getting ready for the party." She flicked a glance at the wall clock over the kitchen door and breathed a sigh of relief that she still had plenty of time before guests started arriving. "I was looking in the window of the apartment over Sliced. I was surprised someone had moved in already. And I saw a man stab another man." She scrunched her brow. "Well, I think they were men, anyway."

"That's far enough away that you could easily have been mistaken about what they were doing." Jason spoke in an understanding tone. "There's no way you could have seen clearly from that far away at that angle. You probably just saw—"

"I was looking through binoculars." Heat rose to her cheeks.

"Uh, you were spying on your neighbors with binoculars?" Jason looked at Kyle as if he expected her to look surprised.

She didn't. Instead, she glanced out the front window to where Giselle stood, waving her arms animatedly as she spoke with Orlando, who kept looking back and forth between Giselle and the loft.

Then Kyle looked back at Blake with an arched brow. "Shirtless pull-ups?"

"Yeah, pretty much." Despite the gravity of the situation, Blake felt like giggling.

Ryan shook his head next to her. "I'm not even going to comment on the number of men you have on deck, sis. Now you're adding Merryfield?"

Before Blake could respond with righteous indignation, Kyle broke in. "Okay, so aside from Orlando's abs, what did you see?"

She elbowed her brother. Satisfied with the "oof" he made, she turned back to Kyle. "I saw a clown and the Phantom of the Opera. They were arguing." She chewed on the inside of her cheek as she tried to visualize the details. "I mean, I assumed they were arguing. They seemed really intense, and even though I couldn't hear them, they looked like they were yelling at each other. And then…" She bit her lip.

"A clown and the Phantom of the Opera?" Jason prompted. "You sure you weren't drinking Irish coffee?" When Blake shot him a death glare, Jason cleared his throat. "Sorry. Go ahead. You were saying?"

"I am absolutely certain about what I saw. I haven't been drinking, and I haven't taken any sort of medication that might make me drowsy before you even ask." Blake closed her eyes to block out the people in front of her and let the memory wash over her. "They started struggling, then the Phantom threw a punch. The clown fell against the table where the flowers and the dagger were. Then he picked it up and…" She raised her hand and brought it down in a stabbing motion. "Right in the Phantom's chest."

Jason's hands flew over his tablet as Blake's mind sped up. Maybe even though they hadn't found the body, they'd found other clues. "What about the dagger or the flowers? Maybe you could get fingerprints off of them or something."

Jason shook his head, his tousled caramel-colored hair falling forward as he continued to tap away. "No flowers. Nothing like that, Blake."

Kyle leaned forward and rubbed her hand on Blake's knee. Even though Blake was sure she meant it to be reassuring, it just seemed condescending. "Blake, it looks like the place hasn't been lived in since it was remodeled."

"You talked to Micah, right?" Blake asked Jason. "Did he rent it out yet? He has to know who has access. Did he see anyone go up before he left for the day?"

Jason shook his head. "He closed up shop early and went home to try to finish the paint job on his house. Silas went with him to help."

Kyle sat up and rolled her shoulders. "Silas? That's Eli's friend, right? He works for Micah?"

"That's right. He's my best bud." Eli walked over, carrying a tray with a pot of coffee and four mugs. He set it down on the table next to Blake, tossing back his bleached-blond hair that was just long enough to cover his eyes. "Hey, Boss Lady, I thought you all might want some coffee."

Everyone blinked as they took in his costume. He had the word "Book" written across his face, and he wore a white T-shirt with "Timeline" written across the top in Sharpie and different phrases all over the shirt. As he poured coffee, the four of them tilted their heads back and forth as they read "Photos," "About Eli," "Life Events," "Check-ins," and her personal favorite, a crude drawing of a blue-haired woman, followed by the words "Eli tagged Janelle at Mystery Cup." A thumbs-up sign was drawn underneath.

Blake could barely control her laughter, and Jason didn't even try. "Dude, you're dressed as Facebook? Great costume!" He held up his hand, and a grin spread across Eli's thin face as the two men fist-bumped.

At that moment, Giselle walked in with her eyes dancing, leading Blake to guess she'd enjoyed her conversation with Orlando. Her smile faded as she started to read Eli's shirt. When she zeroed in on the drawing of the blue-haired girl, she practically growled. "Seriously? My name's Giselle, not Janelle!"

Eli's whole face sparkled as he winked at her. "Why don't you come help me make more coffee? You can tell me all about your name."

He swaggered off as Giselle looked after him, practically spitting fire. She turned back to Blake and mouthed the words "I'm going to kill him" before she stomped off.

When Ryan spoke in his authoritative big-brother voice, it pulled Blake back to the serious topic at hand. "So you were going to say whether you talked to Micah," Ryan said to their sister. "Has he rented the place out?" The stiff leather of Ryan's T-bird jacket creaked as he lifted his arm to run a hand through his dark-blond hair, but the vat of oil he'd put on it stopped him.

Kyle shook her head, her ponytail swaying around her thin face. "Micah doesn't own the apartment. It's kind of like it is here. The city owns the downtown lofts. They're the ones who'll be renting them out. Blake's situation is a little different because there's no loft, so they let her have access to the roof patio. But most of the business owners don't have anything to do with the upstairs lofts."

Blake blew out a breath. "That's one good thing, I guess. The last thing Micah needs right now is to be mixed up in another murder."

"Omigod, Blake, listen to me!" Kyle sounded exasperated. "He's not going to be mixed up in another anything because there was no murder. There's no body!"

Blake wasn't about to give up so easily. "There has to be some sort of evidence in that apartment. In the twenty or so minutes it took you to get here, the killer disappeared with the victim, and he took the flowers and the dagger with him. He was rushed. He had to have left something or missed something."

When Kyle shook her head, Jason cleared his throat. "Look, Blake, let me give you my take on it. Teens around here like to play pranks. They tend to kick things up a notch around Halloween. I think maybe this was just someone's idea of a joke. Someone was just trying to scare you."

She didn't buy it. There was no way anyone knew she would have been watching the apartment at that exact moment.

Ryan nodded. "I'm sure that's it." As if he could read her mind, he said, "Come on, Blake, everyone knew you were going to be up on the roof, decorating for the party. Someone was screwing with you. I say we start by asking the Brentwood twins. You know those boys get crazy around Halloween."

What they said was rational, but Blake wasn't ready to let it go just yet. "Those two are fifteen. Their crazy consists of toilet-papering and lighting bags of dog poop on fire, not staging a murder." She ran a hand through her hair, tugging at the strands. "Surely you can find out who has access to the place?"

"We're going to keep looking." Jason flipped his tablet closed and slipped it back into the inside pocket of his jacket. "I know the city is going through some sort of management company to rent the lofts. I'll check with Bree Nelson, the city commissioner. She'll know what's going on."

Blake nodded, appeased for the moment. She started to get up, when her sister's hand wrapped around her forearm. "Wait one second. Blake, listen to me. I know how you think. I don't want you going over there. I don't want you checking this out. We will look into it and let you know. Do you understand? I don't want a repeat of what happened last spring."

She should have been offended, but the worry on her sister's face told her that Kyle's concern only came from a place of love. "I won't." At least she would try really, really hard not to.

When Kyle didn't let go of her arm, Blake laid a hand on her sister's and squeezed gently. "I promise."

With a curt nod, Kyle let go, and they all rose before Kyle wrapped her arms around her sister. "I love you, sweetie."

Blake squeezed back. "You guys are coming back, right? Later?"

Kyle and Jason were still in their regular detective clothes of dark slacks and button-down shirts even though their shift had already ended. Unless they were going as cops, they didn't look ready for a costume party.

"You know it." Jason tossed an arm around Kyle's shoulders. "Wait 'til you see our costumes. You're going to be super impressed."

Kyle pressed her lips together and studied Blake. "You sure you're still up for this party? I know you're upset. No one would blame you if—"

Blake held her hand up. "I'm fine. Really." *Kind of.* "You know Halloween is my favorite time of year. Besides, I think I'll feel better having a lot of people around. Going home by myself right now might freak me out." She walked Kyle and Jason to the door and gave her sister a tight hug before she watched them get into their unmarked car and drive away. Then she glanced up across the street at the loft window, which was dark.

"Come on, sis." Ryan tugged lightly on her arm as he adjusted his glasses. "I'll finish helping you get ready. Rachel will be here soon to help with anything last-minute."

"Did you fill her in on everything?"

"Just the basics. I thought I'd wait to give her all the details when she gets here." He motioned in the direction of the kitchen. "Come show me what else we need to take up."

"I'll be right there. Just give me a sec." She smiled at Ryan but didn't miss the look of uncertainty he gave her as he slowly walked to the kitchen.

She turned her gaze back up to the window. It was a prank. Jason's theory made complete sense. If it had been real, Kyle and Jason would have found something. But even as she told herself that, something didn't ring true. Something in her gut told her it wasn't a prank at all. And if no dead body had left that loft, that could only mean it was still there.

Chapter Three

The voice of Vincent Price emerged from the strategically placed speakers as the party guests wiggled to "Thriller."

Blake stood at the corner of the patio and blew a feather away from her mouth as she tried to beat down her fluffy white scarf with one hand. She really hadn't thought the costume through. Even though she was enjoying watching her guests dance and eat and laugh, she was having a difficult time getting into the party spirit. The jovial mood she'd been in earlier in the day had apparently gone trick-or-treating after she'd witnessed the scene across the street, leaving her feeling discombobulated.

The "scene she'd witnessed" was how Kyle had put it. At least her sister believed that she had indeed witnessed something. Blake didn't think she would be able to handle it if Kyle and Jason had written her off as being completely delusional. Still, no matter how many times she tried to tell herself it was a prank, her intuition reared its head in disagreement. She knew what she'd seen, and it wasn't a joke. The shiver that went through her had nothing to do with the cool night air.

"Hey, Coffee Goddess, nice costume."

Blake's head jerked back around at the deep voice that made her knees quiver. When she saw Sean Larson standing in front of her, decked out in his Halloween garb, she couldn't control the giggle that erupted.

Sean wore all black except for the red bib apron sporting the Mystery Cup logo. With his name tag in place, he looked exactly like one of her employees. The coffee cup he held completed his ensemble.

She looked up into his sparkling green eyes. "That is some costume. Definitely realistic."

His mouth twitched into a grin. "Tell me about it. Four people have already stopped me, trying to order mochas. I might not have thought this all the way through."

If she thought for a moment that he *would* work for her, Blake would have hired him in a second. It would definitely increase their female clientele. But Sean was busy with the bookstore he owned next door. Macabre Reads had opened last spring, and his business had steadily increased once everyone in town realized he wasn't a psycho killer.

Sean stepped closer and reached up to toy with a white feather at her neck, slipping it between his fingers as he met her gaze. "I'm sorry I wasn't able to help you set up. The meeting with Jamison went long. Did everything go okay?"

She hadn't expected Sean to help her set up since he'd had a meeting with an antique book dealer, but she would have given anything if he would have been with her. Then she wouldn't have been looking through those dumb binoculars. She would have been way too busy looking at him.

The scent of pine from Sean's aftershave wafted over her, making her knees weaken just a little. She always found it interesting that he smelled like aftershave, even though he had that perfectly landscaped dark stubble along his jaw. She swallowed thickly and tried to bring her thoughts back to the present. Since Sean had been gone most of the day, he probably didn't know about what had gone down. Even though a big part of her wanted to spill and get his opinion, a bigger part of her wanted to try to forget it. Plus, there was no need to worry Sean with her overactive imagination.

"Uh, yeah," she said. "Everything went smoothly. No problems."

One dark eyebrow shot up, then Sean slowly turned his head to look across the street then turned back to her and focused on her face. "You sure about that, Batman?"

Crap! He knew. He only called her Batman when he was referring to her crime-fighting skills. "Rachel has such a big mouth."

"I heard that!" Rachel walked up holding her husband's hand. Her dark wavy hair was pulled up into a high ponytail, and a pink silk jacket covered her white blouse. The highlight of her costume was the full black poodle skirt, finished with Mary Janes and bobby socks. Blake's sister-in-law made a great Pink Lady. "Hey, watch this." She stepped back and began twirling. Her skirt flew up in a perfect circle, and the men standing near her backed up so it wouldn't hit them as she spun. "So cool, right?"

Before Blake could answer, her sister-in-law kept talking. "And don't even start in on my big mouth. People need to know what happened so they can watch out for the two *idiotas* who pulled that sort of joke. Those kinds of pranks can get someone hurt."

"Rach, please." Blake stepped closer and lowered her voice. "I'd rather this not get around. The last thing I need is to be associated with any sort of scandal. After last spring, I've had enough to last me for a while."

"Good idea." Ryan plucked a comb out of his back pocket and ran it through the oil slick that was his hair, even though it hadn't moved. "Let's just forget about it and have a good time."

"I think that's a great idea." Sean looped one of his strong arms around Blake's shoulders and pulled her closer. "Come on, Coffee Goddess, dance with me."

The flutter in the pit of her stomach turned into a full-fledged flapping as she followed him onto the dance floor. If anything could take her mind off the evening's previous events, it was dancing with Sean.

She didn't miss the quirk of Rachel's eyebrow as Sean took her into his arms. Rachel was most definitely Team Adam. He and Ryan worked together at the hospital, so Rachel knew him well. Blake could understand why she was a big fan of the good Dr. Bryant. He was kind, funny, and crazy hot. But she had to decide whether she had as much chemistry with him as she did with Sean.

At the moment, Sean was her main focus. They hadn't taken a full spin around the floor before a female voice interrupted them. "Excuse me! Excuse me!"

They turned to see Ruby Cross running up to them with a coffee mug in hand. She shoved it at Sean. "When you're done dancing, can you get me another one of those caramel-pumpkin lattes? I just can't get enough."

"Now Ruby, you know Sean works at Macabre Reads," Blake said firmly, trying not to admonish the seventysomething-year-old woman.

"Yes, dear, isn't he so lovely to work the party for you?"

"Ruby, he's not—"

Sean's hand on her arm stopped her, and he chuckled. "I'd love to get you a caramel-pumpkin latte." He took the cup from Ruby and gave her a little bow. "Be right back, ladies." He gave Ruby a wink. "Great costume," he said before he sauntered away.

Blake could have sworn Ruby blushed enough that her cheeks matched her bright-red lips. She could relate. Sean could throw a woman off-balance without half trying. And he was really good at trying. Luckily, his flirting seemed to be reserved for her and women old enough to be his grandmother.

She tilted her head as she took in Ruby's outfit. For the life of her, she couldn't figure out what the lady's costume was. The white-haired woman looked the same as she did every day when she came into Mystery Cup. She wore black slacks and a lavender blouse. The only thing out of the ordinary was an old cell phone that was taped to her rear end.

Blake furrowed her eyebrows as she studied the cell phone. "I'm sorry, Ruby, but what exactly is your costume?"

Ruby was probably five feet tall if she was an inch, but her larger-than-life personality made up for her small stature. Her blue eyes twinkled as she looked up at Blake. "I'm a booty call, dear."

The laugh caught in Blake's throat. She didn't think the ladies of Murder She Read book club could surprise her anymore. She should have known better.

"Penny and I decided to go simple this year." Ruby motioned across the patio. "Although I think her costume was much more trouble than mine was."

Blake followed Ruby's eyes until they landed on the long silver hair of Penny Driver, who stood by the snack table, loading up a plate with brownies. Her costume was so subtle that Blake had to squint a little. "Does she have quarters glued all over her back?"

Ruby shook her head. "They're nickels. She decided to come as Nickelback. I told her no one was going to get it."

"Wow, I am totally coming to you all for my costume next year. You're way more creative than I am." Although "coffee goddess" had gotten a good reaction from Sean. She just hoped his positive reaction would lead to a kiss later.

Blake started to ask what the other two ladies in the book club were dressed as when a flourish near the snack table caught her eye. She looked to see a man flare out his black cape and fling it behind him. She gasped as saw the white mask over his face. Phantom of the Opera. Sean came back with Ruby's coffee as Blake stared. Ruby didn't seem to notice her lack of focus as she began animatedly telling Sean how she'd almost come as a serial killer but she didn't have enough cereal boxes.

"Sean, I'll be right back," Blake said absently before making her way over to the snack table. Part of her was relieved the murder victim was alive and well. The other part of her was ready to put the smackdown on the guy for playing such a bad joke.

The Phantom had his back to her, talking to a pretty blonde who couldn't have been any more than eighteen. "Excuse me." Blake reached to put her hand on the Phantom's shoulder, when he turned.

When he saw her, his mouth—which wasn't covered by the mask—broke into a big grin. "Hey, Ms. Harper. You like my costume?"

She blinked a couple of times. "Silas?" In addition to being Eli's best friend, Silas worked as an assistant manager at Sliced, across the street. Even though Sliced had closed early that day, Silas could have put on his costume and gone upstairs. But he didn't seem like the kind of person to play a twisted joke like that.

"Yeah, except tonight"—he deepened his voice—"I'm the Phantom."

The girl next to him giggled. "He can even sing 'Angel of Music.' He's really good."

"Um, Silas, did you have your costume on... earlier this evening?"

A bubble of laughter from the opposite side of the table pulled Blake's attention, and she glanced over to see Spider-Man chatting up a pretty brunette. For a moment, she wondered who Spidey's alter ego was, but then she refocused on Silas, who was pulling off his mask. Blake was surprised to discover the mask was connected to a dark wig that covered his close-cropped strawberry-blond hair.

Silas knitted his brows in confusion. "No. I was at Micah's, helping him paint. He's determined to get the final coat on his house before the first frost hits."

"Oh, shoot, that's right." She was surprised by how much that disappointed her. She would have been upset if Silas had been the one playing a joke, but at least she would have known that it *was* a joke, and she could have forgotten about the whole thing. "Well, how long have you had your costume? Did you just pick it up recently, or did someone else borrow it?"

His brows drew together. "Uh, I picked it up at the Twisted Halloween yesterday. There were like three Phantom costumes left." He looked back at the blonde and grinned. "But I'm the one true Phantom. Want to hear me sing 'Music of the Night'?"

She looked at the mask he held in his hand. On further inspection, she realized the mask was only made to cover the right side of his face, not the eyes and most of the left half like the mask she'd seen earlier. *Crap!* He wasn't her Phantom.

"Blake! I see you met my granddaughter!" Red Montgomery, another founding member of Murder She Read book club, walked up and put her arm around the blonde that had been the object of Silas's attention. "Elizabeth is a nursing student at MU. She's insanely smart, aren't you darling?" She squeezed her granddaughter's shoulders.

The girl blushed furiously. "Yes, Grandma," she mumbled as Silas grinned at her.

Blake hadn't quite appreciated the effect of the girl's costume when she'd approached, but now that she saw Red standing next to her, she totally got it. Red Montgomery's normally bright-red hair was covered with a black-and-white wig. She held a cigarette holder that must have been about a foot long, and a black-and-white faux fur covered her shoulders. She leaned in to her granddaughter, who wore a white dress with black spots.

Man, in Blake's next life, she really hoped she came back as Red's granddaughter. She started to comment on how clever their costumes were when she spotted someone over Red's shoulder who made her stomach drop. The person stood at the edge of the patio, right next to the wooden staircase where guests were coming and going.

Time seemed to slow as the party around her faded away. Blake's jaw dropped in surprise as the clown stared at her. For several moments, the only movements she registered were the feathers of her scarf dancing in the breeze. She should scream—for Kyle, for Sean, for anyone. But all she could do was make a squeaking sound as Red kept right on talking to her.

The clown was tall, six feet at least, and wore a red polka-dotted clown suit. He didn't wear clown shoes, but rather what looked like normal men's dress shoes, except they were bright red instead of the usual black.

The mask covered his features, so she couldn't make out who was actually under the mask. But she knew the mask. That mask would forever be ingrained in her memory. The overexaggerated plastic smile made her shiver. Dark eyebrows were painted on in downward slashes, making the clown face look angry. And the billowing red hair of the wig just added to the creepy factor.

She had never been afraid of clowns before. And on Halloween, she was used to scary clowns, but this was the first time that a menacing mask made her back up a step. Because deep down, she knew she was looking into the eyes of a killer.

Chapter Four

When her senses came back to her, time seemed to fast-forward. The people, the party, the music—everything faded away as Blake made a beeline for the creepy clown, who stood by the stairs on the other side of the patio. As soon as she started in his direction, he turned away and began to jog down the stairs. In only a few steps, he was out of her sight. She strained her neck to look over the side of the roof as she quickened her gait, weaving through partygoers as fast as she could. She needed to get to him. She had to find out who it was.

When she was only a few steps from the stairs, a hand landed on her arm and forcefully turned her around. It was on the tip of her tongue to excuse herself, when she came face-to-face with Sabrina Lang.

"I can't believe you invited all those young girls. Did you do it to tempt him? You just have to do anything you can to make my life miserable." Fire shot out of Sabrina's eyes, but Blake found it difficult to feel too intimidated as she eyed Sabrina's bunny ears.

"Sabrina, as usual, I don't know what you're talking about. Now if you'll excuse me..." She tried to turn in the direction of the stairs, but Sabrina jerked on her arm, yanking her back. As much as Blake tried to tamp down her anger when it came to Sabrina, sometimes it was harder than others. Given the day she'd had, it was one of those times when she needed to bite her tongue. Narrowing her eyes, she met her rival's gaze. "Let. Me. Go."

The pointed red nails dug into her arm as Sabrina squeezed tighter. "Not until you tell me what the big idea is of inviting my ex-husband and then inviting every girl in Wilton for him to hit on. First, you steal my best barista, and now you want to make things even more difficult for me. What did I ever do you, Blake?"

Oh gee, where do I begin? There was the bullying all through elementary and high school and Sabrina's obsessive need to acquire Blake's boyfriends. And she'd opened up a rival coffee shop. Sabrina Lang seemed to do her best to make Blake's life as miserable as possible at every turn.

"The party is open to the public. I didn't invite anyone. Trust me, I certainly didn't go out of my way to invite Todd." Sabrina's on-again, off-again relationship with her ex-husband created more drama than Blake needed at her Halloween party, but if she'd known a personal invitation to the man would make Sabrina so mad, she would have considered it. "Why are you even here, anyway? I would think you'd be getting ready for your own festivities at Café Muerte." Blake tried to pull her arm from Sabrina's grip so she could look down at the street. She didn't want to lose sight of the clown. But Sabrina's clamp tightened, her nails digging further into Blake's bicep.

Jason Hart sidled up to Blake, quickly followed by Kyle. "Is there a problem here?"

Blake barely had a chance to admire their striped prisoner outfits before Kyle was in between her and Sabrina, her face as close to Sabrina's as it could be without touching her.

The woman immediately backed up a step when she was faced with Kyle's intimidating glare, but she still didn't let go of Blake's arm.

"I don't know what your problem is, Sabrina," Kyle said through clenched teeth, "but if you don't let go of my sister right now, I'm going to arrest you for assault."

Sabrina may not have been intimidated by Blake, but Kyle seemed to scare the hell out of her. She quickly dropped Blake's arm and adjusted her bunny ears before she flipped her long blond hair extensions.

The sting from her nails was still prominent, and Blake rubbed her arm, wincing, as she bolted to the nearby edge of the roof. But she was too late. She looked up and down the street and along the side of the building, but she saw no one.

Sabrina didn't seem to notice her preoccupation as she prattled on. "I certainly didn't come here to see how lame your party is. I came here to meet my husband and—"

"Don't you mean *ex*-husband?" Kyle sniped.

The daggers from Sabrina's glower were sharp. "*And* to get my barista back," she said, not responding to Kyle. "Now that Café Muerte is busier than this place"—her eyes flicked around the patio, and she gave a disdainful sniff—"I need the extra help. I didn't expect to see my ex schmoozing all over the jailbait." She glared at the gaggle of teenage girls in front of the snack table, where Eli, Silas, and Spider-Man stood talking to them.

Blake hadn't pictured Todd as the Spider-Man type, but the man did have a habit of surprising her. So did Sabrina, for that matter. Saying she had a flare for the dramatic was a mammoth understatement, and Blake honestly didn't know if Sabrina was truly upset or if she was just trying to cause trouble. Sure, Todd had been known to date younger women, but Blake couldn't imagine him hitting on girls who didn't even look to be eighteen yet, even if the man did have questionable morals.

Really, Sabrina's little outburst boiled down to one thing—she was jealous. It didn't seem to matter that she and Todd were divorced. Sabrina obviously wasn't ready to let him go. Oddly, Blake's annoyance toward her rival vanished, and she was left feeling sorry for Sabrina.

"Sabrina, I think you're mistaken." Sean's hand landed on the small of her back, sending heat radiating through her whole body.

She hadn't even heard him walk up. "I haven't seen Todd, and I've been here since the beginning of the night."

"Of course you haven't seen him. He's in costume, you nitwit. Besides, I saw him, talking to those... those... *girls.*" She waved her hand in the direction of the snack table.

Sean's eyes traveled to the same group of teenagers, and his forehead crinkled in obvious confusion. Blake could tell he also didn't think Todd would be hitting on girls so young.

Sabrina huffed. "Just forget it. I didn't come here for him. I came here to get my barista back."

Blake crossed her arms over her chest. "Eli has been here since the spring. What makes you think he's going to up and come back to Café Muerte after six months?"

Sabrina lifted her nose so high in the air that she probably would have drowned if it started raining. "Because it's obviously the better place to work."

Kyle gave a low growl, and Blake put a hand on her sister's arm. It was funny how things had changed. Six months before, Sabrina would have gotten under her skin even more, but Blake was getting better at thinking of the woman as a fly she wanted to swat. After it had become common knowledge around Wilton that Sabrina's husband had been cheating on her, Blake actually felt sorry for her. She only wished it hadn't taken that for her to finally realize that Sabrina didn't have a thing she wanted.

"Hey, there's a crowd gathering over here. Anyone want drinks?" Eli walked up, his lanky frame relaxed as he eyed his old boss. "Hey, Serena. Whatcha doin' here? Did you come to try our famous caramel-pumpkin lattes?"

Blake's eyes widened as Sabrina stomped her foot in frustration. "My name is Sabrina, you twit." At her raised voice, the conversations around them died to a whisper.

People turned to watch them. It seemed Sabrina had also garnered the attention of Ryan and Rachel, who had been dancing. When Rachel spotted the blonde, she dropped her arms from her husband's shoulders and marched in their direction, her poodle skirt swaying with each purposeful step.

Oh lord. The last thing Blake needed was for Rachel to get mad and start cursing in Spanish. "Sabrina," she said in as kind a voice as she could muster, "why don't we go someplace else to talk about this? There's no need for you to get so upset." She reached for Sabrina's arm, but the woman jerked back as though Blake were trying to set her on fire.

"Just forget it. Coming here was a mistake. Todd can screw whoever he wants. And you!" Her dark eyes glittered with fury as she turned back to Eli. "There are way better baristas out there than you." With a *humph*, she turned on her heel and headed for the stairs—the same stairs the clown had disappeared down only moments before.

"I guess she didn't want a latte," Eli said, his eyes twinkling.

Blake sighed. *So much for finding out who was behind the clown mask.* She looked over the ledge again, her eyes trailing up and down the street. Whoever it was was long gone.

As Sabrina made her way to the stairs, she bumped the arm of a man who stole Blake's breath, only this time it wasn't because the man was wearing a mask. Adam Bryant caught her eye and offered her a wide grin. He'd said he was coming right after work, so she was surprised to see he'd still managed a costume. He wore a blue Kansas City Royals jersey, and his blond hair peeked out beneath a batting helmet. He had a catcher's mitt sticking out of his wide pocket, and a bat was swung over his shoulder. As good as he looked in scrubs, he looked even better in a baseball uniform.

It wasn't until the hand on her back tightened that she remembered Sean still standing behind her. She quickly looked up into Sean's tense face. Although he and Adam both knew she spent time with each of them, they were still normally friendly. However, an icy undercurrent that she couldn't figure out how to thaw had started to grow between them. Defrosting probably wasn't going to happen until she completely figured out her feelings for the two of them.

Adam reached them at the same time as Ryan and Rachel, who leaned in to give him a hug. "Love your costume. If you had vampire teeth in, it would be the same costume my son is going to wear for Halloween."

Amusement lit Adam's face. "A vampire baseball player?"

"My boy's creative." Ryan reached out to slap a hand on Adam's back. "Hey, man, glad you could make it. You've missed quite a night so far."

He turned those scrutinizing blue eyes to Blake. "Oh? Is everything okay?"

"Everything's fine." She smiled, hoping to relieve some of the tension she felt around her. "Just a little crazy." News of the homicidal clown could wait. She didn't have a desire to launch into the whole story where there were so many prying ears.

He stared at her for a long moment as if trying to decide whether to believe her before he nodded. Then he turned his attention to her sister and greeted Kyle and Jason. "Nice costumes." He laughed, eyeing the ball and chain attached to Kyle's ankle.

Eli seemed to decide that his presence was no longer needed. "Hey, doc, I have a caramel-pumpkin latte coming your way," he said before heading over to the table with the Crock-Pots and coffee carafes.

Finally, when Adam had greeted everyone else standing around them, he turned his attention to Sean. His smile remained in place, but it didn't reach his eyes. "Hey, man."

Sean inclined his head. "Doc. Glad you could make it." But the tone of his voice made his words sound far from sincere.

Ugh. The cordial tone between the two was really starting to grate on Blake's nerves, but she supposed it shouldn't surprise her.

"Hey, sis, I want to talk to you for a sec." Kyle jerked her head as an indication that Blake should follow her, and she did, grateful to leave the tension behind. When they made it to the ledge of the patio, Blake couldn't help but cast a glance over the side of the building and down the heavy wooden steps again. Jax Talon and his partner, Jeremy, ascended the stairs, waving excitedly in their costumes—Captain America and Thor—as they headed up to the party. Blake returned their greeting before focusing her attention back on her sister.

Kyle's steady gaze held hers. "Talk to me, Blake. I can tell you're distracted. What's going on in your head? Are you still thinking about the scene across the street? Or is it the wicked witch of Café Muerte that's bothering you?"

She blew out a breath as she scanned the happy faces around the roof. Eli was ladling coffee drinks, and the group of teenage girls standing nearby eyed him and giggled as Lady Gaga's "Monster" began playing through the overhead speakers. The crowd seemed to be growing, and Blake noticed the faces of several of her regulars. The party looked to be a huge success. Silas and Spider-Man were still in their same spots. Silas was attempting to drink a cup of coffee without hitting his mask, and Spidey was demonstrating how he could shoot webs from his wrists.

Blake shook her head. "I didn't really picture Todd as the Spider-Man type."

Her sister rolled her eyes. "I've given up on trying to figure out Todd and Sabrina, but I still think Sabrina is smoking something. I seriously don't think Todd was coming on to those girls. She pointed to the pretty blonde in the group of teenagers. "Red's granddaughter is only seventeen, for goodness sake. Surely, Todd has more sense than that."

"Red's granddaughter..." Something was off, but Blake couldn't quite put her finger on it.

Kyle snapped her fingers in front of Blake's face. "Hey, focus. Shake off Sabrina and Todd and their dysfunctional problems and tell me why you were heading for the stairs earlier, looking like you'd seen a ghost."

"Kyle, I saw him!"

Her sister looked confused. "Todd Lang?"

"No, the clown. I saw the clown. He was standing by the stairs, but he took off before I could get to him." Blake jabbed her finger in Kyle's face when her sister rolled her eyes. "Don't look at me like I'm nuts. It was him! It was the killer. The same guy I saw across the street!"

"Shhh!" Kyle grabbed her arm and yanked her closer. "Keep your voice down. Good lord, Blake, you start talking killers around here on Halloween, you're going to cause mass hysteria."

She looked around to the partygoers, who seemed to be paying little attention to them. "You have to believe me," Blake pleaded.

Kyle searched her face and finally let out a long sigh as her eyes drifted to the crowd and watched as the dancers formed monster claws with their hands. "There." She pointed with one hand and grabbed Blake's chin with the other, turning her head so she faced the crowd. "There by the DJ, look."

Standing by the DJ was Derek Preston, her delivery man, with white paint on his face and a big clown nose. He wore a Bozo the Clown wig and a blue clown suit with big white pom-poms on the front.

"The clown is right there," Kyle said. "Are you trying to tell me that Derek is a killer?"

"No!" Blake batted her sister's hand away then pinched the bridge of her nose between her thumb and forefinger. "There was another clown. Mine wasn't dressed as Bozo. It wasn't Derek. I'm not lying, Kyle."

Kyle threaded her fingers through Blake's. "I don't think you're lying, but I do think you're upset. Blake, listen to me. Forget about the prank, forget about clowns, and forget about the Langs. Grab one of your hot guys and dance. Hell, grab both of them."

As Kyle smiled widely at someone over Blake's shoulder, she turned to see Sean walking in her direction. Adam was preoccupied talking to Ryan, so at least she didn't have to choose which one of them to dance with. She hoped that if she took turns dancing with both of them tonight, neither of them would get upset.

"There. Book Hottie's on his way over. Have fun with him, Blake. Enjoy the party. Once you've calmed down and gotten some rest, we'll talk. Tomorrow."

"But—"

"Blake! There you are!" The friendly voice of Mr. Hamilton interrupted further argument, and she had to stifle a groan. The Wilton Chamber of Commerce was in the midst of arguing with some of the downtown business owners who were requesting more money for renovations. Mr. Hamilton was against it. Thank goodness she wasn't involved in that battle. She was more concerned with Mr. Hamilton's new tirade—he wanted the businesses to pay half of the fees for the Christmas decorations that went up downtown every November. Blake loved the man, but he was cheap.

Mr. Hamilton walked up to her with his arm around a younger version of himself. The younger man had dark hair, where Mr. Hamilton's was graying, but they both had the same silver eyes. "I wanted to introduce you. I don't think you've met my son, Whitley. He's just moved back to town from Miami."

Whitley Hamilton reached out to shake her hand. "It's just Whit," he said with the slightest hint of a regional accent that she couldn't quite place.

Blake raised her eyebrows. The man was handsome. Without the skeleton makeup on, he might even be gorgeous. She wondered if Giselle had had the pleasure of meeting Whitley Hamilton yet or if her steampunk vampire assistant was chasing Orlando around the party.

Whit's brown hair fell in waves to the collar of his black leotard, and his silvery-gray eyes sparkled in a face that had been artistically made up to look like a skull.

"It's nice to meet you. Mr. Hamilton said he had a son who lived in Miami."

"But he's back now"—Mr. Hamilton clapped a hand on his son's back—"and bringing his business expertise to Wilton. With his help and the renovations currently underway, we're really going to put Wilton on the map."

Whit smiled back at his dad. "I'll do whatever I can to help."

A stab of guilt made Blake regret her earlier thoughts about Mr. Hamilton being a nuisance. He just wanted to better Wilton, and he took that very seriously. His jovial attitude seemed to be a magnet for new business owners, and the town's revitalization was largely due to his efforts. Blake admired the man and everything he'd done for Wilton, Missouri.

She leaned in and gave Mr. Hamilton a hug, careful not to disturb the fireman's helmet perched atop his head. Silvery eyes twinkled, and she could have sworn he blushed as she kissed his cheek.

"Oh my. What's that for, dear?"

"Just happy to see you." It was because of him that Blake now had the rooftop patio, and Mystery Cup had seen huge growth because of it.

The man looked around the party with pride on his face. "You've really done great things up here. I just can't get over the transformation. Whit, you should have seen this place before Blake got ahold of it."

As he went on to explain to his son how they'd renovated the rooftop, warm hands slid around Blake's waist and pulled her back into a rock-hard chest. "Didn't we leave off in the middle of a dance?" Sean whispered in her ear.

Tingles shot through her as he began to sway.

"Isn't that right, Blake?" Mr. Hamilton asked. "Blake?"

She blinked rapidly. "I'm sorry, what?"

Whit chuckled and gestured to the corner. "Come on, Dad, let's get you something to drink. Let Blake enjoy her party."

"Of course, of course. Have fun, dear!" Mr. Hamilton and his son walked off, and Blake turned in Sean's arms to look up at him. A cool breeze ruffled his hair, and his eyes sparkled in the moonlight as they traveled over her face. When his gaze settled on her lips, her entire body quavered.

For the first time that night, all thoughts of masked men, daggers, and murder completely left her mind.

Chapter Five

The stepladder wobbled a little under Blake's feet as she reached to put the mystery cup back on the high shelf above the kitchen to display.

"You have next month's offering picked out already?" Giselle eyed her with curiosity.

Blake held on tightly as she descended the ladder. "Yeah, we're close to the end of October. I have to give people time to guess before I reveal it on November first."

Giselle's eyes flitted around furtively before she leaned in, tucking a blue strand of hair behind her ear. "So what is it? Cranberries? Sweet potatoes? Turkey?"

Blake laughed as she folded the ladder and pushed through the swinging door to the kitchen. "You have to wait until the beginning of the month just like everyone else." She cast a glance back at Giselle. "And I don't think turkey would go great in a dessert pastry."

A pierced eyebrow arched as Giselle gave her a considering look. "You never know," she said in a singsong voice as she turned to go back out front.

Blake thought about it as she stowed the ladder in the supply closet in the kitchen. "Huh. Turkey."

She backed out of the closet, swung the door shut, then breathed in the intoxicating aroma of sugar and caffeine always present in her kitchen. Coffee sat in a French press on the industrial kitchen island that took up the center of the room, and five loaves of pumpkin bread baked in the oven. Blake inhaled deeply. "No better smell in the world."

"Talking to yourself, Goddess?"

Whirling around, Blake clutched a hand to her chest. The anxious thumping of her heart pounded in her ears. "Sean! Don't do that! You scared me half to death."

He swiped a hand across his beard and smiled, his dimple making an appearance. He looked way too pleased with himself.

Oh man, he could use that dimple as a weapon. Blake put a hand to her chest, knowing that the surprise wasn't the only thing that'd made her heart rate speed up. "Has Giselle made your morning coffee yet?" Sean came in every morning for a black-and-white mocha before he opened Macabre Reads, even though she'd tried to get him to branch out and try something different.

"Uh, no, not yet. I wanted to talk to you first." He looked down and shuffled his feet. "About last night."

Last night. The party had been a huge success, but there were certain things about the evening that she'd rather not dwell on—besides the mystery clown going all Pennywise on the Phantom of the Opera. Nope, all she could think about was Sean walking her to the door. He'd said goodnight and leaned in, and she'd thought to herself, "This is it! He's finally going to kiss me after six months." And he *had* planted a kiss on her—firmly on the cheek. Yep, total friend zone. Kyle or Rachel would have just grabbed her man and planted a big smooch right on his lips. But Blake had a tendency to play it safe. And she could kick herself for that.

She took in Sean's guilty expression. The last thing she wanted at that moment was him trying to let her down easy. *Swerve and deflect. That's the key.* She walked around him and over to the smaller espresso machine that sat on one of the large stainless-steel kitchen countertops by the stove.

"Yeah, last night was great, wasn't it? Everyone really enjoyed the party, don't you think? I think the highlight was when Red spiked her coffee with Kahlua and started rapping on the dance floor. I thought she was pretty impressive. What do you do think?" She pressed freshly ground espresso beans into the portafilter before fitting it to the machine with a quick jerk. She gave Sean a quick glance as she reached for the dark-chocolate and white-chocolate syrups.

His brows were drawn together in confusion. "Uh, yeah, but that's not what I was—"

"Look what just came!" Rachel breezed in the kitchen, her arms carrying a huge vase filled with a dozen long-stemmed red roses.

Blake blew out a low whistle as she set the paper cup under the spigot and pressed the button. "Boy, my brother really loves you."

"Oh, they're not for me." Her smile grew wide as she waggled her eyebrows. "They have your name on them."

She blinked, confused as to why someone would send her flowers. "My name? I don't remember the last time someone sent me flowers."

Rachel held out the card, and Blake snatched it out of her fingers, opened the small envelope, and pulled out the small white card. Frowning, she read the message. "Happy Halloween." It wasn't signed, and there was no name on the front of the envelope. She flipped it over. No name was on the back, either. "That's weird. It's not signed." She looked up at Rachel, then both women turned their gazes to Sean. Hope bloomed for a brief second before he shook his head.

He held up his hands, palms out. "Don't look at me. Maybe you have a secret admirer." Even though he tried to keep his voice light, the muscles in his jaw tensed. There was only one other logical person who would send her flowers, and Sean knew it. He blew out a breath, heading for the door. "Look, I gotta go open the store. Rain check on the coffee, okay?"

Before she could answer, he slipped out the back door and shut it behind him.

Rachel bit her lip. "Sorry, I would haven't brought them in if I'd—" She shook her head. "I thought they were from him. I thought maybe after your big date last night... Uh-oh. The look on your face tells me things didn't go great when he took you home. No kissy smoochy?"

Blake tossed the card on the counter. "Kissy smoochy? You have a way with descriptions, Rach." She really didn't want to go into Sean analysis mode with Rachel. The last time she'd laid everything out, her sister-in-law had written down a list of pros and cons and talked about putting the whole thing into a graph for visual illustration. "I don't want to think about this right now." She had other things on her mind, way less emotional things, like this whole murder thing that no one seemed to believe she saw. At the moment, thinking about that seemed less dangerous than thinking about her love life.

She looked at the wall clock over the door. Sliced should be open, so she could go over and talk to Micah to see what he knew about the upstairs loft before the place got too busy. "I'll call Adam later and thank him for the flowers. Right now, I'm kind of craving quiche."

"Quiche? But you just ate. You had a pumpk—" Rachel stopped and shook her finger in Blake's face as her voice went into mom tone. "Wait a second. Blake, no. I know what you're up to."

"Hey, last time someone was killed, you were all for me investigating, remember? You told me to go for it."

Her sister-in-law perched her hands on her hips. "Yeah, well, that was before you almost got yourself killed. *Déjalo ir,* Blake! Let it go! The police will talk to Micah."

"Omigod, you're starting to sound like Kyle. And the police aren't going to make this case a priority when they're not even convinced there was an actual murder. So don't get your bra in a twist. I'm talking a piece of quiche and a couple of questions. Not a big deal."

Rachel sniffed and crossed her arms. "I am not nearly as uptight as Kyle, but I'm also not covering for you if she comes in looking for you."

Blake quickly untied the red apron and lifted it over her head. "And I wouldn't expect you to," she said as she draped the apron over a hook on the wall. She pushed the swinging door and headed into the café, on her way to the front door. "I'll be right back."

As she walked out from behind the counter, she cast a glance at Eli, who was holding a cup in his hand and shouting out the name "Ellen" as Elaine Page stood in front of him, looking very confused.

The crisp morning air was chilly as Blake rushed out of the café, and she immediately wished she had thought to grab her jacket. The gray skies didn't offer any sunshine for warmth, and she shivered as she walked by Macabre Reads. Glancing in the front window, she saw Sean talking to his newest employee, Ashley, as he pushed a few buttons on the cash register. Then, as if he felt Blake's eyes on him, he looked up. He started to smile, but then he seemed to notice which direction she was going and frowned. He looked at her then across the street and back at her before shaking his head vehemently.

People around here are way too judgy.

Blake rushed across the street and pushed open the door of Sliced, hoping Sean didn't jump on the let's-stop-Blake bandwagon. The breakfast crowd was already there in full force, filling many of the tables around the restaurant. The place was getting busy quickly, and they'd only been open for twenty minutes. Inhaling the aroma of coffee and bacon, Blake put a hand to her stomach as it started growling. She walked up to the register, where Silas was pouring a cup of coffee, swaying to the music in his head.

When he spotted her, the boy smiled. "Hey, great party last night, Blake. Your costume was lit!"

Oh crap, it looked like she was going to have to learn new slang again. "Lit?"

"Yeah, just go with it," Micah said as he came around the corner, holding an order pad. "Everything's lit these days."

"Right." She turned back to Silas. "That's, uh, tight."

He grinned and gave her a thumbs-up.

Micah laughed and gave her a hug, his tousled red hair tickling her nose. "I know you didn't come over here for the coffee. Quiche?"

She pulled back. "Actually, I was hoping to talk to you for a second. But okay, yeah, I wouldn't turn down a piece of quiche."

"Sure." Micah put his order pad on the counter, instructed Silas to get her a slice of quiche to go, then led her to a booth away from where most of the patrons were seated. "So what's up?" he asked as they slid in to the booth. Before she could answer, he smirked and leaned back in his seat. "As if I didn't know."

She could feel the heat rise in her cheeks. Micah knew all too well Blake's fascination with a good mystery, and she wondered if going over there to question him was in poor taste. "I'm sorry, Micah. I was going to ask you some questions about last night, but I realize that's probably... I'm sorry."

She started to get up when Micah rested a hand on her arm. "Blake, don't. Don't try to change who you are. I feel like we're finally getting into a groove again. I don't want you to walk on eggshells around me."

"I know, and I don't want to. But with the topic at hand, I just don't want to open up any old wounds."

A shadow passed over his face. "There's only one person who's good at opening up wounds, and it's not you, so please don't worry about that." Micah released her arm and clapped his hands together. "Now, the topic at hand." He slid his hand into the pocket of his jeans, pulled out a silver key, and slid it across the table to her.

She frowned. "What's that for?"

He grinned. "The upstairs loft. I figured you'd ask to look around eventually. I just thought I'd save you some time."

Her mouth dropped open. "I... okay, well, fine." He obviously knew her too well—or he just knew she was super nosy. She picked up the key. If he had the key, she wondered if he knew more about who'd rented the apartment. "Wait a second. How do you have a key? Kyle said you didn't have anything to do with the loft upstairs, that it was owned by the city."

He bobbled his head from side to side. "It is, but all of the shop owners have keys to the second-floor lofts in their building. That way, if we ever need to get in for an emergency, a burst pipe or something like that, we can. Especially now, when a lot of them are empty."

Blake drummed her fingers on the table. "Does anyone else have access to your key?"

"Nope." Micah reached into his pocket and pulled out a key ring with half a dozen keys dangling from it. "It stays on this, in my pocket. I only took it off to give to you."

"Okay, well, I heard through the grapevine that the place was rented, but no one seems to know by who. I thought I'd call Bree Nelson and see if I could get any information out of her about it." If anyone knew who was renting out the buildings, it would be the city commissioner.

"I saved you the trouble." Micah's cheeks flushed as red as his hair. "I'm in pretty good with the city commissioner, so I asked for you."

Blake widened her eyes "You and Bree?" She didn't know the new commissioner that well, but Bree seemed to be very type A. She came in every afternoon in her perfectly ironed pantsuit and ordered a half-caf, no foam, skinny-vanilla latte. She wasn't at all like the rocker chicks Blake was used to seeing Micah with.

He lifted a shoulder and looked down. "She was in a lot when we were renovating."

When the upstairs loft was being laid out, Micah had decided to update Sliced as well. Blake looked around at the freshly painted walls and new industrial carpet. The result was fabulous. "New beginnings," Micah had said.

"I'm happy for you. From what I know of her, she seems nice." And that also explained why Giselle had been so mopey anytime Micah's name was mentioned for a few weeks. He never had reciprocated her crush, but luckily, he'd found somebody that seemed to make him happy.

His face lit up. "She is. You'd like her."

"Hey, Micah," Silas called from the counter as he lifted up a phone receiver. "Mr. Hamilton for you. Something about damage control."

Micah's brows drew together. "I wonder what that's about." He scooted out of the booth. "Anyway, go look around. As soon as I hear back from Bree, I'll let you know." He pointed to a Styrofoam to-go box on the counter by the register. "Don't forget your quiche. It's on the house."

"Thanks, Micah." She fisted the key in her hand then got up and grabbed her quiche before scurrying out the front around to the side of the building where the wooden staircase led to the overhead loft. After two steps up, Blake paused, nerves washing over her. *Maybe this isn't a good idea. If I'm right, there could be a dead body in that apartment.*

As she debated whether to keep going or turn around and head back to Mystery Cup, an arm hooked around her waist from behind.

Blake screamed.

Chapter Six

"Shhh, you're going to wake the dead."

"Sean! Omigod, that's twice in less than an hour. Are you trying to kill me?" She clutched a hand to her chest, rubbing the spot where she was certain her rapidly beating heart was going to burst right through. She totally should have checked to make sure no one was behind her before she ventured up the stairs. "What are you doing here?"

"I'm here to save you from yourself. I sure as hell don't relish seeing you get into a situation that's going to get you hurt. I've been through that last spring, and I don't want to do it again." He took the Styrofoam box from her and hooked his arm through hers. "Come on, let's go back across the street."

"What? No!" She batted at him with her hand. "I can take care of myself. And it's not like I'm breaking and entering." She waved the key in front of his face. "Micah gave me a key. I'm totally authorized to go in, so suck it."

Sean let his head fall back and let out a sigh. "Blake, just because you have permission to be there doesn't mean you *should* be there."

Her lips pursed in annoyance. Sean was beginning to sound way too much like her sister. She needed to make it clear that she was a strong, independent woman, and she could do whatever she darn well pleased. Standing on the second step of the staircase brought her to eye level with Sean. Standing so close, she could really make out the flecks of gold in the bright green around his pupils.

She gave her head a little shake. *Focus, Blake.* Planting her hands firmly on her hips, she lifted her chin in defiance. "You're not the boss of me, Larson." Well, that sounded way lamer out loud than it had in her head.

Sean's eyes lit with mirth as he crossed his arms over his chest. "Really? Next, are you going to say, 'I know you are, but what am I?'"

With a huff, Blake spun on her heel and grabbed onto the railing to steady herself. She was really getting tired of no one taking her seriously. After two more steps up, she heard the stairs creak behind her.

"Don't try to stop me, Sean," she called over her shoulder.

His footsteps fell heavily behind hers. "I'm not going to try to stop you. But I'm also not going to let you go up there by yourself. If your secret admirer's not here to join you, then I will."

"Secret admirer?" Then it dawned on her. "Oh, sweet cheese, are you talking about the flowers?" She rolled her eyes. "I cannot believe we're doing this right now. I don't even know who they're from." *Wait. Is he jealous?* That was something she really wanted to explore in more detail.

"Really?" He crossed his arms, and sarcasm tinged his voice. "The good doctor didn't send them?"

"I... uh..."

"You didn't ask him?"

"Well, no, but—" A truck roared by, cutting her off. "Crud, I really don't want to stand out here on the stairs to the loft where everyone can see me having this conversation." *Because someone might tell Kyle, and then I'll be in big trouble.*

Sean gestured up the stairs. "Lead the way, Coffee Goddess."

"If you can't beat 'em, join 'em?" she asked once they reached the landing.

Sean took the key from her hand and shoved it into the lock on the doorknob. "Something like that." He turned the key and pushed the door open, and they were faced with... a nondescript apartment. The smell of fresh paint and cleaner was almost overwhelming. She wondered if the person who'd rented the place had been in there cleaning. If not, someone had been there recently with a potent chemical.

Blake didn't know quite what she was expecting, but she was disappointed that the place looked so plain. The furniture still remained—the big wooden desk, the dinette set, and the red futon. Otherwise, there was nothing remarkable.

Sean nudged the door closed behind them as his eyes darted all over the small space. "Tell me exactly what it is we're looking for." He stepped inside and moved to the window to look out at Mystery Cup. "Where exactly was everyone positioned when you were watching them?"

His voice calmed her unease, not only because of its warmth, but because he wasn't talking to her as if she were some kind of loon.

She looked up at him. "You believe me?"

His face softened. Sean walked over to her and reached up to cup her cheek in his palm. "Of course I believe you. That was never the question. I told you—I just don't want you to put yourself in a dangerous situation like you did a few months ago. I don't want to think about anything happening to you."

He cares about me. Her stomach fluttered, and she could barely control the smile that tugged at the corners of her mouth. She cleared her throat and tried to focus on the matter at hand. "So you don't think it's a prank, like Kyle said?"

"I don't know. But as long as we're here, let's see if we can find anything to prove it one way or another." He dropped his hand and watched her as she moved across the room to the dinette table, taking everything in. "This place reminds me of my dad's apartment back when I was in junior high."

Sean had only mentioned his dad a few times. Blake knew that his parents had split up when he was twelve, but he didn't seem bitter about it. He just talked about it very matter-of-factly.

"Did your dad live close to you after the divorce?"

"Yeah, for a while. My sister and I would go over every other weekend. Kind of weird, though. Two-bedroom apartment, and I was sharing a bed with my little sister. She could never sleep very well at my dad's, so she would wait until I fell asleep then paint my nails." He chuckled, looking lost in thought for a moment before he focused back on Blake. "You'll meet her soon. She's coming to town over the holidays."

"I can't wait to meet your family." She held Sean's eyes for a long moment, feeling something strong between them. He had to like her as more than a friend if he wanted her to meet his family.

Finally, Sean cleared his throat and broke eye contact. "So, back to our search here. Tell me what you saw."

"Right." She ran her fingertips across the center of the dinette table. "Here. There was a bouquet of daisies right here, wrapped in green paper. And a dagger. It was big and ornate." With her hands, she outlined the dagger in the air in front of her. "Medieval, almost. Like something you'd see on *Game of Thrones*."

"Okay." He walked slowly toward her. "And you said the clown fell into the table? Where was the Phantom standing?"

"Right there." She motioned to the area between the big wooden desk and the kitchenette. The red futon sat by the front door, and the dinette blocked the path from the desk to the doorway that she assumed led to the bedroom. "He was backed in. The desk on one side, the kitchenette on the other, and the clown in front of him."

Sean stood in the exact spot the Phantom had. "Okay, so if you're the clown, I punch you, and you fall into that table. Then what?"

Blake semi-crouched in the position she remembered the clown taking after he'd stumbled. "He was hanging onto the table to steady himself, and when he stood up, he grabbed the dagger." She mimicked the motion and stood, pretending to hold a dagger in a stabbing position. Then she walked toward Sean. "He walked to the Phantom, who started shaking his head."

"He didn't throw another punch?" Sean asked.

She shook her head. "I think he was trying to figure out if he could get by the clown, but he was trapped. He was looking all around—for an escape route, I suppose. That's when the clown stabbed him." Her hand came down in a stabbing motion, and she rested her fist against Sean's chest over his heart. "Here."

He let out a low whistle. "If he stabbed him right in the chest, the Phantom wouldn't have walked away from that."

She dropped her hand. "No, he wouldn't have."

Sean looked at the hardwood floor beneath where he stood and at the wall behind him. "There's no blood. You'd think there would be something."

Blake knelt down to examine the floor and took a deep breath. "Did you notice that the smell of Pine-Sol seems stronger right here? If there wasn't much blood, he could have cleaned it up quickly."

Sean leaned against the desk and crossed his gloriously tattooed arms over his chest. Blake tried to focus on the discussion rather than his massive biceps.

"So from the time you saw this, it took how long for Kyle and Jason to arrive?"

"Uhh..." She thought back. "I was stunned for a minute. When I finally gathered my senses, I ran downstairs, grabbed my cell phone, and called Kyle."

"You called her directly? You didn't call 911?"

Blake nodded. "I probably should have called 911, but I wasn't thinking. I just automatically called her cell phone."

"Okay. Did she and Jason come right away?"

She shook her head. "They were on another call somewhere outside of town, in between here and Colombia. So it took a while for them to get here, about twenty minutes or so. And before you ask, they called the station to try to get someone else over here, but apparently the only other unit on duty was investigating a domestic-violence case."

"Only two units were on duty?" He shook his head. "Gotta love small towns. Okay, so including the time it took you to get downstairs, make the call, talk to Kyle, and for them to get here, we're looking at… twenty-five, thirty minutes?"

She lifted a shoulder then let it drop. "Yeah, that sounds about right."

Sean looked around, studying the room as he spoke. "So your clown had half an hour to get a body out of here. That's more than enough time." When he looked back at her, his expression was serious, and Blake could tell the gravity of the situation was getting to him.

She shook her head vehemently. "No. Giselle was at Mystery Cup, watching. As soon as I came down and got on the phone with Kyle, she ran to the front window. She had her eyes on that staircase"—she pointed to where they'd entered—"on the side of the building until Kyle got here. She tried to look back in the window, but the blinds were closed." She shoved a hand through her hair. "I could kick myself for screaming. If he heard me, that's probably why he closed them. But Sean, I'm telling you, no one left this apartment." Her insides started to tingle as the anxiety began anew. The lack of evidence was going to be enough for him not to believe her.

"Look, Goddess, calm down." Sean seemed to be getting really good at reading her and heading off her mood swings. He stepped forward and grasped both of her shoulders. "I'm just playing devil's advocate so we can cover all our angles. We have to figure out how someone got a body out of here without going down that staircase, which is the only exit. We also have to figure out how they managed to move a body—which had been stabbed—without getting blood everywhere."

"That's why my theory was that they still had to be here some-where. The killer and the body." She pulled away from him and turned in a slow circle. "But now that I see the place, that seems unlikely." The apartment definitely had a minimalist thing going on—no big trunks or chests, no garbage chute, no nothing. "It's not like there's really anywhere to hide."

Aside from the living-room-kitchenette combo, there was a doorway leading to the bedroom-bathroom area. Unless the killer and the body had disappeared into thin air, Kyle and Jason would have found them. Blake rubbed a hand over her face. Maybe she *was* nuts.

"Well, let's make sure." Sean walked past her into the bedroom.

Blake followed him into the pale-yellow room. The Venetian blinds were closed on the one window that overlooked the street. A queen-size bed with a blue quilt took up most of the space, and a dresser, which looked to be secondhand from the scuff marks, stood against one wall. Sean fell to his knees and lifted the quilt to look underneath the bed. He quickly dropped it and stood up.

"No dead body popping out at you down there?"

He grinned. "No, but no one ever hides a body under the bed. Too obvious. Don't you watch horror movies?"

She gave him the side-eye. He knew she loved horror movies. And he was right. The first place in an apartment that size to hide a body would be under the bed. The second place would be... Her eyes drifted to the closed door that most likely led to a closet. Blake walked past the dresser and reached for the closet door. She paused with her hand on the knob and had the fleeting image of a body falling out on her when she opened the door.

"Let me guess." Sean came up behind her. "You're thinking of *Wait Until Dark,* the part where Audrey Hepburn opens the closet door, and there's a body hanging there, encased in plastic."

She thought of the movie night she'd had with Sean a couple of weeks ago. He'd invited her over, but rather than sitting on the couch next to her, he'd sat in a chair by himself while they watched the film, which was one of her favorites.

A shiver went through her, and her hand tightened on the knob. "Great movie. Not nearly as thrilling a scenario when you're the one standing in front of the closet."

He gently removed her hand from the doorknob. "Here, let me."

Blake stepped back as Sean gripped the door handle.

He turned it and quickly pulled the door open then stuck his head inside. "Nothing. No bodies." Relief filled his voice.

She peered past him into the small walk-in closet. It was completely empty, with not even a hanger, only a pull chain hanging down to turn on the light. She blew out a breath she wasn't aware she'd been holding and noticed it didn't smell like cleaner in there like it did out front. "So, nothing under the bed, and nothing in the closet. That leaves the bathroom."

Sean followed her around the bed and through the open door of the bathroom. There was nothing remarkable about the black-and-white tiled floor, toilet, pedestal sink, bathtub, and no windows. Except...

"Nothing here, either." Sean opened the mirrored medicine cabinet and peered in, but it was empty. "I think this visit was a bust." Blake couldn't tell if he sounded relieved or disappointed.

"Not necessarily." Blake stepped closer to the bathtub and reached up to finger the hooks on the shower rod.

Sean leaned a shoulder against the doorjamb and crossed his arms once again as he studied her. "What's going through your head?"

"You said one of the things we had to figure out was how the killer managed to get a body out of here without getting blood all over the place."

"Yeah..." Sean drew out slowly.

A thrill went through Blake as things started to come together in her head. "Well, don't you think it's a little odd that this place is completely furnished down to the bedspread and dainty curtains, but there's no shower curtain?"

A muscle worked along Sean's jaw as he pondered what she was saying. "Maybe whoever decorated hasn't gotten around to picking it out yet."

That gave her another thought. "Who exactly *was* the person that had decorated the apartment, though? The apartment manager or the person who rented the place?" She tore her eyes away from Sean and crouched down so she could get a closer look at the tiled floor.

"What are you looking for?"

Her mouth quirked in thought as she inspected the tile closely. She turned her gaze to the bathtub, and her eyes lit up. "Aha!" She reached into the tub and pinched a couple of little plastic dots. "You know when you buy a new shower curtain and you hang it up, you have to punch through the little plastic holes with the hooks? I replace my shower curtain every couple of months, and every time I do, I have these little plastic dots all over my bathroom." She held them up for Sean to see, and his dazzling grin made her smile.

"Coffee Goddess, you're a genius."

She rose, still looking around at the tile. "That means there *was* a shower curtain. That's it, Sean. Why would someone have taken it down? They wrapped the body in it. There's no other explanation." She leaned forward so she could look around the toilet and vanity. "The killer came in here and—wait a second." Her eyes zeroed in on a foreign object behind the pedestal sink. "What's that?"

Sean leaned forward, trying to see. "What?"

"That!" She braced one hand on the sink as she reached down with the other and plucked a black square off the floor.

She stood back up and held it out to Sean.

"A matchbook?" He glanced at her face then back at the black matchbook in her hand. "Who still has matchbooks? You can't smoke anywhere anymore."

"Oh yes, you can." She turned the matchbook over to reveal the skull on the front of it. "Crossbones has an outdoor patio for smokers. It's about the only place in town someone can smoke except for their own home."

"So the killer is a smoker who hangs out at Crossbones?"

She offered Sean her biggest smile. "We're going to find out."

Chapter Seven

"So Sean is the Robin to your Batman now?" Kyle plopped herself on a tall stool at the kitchen island while Blake turned on Mystery Cup's convection oven to preheat.

"No... heck, I don't know. Sean is so confusing. First, he's mad about the flowers, then he's all protective, then he rushes back to the bookstore just when we're connecting. I need an interpreter to figure out the men in this town."

"Well, I'm just glad he talked you out of going down to Crossbones and interrogating every smoker on the patio." Kyle bit into a big espresso brownie and chewed thoughtfully. After a moment, her eyes narrowed at Blake. "Who am I kidding? They're closed today, aren't they? That's the only reason you're not there right now."

Dang it, Kyle was too smart. Blake averted her eyes from her sister as she leveled off a cup of sugar, dumped it in her mixing bowl, and turned on the industrial mixer to begin blending the batter for the pumpkin bread. She was hoping to play it off as though she were following the rulebook rather than going rogue like last time she'd happened across a murder. "I would never step on your toes... You are going to question the people at Crossbones, right?"

Kyle snorted. "Blake, I need a little bit more to go on than a matchbook and a missing shower curtain." She reached for her mug of coffee and took a large gulp. "Chief Raimy would have my hide if I started interrogating people based on that. Besides, I'm still not convinced it's not just a prank."

"Omigod, Kyle!" Blake wiped her floured hands on her red Mystery Cup apron. "I can't believe you still think that. Sometimes I could shake you." She clenched her hands in front of her as if she were shaking an invisible person.

Kyle grinned. "Try it, and I will flick you in the head."

Blake had experienced Kyle's head flicks many times. They didn't feel good.

"Look at what we have so far." Kyle cupped her hands around her mug. "You said yourself the clown was at the party. What do you think he was doing there? Because he just made sure you saw him and left, so I'm guessing he didn't come for the pumpkin bread." Her short, clipped nails tapped furiously against her mug, the only sign of her inner turmoil.

Blake knew that meant her sister was thinking the same thing she was. "He obviously knows I saw him. He was trying to scare me." She hoped that was all it was and that his appearance wasn't some kind of threat.

Kyle's gaze snapped to hers. "We don't know that." She set the mug down. "But it wouldn't hurt to watch your back in case someone out there is trying to keep you off-balance. And you're absolutely sure it was the same clown that—"

"I'm sure. Very sure."

"Okay. Well, I didn't see him, but I saw the Phantom. He was there too."

She was shaking her head before Kyle even finished. "That was *not* the same Phantom. Silas was dressed up as the Phantom at the party. Plus, he had a different mask than the one I saw on the murder victim."

"Blake, just let me handle this my way. I have a call in to Bree Nelson's office so we can find out who rented the apartment. Once we know that, we'll go from there. I can interview the person, and we can find out who has access to the place. I'm not ignoring this, but I'm going by the book. I can't follow up on every crazy theory you have when you don't have anything to back it up." Kyle took another bite of her sweet bread, and Blake could tell from the closed look on her sister's face that Kyle thought the conversation was over.

"Okay, I can live with that, but hopefully my source is quicker than yours."

Kyle stopped chewing, and her eyebrows rose. "Whaddya mean?" she asked with a full mouth.

Blake shrugged as she turned off the mixer and began cracking the eggs to add to the batter. "I talked to Micah. He's dating Bree, so he might be able to ask a couple of questions for me."

Kyle let out a groan and pinched the bridge of her nose. "Do not conduct your own investigation, Blake."

"Well, if it's a prank like you say, then I don't have anything to worry about, right?" *As if!* She reached for a third egg, but Kyle was off her seat in a heartbeat and standing in between Blake and the counter. "Hey, what are you—"

"Listen to me." Kyle's face was tense, and her blue eyes were hard. "I know you saw exactly what you're telling me. I never said I didn't believe you. Hopefully, this is a prank, but if it's not, I don't want you anywhere near this. Not this time. I almost lost you last spring because of your curiosity. I do not want to go through that again, okay? I can't lose you!"

Blake's stomach tightened as she looked into her sister's face. For years, it had been her, Ryan, and Kyle against the world. After their dad had taken off when they were kids, the three of them had leaned on each other. They'd lost their mom to breast cancer three years ago, but she'd been sick long before that. She, Ryan, and Kyle were a unit. All they had were each other, and she knew how gutted she would feel if anything happened to one of them. Suddenly, she felt bad for making Kyle worry. "I'm not going to do anything stupid. I promise."

Kyle opened her mouth to speak, but the buzzing of her phone stopped her. She pressed her lips together then grabbed it from the island, where it was lying next to her purse. "Crap, it's the chief. Hang on." As she answered, she stepped out the back door to take the call in private.

Just then, Giselle came in, looking flustered and carrying a rectangular plastic basket filled with dirty dishes. Blake was about to ask her what was wrong, when Eli followed her through the door a second later.

"I'm still not sure why exactly you're upset, Janelle." His eyes twinkled. "You're not jealous, are you?"

"Jealous?" Giselle spun around to face Eli, two red dots staining her cheeks. "You are crazy if you think I'm jealous!"

"Whoa." Blake stepped forward, her hands up as if her presence could calm the storm between the two of them. "What's going on with you two?"

Eli turned to her. "Not a thing. I have a blind date. Silas asked out Lizzie Montgomery, and she's setting me up with her friend, Missy."

"Lizzie Montgomery? Elizabeth? Red's granddaughter?" Lizzie was still in high school, which meant her friend probably was too. Despite Eli's quirks, he was one of the most responsible employees Blake had ever had, so she forgot he was only nineteen. Still, she was surprised he would date a high schooler.

"Yeah." Eli bobbed his head. "Her and Silas hooked up at the party. Anyway, they're setting me up. We're going to the haunted house they have set up over by the gym." He glanced over to where Giselle stood with a clenched jaw, and he grinned. "Janelle's jealous I have a date."

"My name is Giselle," she said through clenched teeth. "And I am *not* jealous. All I said was that Lizzie and Missy are still in high school. They're seventeen."

"And me and Silas are nineteen." He chuckled. "I think we can deal with the age difference." He took a step closer to her. "Unless you can think of a reason I shouldn't go out with her."

Giselle lifted her chin and crossed her arms. "I don't have time to think about your love life. I told you, I have a date with Orlando."

"You do?" Blake tried not to look surprised, but she wouldn't have guessed the two of them would have much in common aside from the whole Giselle-liking-to-ogle-him thing.

"Yes! He's taking me out to dinner." She said it almost like a challenge, but Eli didn't seem fazed at all.

"Great," he said. "I hope you have a good time." He walked out of the kitchen and back into the café, leaving Giselle seething.

"I'm sure we will!" Giselle hollered behind him.

The door swung behind Eli, and Blake turned back to her assistant. "That's great that Orlando asked you out." When Giselle stood there, fuming, Blake asked, "What's wrong? Isn't that a good thing?"

"Okay fine, he actually asked me to come to his new spin class and then we could go to the snack bar, but that's kind of like a date." She gave Blake a pointed look. "But whatever you do, do *not* tell Eli that!" She swung around to the sink and started rinsing the dishes without another word.

Blake's head spun for a moment. She knew Eli liked to tease Giselle, but that was the first time she thought there actually might be something between the two of them. That was the only reason she could think of to explain why Eli would be trying so hard to get a rise out of Giselle. The girl was twenty-two, which really wasn't much of an age difference in the long run. In Blake's opinion, they were very well suited for each other.

Kyle cleared her throat from behind Blake. When she turned back around, her sister flicked her eyes at Giselle, obviously wondering why she looked so upset. Blake just shrugged.

"Okay, well, that was the chief." Kyle shoved her phone back in her purse then hiked it over her shoulder. "I need to get back to the station." She grabbed Blake in a fierce hug. "If you hear anything, you call me and let me know, okay." She didn't even try to make it a question.

Blake promised she would call with any new information then watched as her sister walked out the back door of the kitchen to where she'd parked in the alley behind the café.

BY THE END OF THE BUSY day, Blake was ready for a nap. The café was always crazy on Mondays, but the traffic through the shop that afternoon had been off the charts for some reason. With only an hour until closing, the flow of customers had finally started to wind down, and Blake was more than ready to head home and relax.

"Auntie B!"

At the sound of her niece's sweet voice, Blake's head popped up from where she was wiping down the shelves of the pastry case. "Emma! Hey, little one, come here." She stepped around the counter, and a six-year-old bundle of energy ran straight into her arms. "Where's your daddy?"

The little girl waved a hand in the direction of the door. "He's coming. Him and Aiden are slow. But guess what? Daddy bought my Halloween costume. I wanted to be a princess, and then I wanted to be a ninja, and then I wanted to be a monster, but then I thought I wanted to be a bride 'cause they get to wear a poufy dress. I told Daddy I could be a monster with a poofy dress, but he said monsters don't wear dresses. I think monsters could wear dresses, don't you?"

Blake laughed at the six-year-old's stream of thought. "Slow down, Emma Bemma." She dropped a kiss on top of Emma's head as she lifted the little girl into her arms. Her thick black pigtails bounced as she wrapped her chubby little arms around Blake's neck. "I think you can be whatever you want for Halloween. If you want to be a monster with a poofy dress, then you should go for it."

Emma's blue eyes sparkled. "That's what I said, but guess what I finally decided? Guess, guess, guess!"

Rachel came out of the kitchen door behind Blake. "Uh-oh, what did you decide on, *mariquita*? Is it going to scare me?"

"Mommy!" Emma reached for her mother and began speaking in rapid-fire Spanish.

"English, Emma. It's not polite to speak Spanish in front of people who don't know the language. Auntie B will think you're talking about her." She winked at Blake as she hefted her daughter into her arms.

"Hey, I'm getting better. I heard '*zombi princesa.*' Is that a zombie princess?"

"Yes!" Emma bounced in Rachel's arms as she giggled. "I get to be scary and wear a pretty dress!"

"Well, I can't wait to see that." Blake closed the pastry case and took in Rachel's expression. Her sister-in-law seemed uncertain about Emma's costume choice. "I'll bet you're going to be the best zombie princess ever. What about your brother? What's he going to be?"

The little girl crinkled up her face. "A baseball player. Boys are so boring. He gets to dress up like a baseball player every week for T-ball practice, anyway."

"I'm not boring!" Aiden stood in the doorway, holding his father's hand. "And I'm not going to be *just* a baseball player. I'm a vampire baseball player!"

Ryan poked his glasses up on his nose. "Yes, now we just have to figure out how to zombify a Cinderella dress."

Blake was about to offer to do makeup when the bell above the door jingled and a couple came in behind Ryan and Aiden.

"Hi, Blake!" Bree Nelson, Wilton's newest city commissioner, had one arm around Micah's waist and waved at Blake with the other.

She wasn't sure what had happened between Giselle and Micah, but she was glad her barista had already left for the day. It seemed as though she was having enough man trouble without seeing Micah walk in with his arm around another woman.

"Just who you were waiting on," Rachel hiss-whispered. "Go. You can get your info right from the horse's mouth." Then she motioned for her husband and son. "Hey, you two, come back to the kitchen. I just took a tray of cookies out of the oven. You can visit with Auntie B in a little bit."

Blake smiled, appreciating the fact that Rachel wasn't throwing up obstacles as far as her independent investigation went. Well, she hadn't yet, anyway.

After Ryan and Rachel disappeared into the kitchen with their children, Blake turned her attention to Micah and Bree.

Micah gave the woman on his arm a squeeze. "I told Bree you had a couple of questions, so—"

"So I thought that would be a great excuse for me to come over and score some espresso brownies." She grinned. "What do you say? Info for chocolate? That sounds like a good trade."

"Absolutely. You two have a seat. I'll grab the chocolate and caffeine." She started to go back behind the counter, but Eli waved her away. "It's okay, Boss Lady. You go sit. I'm on it."

She thanked Eli then led Micah and Bree to the big couch in the corner of the café, happy they'd come into the shop. No one could give her crap for talking to them when they came into Mystery Cup for coffee.

Bree settled in and crossed her long legs, looking totally relaxed. Her crisp white pantsuit contrasted perfectly with her smooth skin, which was the same color as a perfectly crafted caramel mocha. She was a brave woman in Blake's book. Tackling brownies and chocolate while wearing all white screamed confidence.

Bree rested her hand on Micah's denim-covered thigh. Even though he wore jeans and a T-shirt with the Sliced logo, the two of them just looked like they... fit. Blake was thrilled to see the smile on Micah's face when he looked at the woman next to him.

"So!" Bree turned her big brown eyes to Blake. "Micah says you have questions about the lofts downtown. What do you want to know?"

Her face fell as her mind turned back to more serious matters. She blew out a breath and decided to lay it all out. The worst that could happen was they would just tell her to mind her own business. And it wasn't as if that would be the first time someone had said that to her. Heck, it wouldn't be the first time *today* someone had said that to her. "Okay, here goes..."

They listened to her rundown of events, from the night of the party to looking around the loft apartment, with slowly widening eyes. They didn't even speak when Eli came over to deliver coffee and a plate filled with espresso brownies and pumpkin bread. Blake kept close attention on Micah, making sure not to upset him. But other than becoming a little pale—most likely at the details of another murder occurring in such close proximity to Sliced—he didn't say a word. It seemed to help that Bree had a hand on his thigh, rubbing up and down in a gentle, comforting motion.

When she finally finished, she sat back and gave them both a moment to process the information. "So you can see why I'm anxious to find out who it was that had access to that apartment. I mean, if it's not a prank, then I want to get to the bottom of it." Blake held her breath, preparing herself for Bree's reaction.

Bree picked up her coffee, her black curls falling around her face. She took a sip and looked at Blake thoughtfully. "But you don't think it's a prank."

"No. No, I don't."

Bree sipped her coffee slowly. "I wish it were easy enough that I could just give you a list of names of people who are authorized to be there."

A frown tugged at her mouth as disappointment cut through her. "It's okay. I understand that you can't say anything."

"What?" Bree's perfectly arched eyebrows furrowed, and she shook her head. "No, no, no. You don't understand. I will gladly give you the names of all the people I know, but I don't know everyone. I don't know who exactly owns the place."

Micah reached up to brush a strand of hair from Bree's face and tuck it behind her ear. "I thought you were in charge of the downtown lofts. You don't have that information?"

Bree uncrossed then recrossed her long legs. "It's complicated. See, the city needed investors so they would have enough money to renovate downtown. By selling off some of the lofts, we've earned enough money to revamp the buildings and the historical landmarks. We can also now afford to put more money into the places and events that attract the tourists. Selling off the lofts was the best way to make that money."

Blake reached for a brownie, her first one of the day. Of course, she'd had several slices of pumpkin bread, but she was pretty sure pumpkin calories didn't count around Halloween. At least that was what she was going with. "It still seems like you'd know who bought them, though, right?"

"Well, it's not that easy." Bree put some pumpkin bread on a napkin and handed it to Micah. "You see, there were ten lofts for sale, including the apartment over Sliced. We—the city—hired a management group to handle the individual sales of the properties. We wanted to make sure that one person didn't buy up all of downtown, so Ozark Management sold off the properties. The problem is that of the eight properties that have been sold so far, seven of them have the owner listed as a holding company."

"Okaaay." Blake racked her brain, trying to remember the purpose of a holding company. "Is that normal?"

"Not exactly." Bree continued to explain in between sips of coffee. "In this case, a holding company is representing an anonymous buyer. Not a big deal. That's something that happens a lot. And if it were for one property or even two? Fine, whatever."

"But not seven."

"Exactly. Seven properties and seven different holding companies? Something is definitely not kosher with that."

Micah cleared his throat. "You think one person is trying to buy up all of downtown even though different holding companies own the properties."

Bree put a hand over her full mouth as she spoke. "Could be the same person hiring different holding companies to invest in properties."

"And they were trying to go unnoticed by going through different companies?" Blake asked, wondering who on earth would have any interest in gaining that much control of their little town.

"That's my guess. That's why we froze all sales at the last council meeting until we can find out what the heck is going on and find out who the buyer or buyers actually are."

"Wait a second." Blake scooted forward in her chair. "You're still renting the properties. How can you do that if you don't own them?"

"The city owns the rights to rent the properties for two years. It's in the contract. We take care of the rental responsibilities, and we split the rent money with the owners."

It was starting to come together. "So they're a silent partner, basically."

"Basically. For now, anyway." Bree brushed her hands off. "Crap, did I just eat four pastries? This place is dangerous. Now I have to work the calories off somehow."

Micah grinned and put an arm around Bree. When he leaned over and whispered something in her ear, heat rose in Bree's cheeks.

Whoa, they were obviously way more serious than Blake had thought. She rose and picked up the empty plate from the table in between them, feeling a pang of jealousy at their easy affection. She wished she had that in her own love life. Heck, she wished she actually had a love life. "Well, thanks, Bree. I appreciate you telling—"

"Wait," Bree interrupted. "I may not be able to tell you who owns the place, but I can tell you who's renting it."

She sat up straight. The renter could be the clown... or the Phantom. "Who?"

"Do you know the head bartender at Crossbones, the really skinny girl with pink-streaked hair and the big"—she cleared her throat—"uh... ego?"

Micah snorted. "I think you mean Pepper Wright."

Visions of the pink-haired girl with the sour face filled Blake's head. "Pepper?"

Occasionally, she had gone to Crossbones for girls' nights. Most of the employees were friendly, but Pepper acted as if she would rather be anywhere other than bartending and waiting tables. Blake often wondered how the girl kept her job.

"Yeah, but I can't imagine she would have anything to do with the whole buy-up," Bree said. "No offense to the girl, but she seems concerned with way more superficial matters."

Blake continued gathering plates. "Maybe. But one thing I've learned in this town is that people have a tendency to surprise you."

Chapter Eight

"What the hell kind of a name is Pepper? That name should be reserved for dogs and strippers." Kyle tossed herself on the couch next to where Blake sat with her legs crisscrossed and her black cat, Ninja, curled up in her lap. "And I can't believe Bree told you all of this stuff first before she called me back."

Ninja poked his head up at Kyle's bounce and gave a soft little purr-growl of derision before he snuggled his head back against Blake's leg.

Blake ran her hand through Ninja's soft fur. "What can I say? I have coffee and pumpkin bread. I'm always going to win."

Kyle stuck out her tongue but couldn't hide her grin. "You are so lucky you got Mom's baking gene. I tried to make mac and cheese last night, and it turned out all congealed and black on the bottom."

"Black?" Blake giggled. "How do you burn mac and cheese?"

Kyle picked up the bottle of wine she'd set on the table and poured some into two glasses. "I blame the stove. Totally not my fault." She picked up a glass and curled her legs under her. Her blue eyes sparkled, and Blake wasn't sure if it was from the wine or something else.

Either way, she decided to take advantage of her sister's good mood and steer the conversation in the direction of the case. "Sooo... you're not going to get on my case for talking to them."

Her sister's smiled faded, and she sighed. "I just don't want you do anything dangerous. Do I still think you should mind your own business? Yes. But it's not like I can bust your chops for talking to people who come into the café."

Whew! That was relief. "Then we're on the same page. Did you go talk to Pepper after Bree filled you in?"

Kyle's eyes narrowed over the rim of her wine glass. "Not yet. Crossbones was closed today, remember? And since she hasn't moved in to the apartment over Sliced, she's still at her old place, which is about forty-five minutes from here. I'll head over to Crossbones when they open tomorrow around lunchtime."

"Ooh, I could go for a cheeseburger at Crossbones."

Kyle's wine glass clinked against the coffee table as she set it down. "Don't push it, sister."

Ninja purred as Blake absently stroked his fur. "Fine. So she hasn't moved into the apartment yet. But I wonder if she's been there."

Kyle set her wine down and picked up a chocolate-marshmallow crinkle. "What are you getting at?" Her eyes widened as she bit into the cookie. "Oh, holy crap! These are good!"

A grin tugged at Blake's lips. "Marshmallow is my winner for next month's Mystery Cup ingredient. Thumbs-up?"

"Omigod, way up!" Kyle popped the rest of the cookie in her mouth and reached for another one.

"What I was getting at with the apartment was that it was decorated, remember? I guess I thought whoever rented it was in the process of moving in."

Kyle shook her head and swallowed. "Bree said all the apartments come decorated and sparsely furnished. Pepper's not supposed to move in for a couple of weeks."

Clues and possibilities started to run through Blake's mind. She needed to find out if Pepper had been in that apartment. "So if Pepper hasn't moved in, then why was there a matchbook from Crossbones in the bathroom?" After talking to Bree, she had assumed the matchbook came from Pepper. But if it hadn't, maybe it had come from the killer. Or maybe Pepper *was* the killer. She was tall and thin.

Closing her eyes, Blake tried to think back and remember how tall the clown had been.

"I can hear the wheels turning, Blake. Calm down. If Pepper has been in that apartment, she could have easily dropped a matchbook. But I will find out. I don't have to tell you to stay away from her, do I?"

"Of course not." Because it wouldn't really do any good anyway, considering Blake was craving a cheeseburger from Crossbones. And if she happened to talk to Pepper when she was there... well, that wasn't against the law.

"Good. Now, enough talk about this. You said you were going trick-or-treating with the twins on Saturday?"

She nodded, excited about spending Halloween with her energetic niece and nephew, although she was a little worried about the thought of Emma on sugar overload. "Ryan's on call on Saturday night, and Rachel didn't really want to take the kids trick-or-treating by herself. Their neighborhood's so crowded on Halloween, she's afraid of one of them taking off and getting lost in the crowd. That's where I come in. I'm on Aiden duty."

"Divide and conquer." Kyle reached for another cookie. "Cheers to that. Plus, I'm sure you're happy that you get to dress up again. Coffee Goddess?"

"Nah." She shoved down the disappointment that rose. Sean had complimented her on her costume, and he'd seemed to enjoy running his fingers through the white feathers around her neck, but it hadn't gotten him any closer to making a move. "I might do something simple. I haven't decided what yet, though. Are you working?"

"Oh, yeah." Kyle reached over to ruffle Ninja's head, but he pulled back and sniffed her hand before leaning forward once she'd deemed her worthy of petting him. "It's all hands on deck on Halloween every year. You know, this time of year always attracts the tourists who have a real taste for the macabre. Mr. Manson said the hotel's been booked solid for months. Just one more reason I want to get this case wrapped up ASAP. The last thing we need is someone with ill intentions running around when we have an increase in tourists."

"I know the business owners have been enjoying the extra traffic. Sean sold all of the first edition Agatha Christie books he had, and those were expensive! Mrs. Russell has a huge display set up with pictures and news clippings from the Red Rose Murders, and Mr. Jeffries has his ghost tour bus packed full every night, going up and down Main Street."

Kyle snorted. "Yeah, I took his tour just out of curiosity. You know he totally plays up the fact that there was a murder in your café last spring, right?"

Blake's stomach dropped. "He does not."

"Sis, haven't you wondered why you have tourists coming out of the woodwork?"

"Well, crap. I thought it was because I had the best coffee in the Midwest. Or maybe it's the cookies." Although the ghost-murder tour would explain why Mystery Cup had been so busy lately. Halloween was nearly the busiest time of year anyway due to all the tourists coming to town with their Red Rose Murder curiosity. The ghost tour would push even more her way.

"You know you could make him stop. You could file an injunction. But I have a feeling you don't want to lose the increase in business, right?"

Blake rested her head back against the sofa. "Crap. It's a blessing and a curse."

Laughing, Kyle stood and picked up the empty plate. "I'm going to get more, and then we're starting the movie. I was promised Hitchcock, remember? When I get back, no more talk. All I want is wine, cookies, and Janet Leigh screaming in the shower. I'm out of town for weapons training for a few days, and this is the last chance I have to relax before I have to leave tomorrow afternoon."

She padded off to the kitchen as Blake looked down at the cat purring in her lap. "Today's been full of clues, Ninja. But I still don't know who the heck was in that apartment. Do you think I can get any information out of Pepper Wright?"

Ninja blinked up at her with big green eyes and flicked his long tail.

"You're right." Blake lifted him enough so she could drop a kiss on his head. "There's only one way to find out."

TREPIDATION RAN THROUGH Blake as she sat in her Honda Civic outside of Crossbones. The big blue building looked like any bar and grill from the outside. Large tinted windows didn't give anything away. Big posters advertising Bud Light were tacked on the painted-brick walls, and an unlit *Open* sign hung by the front door. The place didn't open for another twenty minutes, but Blake had already watched a slew of employees go in. Still, she had yet to see Pepper Wright.

Kyle had been ordered by Chief Raimy to leave that morning for shooter training or whatever in St. Louis—earlier than expected—so she wouldn't get the chance to interview Pepper until she returned at the end of the week. But Blake couldn't wait that long. If there was a killer on the loose, they could strike again. She didn't want to take the chance of that happening if she could uncover information that could lead them to the killer.

She leaned back in her seat and admired the orange and yellow leaves on the trees that swayed in the fall breeze. A lone orange leaf broke free of its branch and floated down, landing on the hood of Blake's car. She was so lost in her own world, thinking about fall, that she almost missed the thin girl with the cotton-candy-colored hair swinging through the door of Crossbones.

That's her. Blake smoothed back the dark-blond hair that had slipped out of her ponytail. *It's now or never.* She stepped out of her car into the cool midmorning fall air and closed the door. The crisp air was tinged with the smell of grease from the bar and grill's lunch preparations. Blake pulled her jacket tighter around herself and made her way across the lot and through the door, grateful that none of the waitstaff had decided to lock it behind them.

When she walked in, she stepped up to the bar, where a dark-haired man had his back to her. Pepper flipped up a section of the counter, walked behind the big circular bar, and hung her keys on a hook above a shelf of what looked like flavored vodkas. The dark-haired man turned and snagged Pepper's belt loop. The girl giggled as the man yanked her close to him and kissed her deeply.

Whoa. Uh, okay. If that's how you greet your employees these days, my management skills are seriously lacking.

When the kiss ended, Pepper pulled back from the man and spotted Blake. Her face immediately tightened. "What are you doing here? We're not open yet. You shouldn't be in here."

The dark-haired man turned around, and a wave of hair fell over his forehead as his face lit up in a smile. "Blake Harper. That's your name, right? You own the coffee shop, the good one. I'm Whit, remember? We met at your party."

On the night of the party, their meeting had been brief, so she hadn't received the full power of that smile. She also hadn't noticed just how much Whit looked like his father with his kind gray eyes and dark hair, except his wasn't peppered with silver like his dad's. "Oh yeah, Mr. Hamilton's son. I didn't realize you worked here. I thought your dad said something about you offering Wilton your business expertise?"

Pepper sniffed as she walked up to stand across the bar from Blake. "He doesn't just work here. He bought the place. Like I said, we're closed. Come back later."

As Blake looked at the sneer on Pepper's face, she remembered what her mother used to tell her when she'd made that face as a teen. *"Blake Mildred, you'd better fix your face, or I'll fix it for you."* She had to bite her tongue from saying the same thing to Pepper.

Whit frowned. "There's no need to be rude, Ms. Wright. Blake's a friend. She's welcome to hang out until we open."

Ms. Wright? Interesting that he's acting as though he didn't just have his tongue halfway down Pepper's throat.

He turned his warm brown eyes on her. "The kitchen's not open yet, though, but I can get you a cup of coffee or something." The way he leaned forward as he spoke to her made her wonder if he treated all the customers that way or if he was just a classic flirt. Either way, his smile didn't make her insides go all melty like Sean's or Adam's.

Pepper pinched her lips in a firm line and crossed her arms over her medically enhanced chest as she glared at Blake. It was understandable that people described her as having a less-than-stellar attitude.

"Uh, no, thanks, I've probably had enough coffee for one morning." She smiled at Whit. "I actually came in to talk to Pepper."

He raised an eyebrow as he turned his curious gaze to the girl next to him.

The girl flicked her pink hair over her shoulder. "Me? About what? I don't have anything to talk to you about."

"Well, I was just talking to Bree Nelson yesterday, and she tells me you rented the apartment above Sliced."

Pepper narrowed her eyes. "Yeah," she said slowly, "So?"

It was not going well. Blake needed to think of something quickly to get the girl to warm up to her, or she wasn't going to find out any useful information. "I came to welcome you to the neighborhood, and uh"—she opened her purse and dug through it until she found a coupon then slapped it on the bar—"offer you a coupon for a free handcrafted beverage. Come on over anytime."

The bartender's eyes flicked back and forth between Blake and the coupon then back to Blake. "You came all the way down here to give me a coupon for free coffee?" She put her manicured fingers on the coupon and slid it back across the bar toward Blake. "I'm not stupid, Blake. I hear the rumors around town, even the crazy one about you thinking you witnessed a murder in my apartment by a guy dressed as Ghost Face or something. Thanks for that bit of gossip, by the way. The last thing I need is to be a stop on Mr. Jeffries's ghost tour."

Welcome to the club. "It's not gossip," Blake argued, although she knew how fast rumors spread through the grapevine in small towns. It didn't surprise her a bit that word had gotten around.

Whit stopped drying the glass he'd been rubbing with a dishcloth as he watched their exchange. "Wait a second. What? You witnessed a murder?"

"No, she didn't," Pepper answered. "I heard she's losing it, that she's cracked up after she got attacked by a killer last spring."

Blake clenched her jaw, telling herself not to lose her cool. "I just wanted to ask if you've been to the apartment yet. Maybe you came in to decorate or something?"

Pepper shook her head. "Not that it's any of your business, but no. I've only seen the plans. I picked up the keys a couple of days ago, but I don't have my walk-through for a few days."

That didn't make a whole lot of sense. No one rented a place sight unseen. Luckily, she didn't have to ask that question because Whit's curiosity had been piqued.

"You rented a place you've never even seen?" he asked Pepper. "Do you really think that's a good idea?"

Pepper rolled her eyes and uncrossed her arms to perch her hands on her pointy hips. "I've seen the blueprints. The lofts were starting to go, and I wanted to grab one before they were gone. Most of them are all open with exposed brick, but I liked the one above Sliced because it had so much storage space. I have a lot of stuff, you know."

"Storage space?" Now Blake was confused. Maybe Pepper was lying to try to throw her off. "I'm sorry, Pepper, but I don't understand. I've been in the apartment. There's no storage space in there. It just has the one closet."

"And the attic. Duh," Pepper exclaimed, looking at Blake as if she were a moron.

"Attic?" Whit set the glass on the bar, and his brows drew together. "I was thinking of renting one of the lofts. The one I looked at didn't have an attic."

"Yeah, that's why I chose the one above Sliced. Todd pointed me in that direction when I went into Ozark Management to meet with a real estate agent."

Red flags shot up in Blake's head so fast that she nearly jolted in her seat. "Todd? Todd Lang? Sabrina's husband? I mean ex-husband?"

"Yeah, I ran into him the day I went in. He was on his way out, and we talked for a little bit. When I told him I was looking for storage space, he said the apartment over Sliced was the only one with an attic, so I snatched it up. I haven't seen the attic, but I know you get to it in the closet. There's supposed to be pull-down stairs."

Blake's mind raced to try to fit Todd into the existing puzzle. "How would Todd have known that? And what was he doing at Ozark Management?" *And how the actual crap did I miss seeing a freaking attic?*

"Who cares? Look, are we done? I'm not your Ghost Face. I haven't even dropped off my first month's deposit yet. And I have work to do." Before waiting for Blake to respond, Pepper lifted a section of the wooden bar top so she could get out from behind the bar and stalked off, sashaying her skinny hips. She could give Sabrina a run for her money.

"Sorry about that," Whit said. "We've been having some issues with Pepper's attitude. She needs to be friendlier with the customers. I'm not sure how to get that through to her." He picked his dish towel back up and began to wipe down the bar. "Was someone really killed in that apartment?"

"Well, that's what I'm trying to find out."

Whit gave her a disarming smile. "I heard you were kind of an amateur sleuth. Let me know if I can help. I love a good mystery."

Blake returned his smile. "Thanks, but right now, I think I need to pay a visit to Todd Lang." But her curiosity couldn't hold out that long. First, she had to get a look at that attic.

Chapter Nine

"Kyle! Gah, why don't you ever answer the phone?" Blake tossed her phone onto the passenger seat and swung into the alley behind Mystery Cup. She screeched to a halt behind the café and threw the car into Park.

A slew of possibilities ran through her mind. Todd Lang was involved, and that man seemed to attract trouble. His name had popped up all over the place last spring when there were murders in town, and here it was happening again. It certainly didn't seem like much of a stretch to believe that Todd Lang could be right smack in the middle of something unsavory. It could have been a coincidence that he was at the real-estate office when Pepper had gone in, and he was just being nice to her. But Blake doubted it was that simple. She was familiar with his history involving drugs and infidelity, so it didn't really seem like much of a stretch. Plus, Pepper seemed just like his type.

First things first. Before she labeled him "Ghost Face" as Pepper had put it, she needed to find out what he had to do with Ozark Management and whether he was involved in the downtown properties.

Questioning Todd was the second thing on her to-do list. First was getting a look at the attic in Pepper's apartment.

Blake was so preoccupied that when she shoved the back kitchen door open, she nearly slammed right into Rachel, who squealed in surprise.

"Rach!" Blake's hand flew to her chest to calm her rapid heartbeat. "What are you doing standing right in front of the door?"

"Jeez, Blake. Derek just made his weekly delivery." Rachel gestured to the large bags of Death Wish Mountain coffee beans that were stacked on the floor next to the door. Her eyes traveled over Blake from top to bottom. "What is up with you? Your eyes look a little wild."

"The apartment across the street." Blake lowered her voice. "Rach, I think the body could still be there. That is, if the killer hasn't gone back in and moved it out."

Her sister-in-law drew back and looked at her as if she had just sprouted a second head. "What on earth are you talking about?" She raised a brow. "Have you been putting Kahlua in your coffee again?"

"Of course not," Blake said in a defensive tone. "I've only done that once... okay, twice. But I didn't do it this morning."

Rachel eyed her speculatively. "You told me yourself that you and Sean looked through the apartment. It's not that big. I'm pretty sure you would have noticed a body."

The oven buzzed, and Blake practically leapt out of her skin.

"*Dios mio,* calm down. You're so jumpy." Rachel reached for the oven mitts. "Sit down. I just made a fresh batch of cookies." When she opened the oven door, the smell of chocolate and happiness wafted over Blake.

She immediately felt her blood pressure lower a couple of notches. "I swear there's no better aromatherapy than cookies."

Rachel giggled. "Tell me about it. We should start a cookie spa." Her expression was sincere as she bounced on her heels. "Ooh, seriously. We could charge people to sit in the kitchen while we bake. How much do you think people would pay for that?"

Blake grinned. "I don't know, but that's definitely a thought."

After Rachel put the trays on cooling racks, she sat on the stool next to Blake and rested her elbows on the island. "Okay, talk. What has you so sure that the body's still there?"

"Well, I went to Crossbones and talked to Pepper."

"You what!" Rachel's judgy tone made Blake think she was trying to impersonate Kyle. "Are you crazy? Your sister is going to flip!"

"I know, I know. Just listen. Pepper said that the reason she chose that apartment was because it has so much storage space. An attic! She said the access is in the closet."

Rachel's forehead crinkled in confusion. "But you looked in the closet. You said it was empty."

"But I didn't look up." She pointed her finger skyward. "The closet was dark. Sean and I just peeked inside quickly. Don't you see? That's it! No one has ever seen a body removed from that apartment because it's still there. In the attic!" It was so obvious to her. *Why isn't it obvious to everyone else?*

"That's a bit of a stretch, Blake. Just because there's an attic doesn't mean—where are you going?"

Blake had hopped off the stool and was heading toward the front of the café. "Where do you think I'm going? Across the street to see if I can get the key from Micah and check the attic."

"Whoa, Batman! Hold on." Rachel slid off her seat and practically jumped in front of Blake to block her from the door. "Going to talk to Pepper was one thing, but you cannot go over there searching for corpses. You need to call Kyle."

"Kyle is at active-shooter training in St. Louis. She won't be back for two days."

"Then call Chief Raimy," Rachel urged. "I know it's a novel idea, but there are other police officers in this town besides Kyle and Jason, you know."

She gave a huff of exasperation. "Rach, you know I am Chief Raimy's least favorite person. After I sort of did my own investigation last spring, he thinks I'm a nosy busybody."

Rachel bobbled her head in semi-agreement.

"Rach!"

"Oh, I'm kidding. You're not a busybody. Nosy, maybe... okay, definitely. But anyway, you're missing my point. In case you were unclear on everyone's jobs around here, let me give you a rundown. Ryan is a doctor. Kyle is a police detective. And you"—she jabbed a finger in Blake's chest—"own a café. Now, which one do you think should be investigating dead bodies?" She lowered her voice. "I'll give you a hint. It's not you."

"Oh, shut it." Blake took a step back and crossed her arms tightly over her chest. "You're telling me you're not the least bit curious?"

"Of course I am. But Blake, I'm not going to put my life on the line to investigate a possible murder."

Blake fisted her hands in her hair. "Omigod! If one more person says 'possible' or 'alleged,' I might scream. And don't you think you're being just a tad melodramatic? I just want to go ask Micah for a key. What do you think's going to happen? The apartment is right above a restaurant that is currently packed with customers. I can take the big rolling pin if it would make you feel better."

Rachel let out an exasperated sigh. "No, but I'm going with you."

"What? No. Who's going to watch the place?"

"I think Giselle and Eli can handle it for fifteen minutes." She brushed past Blake. "We just have to yank Giselle away from Merryfield, who's out there gulping down an energy drink."

"Oh boy." Blake turned to follow her sister-in-law through the swinging door.

Sure enough, Giselle was leaning over with her elbows propped on the counter as Orlando talked to her, his hands gesturing animatedly. His muscle shirt showed off his bulging biceps, which her barista was openly ogling.

"Blake!" Orlando said in his thick Colombian accent. "I was just telling Giselle about a new self-defense class I'm starting at Buttkick. Kyle and Jason are leading the first few classes. Giselle's going to help me run through a few of the moves they'll be teaching. She's the perfect guinea pig since she loves to work out. You say spin class is your specialty, right?" he asked, looking back at Giselle.

Blake couldn't hide her confusion. "Spin class? Giselle, since when do you—"

"I love spin classes." Giselle turned to look at Blake with a silent plea in her wide eyes. "Remember? I told you."

"Uh, right. Of course, I remember."

Orlando's white teeth gleamed as he smiled. "You and Sean should join us for the self-defense class. You know a workout makes for a great date." He frowned. "Or... sorry. Is it you and Adam?"

Oh, sweet cheese, talk of her love life had even made it to the gym. She certainly didn't think either man seeing her red-faced and sweating at the gym would help her chances of romance.

Rachel unsuccessfully stifled a giggle. "The verdict's still out on that one."

Blake stuck out her tongue. "Very funny. Giselle, I was wondering if you could watch the shop while Rach and I run across the street?"

"Sure," she said dreamily without looking away from Orlando.

Blake and Rachel exchanged an amused glance. "Eli, how about you?" She looked over to where Eli was pulling an espresso shot, and she was very surprised to see a scowl on his usually easygoing face.

"What?" He flicked his gaze to Orlando and narrowed his eyes. "Yeah, sure."

Rachel's eyes widened, and she looked at Blake and mouthed, "Oh my God!"

Blake would have to put the Eli-Giselle drama on hold. "Okay, guys, we'll be right back."

She and Rachel hustled across the street and swung open the door of Sliced. Tables were full, and the waitstaff was bustling with the lunch crowd. They made their way to the counter but did not see Micah's tousled red hair anywhere.

"Hey, Silas," she said to the tall young man at the register. "Is Micah around?"

His face fell a little as he leaned forward and lowered his voice. "Uh, no. He went to Jeff City."

"Oh crap." Blake's face dropped. "It's the last Tuesday of the month. Visitation at the prison."

"Ohhh." Rachel frowned. "I totally forgot."

Micah went every month for visitation. He hadn't missed a Tuesday yet. Still, sadness settled in the pit of her stomach. She knew that couldn't be easy for him.

"Ahem." The person behind them in line cleared his throat, obviously impatient.

Rachel tugged on her arm. "Blake, why don't we just go?"

"Silas." Blake leaned forward, ignoring her sister-in-law. "I was wondering if we could borrow the key to upstairs. Micah let me look around up there the other day, and I realized there was someplace I forgot to look."

"Sorry, Blake. I'd love to 'assist in your investigation.'" He smiled as he made air quotes with his fingers. "But I can't help you."

"Silas, come on. I just need up there for a second. Please. I'll bring the keys right back."

He shook his head. "No, you don't understand. I would help you if I could, but I don't have the keys to the place. Micah keeps them on him. They're on his big key ring."

"Shoot." That meant she was out of luck until Micah got back that evening. "Thanks, Silas." She backed away from the counter.

"I'll tell Micah to give you a holler when he gets back," he called after them.

They walked to the door, and Rachel opened it for Blake. "Thwarted, Batman."

"Ha-ha." Once on the sidewalk, Blake looked up at the window.

Rachel tugged on her arm again. "I don't want you looking for too long. Next thing I know, you'll be busting the door down."

"Oh come on, I wouldn't go that far." Besides, she could totally get arrested if she tried that. She turned to walk across the street and glanced in Macabre Reads, where Sean was putting books on a display in the front window. When he spotted her, he gave her a wide smile, making her heart rate speed up.

Rachel laughed. "Wow, I've never seen you blush that fast," she said as they reached the sidewalk.

"Oh, hush." She waved at Sean. But she knew it was true. She could feel the heat in her cheeks, a common reaction when she saw Sean Larson. Maybe after the Halloween rush was over, she would work up the nerve to ask him out on a real date.

As soon as she walked through the door of Mystery Cup, she was greeted by the smiling face of Richard Hamilton. "Hey, Mr. Hamilton, how goes things at the chamber of commerce?"

"Blake, I'm so glad I caught you. I wanted to make sure you're going to be here Friday night."

"For Trick or Treat Down the Street? Absolutely."

"What's Trick or Treat Down the Street?" asked Orlando, who was sitting at a table near the door.

"Oh, it's so awesome," Rachel said excitedly. "All the businesses are open the night before Halloween, and they pass out candy to the kids. It's a way to ensure a safe environment for your kids to go trick-or-treating. Aiden and Emma love it!"

Mr. Hamilton clapped his hands together. "Yes. Last year, it was a huge success. I think we had every business on Main Street participating. Orlando, you were going to be my next stop. I was hoping you would participate this year as well."

"I would love to." Excitement shone in Orlando's eyes. "I know everyone else will be passing out candy, but I would be happy to provide the kids with a healthier option. We sell carrots in individual bags at the snack bar at Buttkick. I think something like that would be perfect."

Blake exchanged a concerned glance with Mr. Hamilton, and Rachel made a face and backed up.

Orlando's eyes flitted among them. "What?"

Mr. Hamilton offered him a kind smile. "My boy, I know you mean well, but uh... well—"

Rachel interrupted. "Last year, when Dr. Stinnett handed out toothbrushes at the dentist's office, she got egged." When his eyes widened, Rachel offered him a reassuring pat on the shoulder. "I'm just saying, unless you want to see yolk dripping down the windows of Buttkick, you really might want to consider investing in some Twix bars."

Before he could respond, the bell jingled above the door behind Blake. She immediately heard, "You! Two men aren't enough for you? You have to go after *my* boyfriend?"

Fully expecting to see Sabrina—as that was the only person whose screech was usually so shrill—she turned around and was surprised to discover Elaine Page looking back at her.

The buzz of voices in the café died away as all eyes turned to them.

"Elaine?" Blake glanced around at all the people staring at them. "What's wrong? Are you here for book club?"

The woman flicked her auburn hair out of her face. "I just came from Crossbones. Pepper informed me of your little visit. She said you went down there to give her a coupon. That's a pretty lame excuse, don't you think? Everyone knows the real reason you went down there, Blake." Elaine's flaming cheeks nearly matched the crimson pantsuit she was wearing.

Blake backed up a step, a little scared that steam was going to start coming out of Elaine's ears but having no idea why.

Rachel raised her hand as though she were in school. "I know I'm curious what you think the real reason is."

The tone in Rachel's voice hinted that she was trying not to laugh, and Blake glanced at her sister-in-law, hoping Rachel got the message not to try to rev things up.

"Whit Hamilton. That's what you were doing there." Elaine's voice had Blake swinging back around.

If the woman thought she was interested in Whit, she was sorely mistaken. The guy had way too much of a pretty boy vibe going on for her. Plus, he'd seemed to be involved with Pepper.

Mr. Hamilton appeared very confused. "You went to see Whitley?" The man's pocket began to ring, and he fished his phone out of his pocket. "Speak of the devil," he mumbled as he looked at the display. Turning his back, he answered the phone.

At that moment, the bell above the door jingled again, and in walked Jax Talon and Penny Driver. They stopped as soon as they walked in the door, surveying the atmosphere. Jax was their resident true-crime writer, and his eyes gleamed as he assessed the situation. He looked as if he'd just found the subject for a new book.

Some customers had gone back to their normal conversations, but others still had their ears trained on the scene playing out before them.

Jax let out a low whistle. "Talk about cutting the tension with a machete. What the heck?"

Elaine's fiery gaze landed on Jax. "I'll tell you what the heck. You know I've been dating Whit Hamilton, and Blake"—she jabbed a finger in Blake's direction—"is trying to stake a claim on him."

She's dating Whit? Boy, is she in for an unwelcome surprise!

Blake looked at Penny Driver in bewilderment. The older woman was in the book club with Elaine. Maybe she could talk sense into her. Penny nodded in unspoken understanding, but before she could speak, a loud laugh came out of Jax. Then another. Then he was laughing so hard, he was dabbing his eyes. "Elaine, I knew you were paranoid, but I didn't think you were crazy."

Elaine fisted her hands at her sides, and her eyes spat fire. Blake was a little concerned that her final thread of sanity would snap at any moment. And if that happened, God help Jax. The man had no filter.

He reached underneath his thick-rimmed glasses to dab at his eyes. "Blake has eyes for two people, and neither one of them is Whit Hamilton. Besides, rumor has it that boy has given more rides than Amtrak. If you have a problem, then it should be with him, certainly not Blake."

Blake let out a little gasp. Jax obviously hadn't seen Mr. Hamilton. She cleared her throat loudly and jerked her head at the older man, who was putting his phone back in his pocket as he turned to face them. When Jax noticed Mr. Hamilton standing next to her, the laughter died on his lips. "Uh, no offense, Mr. Hamilton. I didn't mean... uh..."

Mr. Hamilton held up his hands and backed up a step. "No offense taken. What Whitley does is his business. But I thought he was dating that cute little waitress at Crossbones."

Blake grimaced and prepared for Elaine's oncoming explosion. Everyone else's eyes widened as they looked from Elaine to Mr. Hamilton and back again.

Elaine's jaw clenched, and she emitted what could only be described as a low growl. "Pepper? That's not true! He's dating me. We've been—" She clamped her heavily glossed lips together, and a muscle flexed in her jaw. Everyone standing around Elaine held their breath as she stood seething for a moment. Then without another word, she turned on her pointy high heel, flipped her dark-auburn hair, and walked out of the café, taking the tension with her.

A collective exhale resounded through the room.

"People don't need TV in this town. They just need to come to Mystery Cup for entertainment." Jax laughed at his own joke.

Blake walked back over to the counter, slowly shaking her head. "I just don't know what gave her the idea that I was interested in Whit. Wait, you don't think she's going to come back and start more trouble, do you?"

"Nah, she's paranoid," said Giselle, who'd been watching the whole scene from behind the counter. "You know she goes after every new guy in town. She'll get bored soon and move on. Whit's just the best prospect she's had in a while. Well, aside from Adam."

Blake was surprised by the jealousy that reared its ugly head, and she tried to squash it down. "Adam?" She hadn't seen him since the night of the party. Poor guy had been so exhausted from the double shift he'd worked, he'd had to leave the party early. They had exchanged texts back and forth since then, but she needed to call him to thank him for the flowers, if he was in fact the one who'd sent them.

Rachel swatted Giselle with the back of her hand. "Yeah, Elaine's a flirt. But Adam's not interested."

"She's right." Mr. Hamilton had finished his conversation with Jax and walked up to the register. "It's very obvious where Dr. Bryant's interests lie." He gave Blake a wide smile, and she felt heat rise in her cheeks. The older man ran his fingers through his thinning hair. "I have a good eye for these things. I can see the good doctor's interested in you, just like I can see who Whitley's interested in." He winked. "And it's not Pepper."

The sparkle in his eyes made Blake laugh. "You sure about that? I saw them kissing."

Mr. Hamilton shrugged. "He did go on a couple of dates with the girl, but he never brought her back to the house. He's staying with me until he can get a place of his own, but he's not much on bringing any women home. I don't think he wants to advertise that he moved back in with his dad. Not that I would mind... unless it's Elaine Page. That woman needs to be taken down a couple of pegs if you ask me. Besides, she wouldn't be my pick for Whitley. Anyway, I hope he was able to help you with whatever you needed."

"Oh, I actually didn't go in to see him."

Rachel started pulling a shot of espresso. "She needed to ask Pepper about her new apartment, to see if she knew anything about a clown and the Phant—ow!" She lifted the foot Blake had just kicked.

Not that it did much good. Everyone probably knew what she had seen, but she didn't need Rachel and her lovable big mouth spreading it any more. If people thought she was nuts, it could hurt her business. Plus, she didn't want the killer knowing just how interested she was in this investigation. Even though everyone in the café had gone back to their own conversations, she was sure they all had an ear open.

"You mean that's true?" Mr. Hamilton's eyes widened. "I thought that was just part of the rumor mill."

Blake waved him off with a smile. "Well, I do have an overactive imagination, so who knows what I actually saw."

Penny and Jax stepped up to the counter. "Can we get our usuals, Blake?" Penny asked.

She glanced at the clock. She was really hoping to get over to Café Muerte and see if Todd Lang was there. But she supposed that could wait for her to make a couple cups of coffee.

"Well, I should go." Mr. Hamilton reached over to pat Blake's hand. "I have a meeting at the office. As always, my dear, it's been entertaining."

Everyone waved goodbye to Mr. Hamilton as he left.

Blake pointed to Jax. "Upside-down caramel macchiato." And then she pointed to Penny. "Half-caf Americano." They both nodded, and Blake set to work. "Is today book club?"

Jax shook his head. "Nope. I have a book signing next door."

"And I'm his assistant," Penny said proudly. The woman tucked a silver strand of hair behind her ear, which sent the large earring she wore swinging back and forth.

"Ah, I forgot about that." Jax's most recent book revisited the Red Rose Murders. Almost fifty years ago, their small town had become famous when twelve women had been strangled, and a red rose had been left with each of the bodies. The killer had never been caught. Nearly half a century later, speculation about the case still ran wild. Jax had timed his book release perfectly since it was coming up on the fiftieth anniversary of the murders. "Maybe I can persuade you to sign my copy."

Jax smiled. "You've read it?"

"Of course I have." She put a lid on Penny's coffee and slid it across the counter. "It scared the bejeezus out of me. Your theory of the Red Rose Killer being alive after all these years? That doesn't help me sleep at night, Jax."

She wouldn't have thought it possible that the killer could still be alive, but the evidence Jax had presented in his book made her think twice.

He grinned. "I think the biggest concern right now is dealing with all the practical jokers around here. I'm guessing you got hit by them too."

She blinked at him. "What do you mean?"

He nodded at the roses she'd received that were being displayed atop the pastry case. "Somebody's been sending roses to female business owners anonymously. You know, just like the Red Rose Killer did. At least they always assumed he was the one sending the roses since half the women who got them ended up dead."

Blake's heartbeat stuttered. Maybe those roses weren't from Adam.

Jax's face fell. "I'm sorry. I didn't mean... Uh, I'm sure yours are from one of your two hot men." He waggled his eyebrows.

Rachel was pouring steamed milk into a cup but paused to glance up at Blake with a concerned look.

Even though a thread of unease went through her, Blake pasted on a smile. "Well, if someone's idea of a practical joke is to send me a dozen roses, I'll take it." But her mind ran rampant. *Could this be a threat from the clown killer? No, don't do that, Blake. Don't jump to conclusions.* She would see if Adam sent her roses and go from there.

Jax took the cup of coffee Rachel handed him. "I better go. I gotta get set up at Book Hottie McBookstore."

Blake laughed. Sean was never going to live down the nickname Book Hottie. She waved goodbye to Jax and Penny then turned and pushed through the kitchen door. She grabbed her purse from where it hung on a hook. She needed to get back to her agenda of speaking with Todd Lang and figuring out what his connection was to the loft across the street. She wasn't sure where he was living at the moment, but he owned half of Café Muerte, so that was a good place to start.

Rachel followed her into the kitchen. "Where are you going?"

"What? This is when we hit our afternoon lull. I thought it was a good time to take a break." She smiled at her sister-in-law. "And I could go for a cup of coffee."

Rachel cocked her head. "A cup of—" She sucked in a breath. "Blake, no. Do *not* go to Café Muerte."

Blake smiled and gave her sister-in-law a wave. "Bye."

"Blake!" Rachel called after her. "Blake!"

Chapter Ten

Knock, knock, knock. Blake stood on the porch of the Langs' two-story brick Tudor and waited to see if Sabrina was going to answer her front door. Even though Todd had moved out after the divorce and into his own place, he still spent an odd amount of time at Sabrina's.

If the rumors around town weren't enough to confirm that, her sister-in-law was. Blake turned around and looked across Sabrina's sculpted hedges and manicured lawn to Ryan and Rachel's sage-green Craftsman. Probably a good thing her brother was at work, or he would be marching over to see what the heck she was doing at Sabrina's.

Just when Blake had assumed that Sabrina either wasn't home or just wasn't answering, the door opened. "What are you doing here?" came the clipped tone.

Blake almost dropped her jaw when she saw Sabrina standing in the crack of the door. The blonde's long hair was knotted on top of her head, she wore no makeup, and her eyes were puffy and swollen.

"Uh... sorry. I didn't mean to bother you. I stopped at Café Muerte, but they said—"

"I don't care. What do you want, Blake?"

Nice to know her attitude hadn't changed. She'd known Sabrina wasn't going to be thrilled to see her, but she'd thought she could suck it up if it meant talking to Todd and getting some questions answered. "I actually need to talk to Todd. They wouldn't tell me what his new address was, so I thought that maybe you could—"

"He's not there. He hasn't been home in days." Sabrina's eyes started to well up, and she backed into the house, leaving the door open.

Blake wasn't sure if that was an invitation to follow, but she figured if Sabrina wanted her to leave, she wouldn't have had any trouble slamming the door in her face. The door creaked as Blake pushed it open to let herself in. Sabrina had retreated into the elegant living room to the left of the large foyer and was sniffling into a tissue.

For as many troubles as the two of them had had, Blake didn't think she'd ever seen Sabrina so upset. "I can go. Really. I'll leave Todd a message or something." She started to back up, when Sabrina swung around.

"Just come in and ask your damn questions." Sabrina perched on a formal blue loveseat with a rich floral pattern.

Blake tentatively walked into the living room but didn't sit down. "What makes you think I have questions?"

Sabrina barked out a laugh. "I listen to the rumors. I know you think you saw a murder. Something about a clown. And your mind went right to us, didn't it? Not surprising after last spring, I guess." She sighed and leaned back against the couch. "It's easier if you just ask now then go away rather than continue to hound us. So just say what you need to."

"Okay." Blake shifted her weight from one foot to the other. "I'm trying to figure out who has access to the apartment above Sliced, and I heard Todd seemed to have information about how the apartment was laid out. I also know he was at Ozark Management the day the place was rented. So I'm trying to figure out the connection."

Sabrina looked at her hands, which were thoroughly shredding a tissue. "He looked at the place. He actually looked at a few of the lofts downtown after he..." Her voice shook, and she cleared her throat before continuing. "After he moved out."

For a moment, the façade Sabrina normally kept in place faded away, and a stark vulnerability shone on her face. She didn't look elegant or superior or put-together. She looked sad, defeated. And despite everything Sabrina had done to her, Blake felt her heart go out to the woman sitting in front of her.

"Okay, so he looked at the place, but he didn't rent it?" That would explain how he knew about the attic, but surely there was more to his involvement. When it came to Todd or Sabrina, nothing was ever that simple. "Did he end up renting one of the lofts?"

Sabrina shook her head. "He rented a bungalow over on Melrose." Something between a smile and a grimace crossed her face. "He said it had more privacy than the lofts. I guess he didn't want the whole town to see all the bimbos he paraded in and out."

Unsure of how to respond, Blake just nodded. She felt bad for intruding, especially since it looked like Todd didn't have anything to do with the downtown loft. "Sorry, Sabrina. I'll get out of your hair." She started to walk to the door, telling herself it was none of her business. But she knew Sabrina's pride. She knew that her rival wouldn't want anyone to see her look weak, even her husband.

Blake swung back to face Sabrina. "You know if you love him, you should go to him. Fight for him."

Sabrina looked up, her eyes filled with the pain of unreciprocated feelings. "He knows how I feel, Blake. He doesn't care."

She blew out a breath. "I find that hard to believe. I mean Todd has made some mistakes, but he loves you."

"Relationships aren't always sunshine and roses."

Roses. "Hey, before I forget, did you get any roses delivered to Café Muerte?" If all of the business owners were receiving flowers, maybe Sabrina had too.

Sabrina rolled her eyes. "I've barely been there lately. Besides, why would Todd send me roses?"

"No, not Todd. I—"

"Look, maybe relationships are perfect in your world, but they're not in mine. Husbands cheat, they do horrible things, and sometimes love isn't enough." Her voice shook on those last words. "I should just let him go. I shouldn't care if the Phantom hits on women more than half his age."

Blake's heart stuttered in her chest. "What did you say?"

"I said he can have all the women he wants. I shouldn't let it bother me."

"No, you said the Phantom." Blake's voice shook. "W-w-what do you mean the Phantom?"

"The Phantom of the Opera. That was Todd's costume at the Halloween party. The night he was all over that blond girl—jailbait, I'm sure."

The room seemed to spin. When Sabrina had spoken of Todd that night, she'd gestured in the direction of the snack table, where a few men had been standing. But only two of them had had their faces obscured by masks. "I thought Todd was dressed as Spider-Man?"

Sabrina's brows knitted together. "Spider-Man? Please, Todd doesn't like superheroes. What would make you think that?"

There was only one person at the party dressed up as the Phantom, and that was Silas. He had been the one hitting on Red's granddaughter, not Todd. But Blake remembered how upset Sabrina had been that night.

"Sabrina, you spoke with Todd at the party, didn't you? Are you sure he was dressed as the Phantom?"

"He was the Phantom," she said bitterly. "He came into Café Muerte before the party started. He told me he had a meeting downtown and that he would meet me at the party. Julie from Kabloom next door had come into Café Muerte and said Todd had ordered a bouquet of daisies, my favorite flowers. I was actually excited. I thought he wanted to—" She shook her head. "I don't know what I thought. I walked up to the roof the night of the party and saw him all over some girl. So I left. His stupid plan was probably just to make me jealous."

Oh God. Daisies? The scene in the loft flashed through her head, and she vividly remembered the bouquet of fresh daisies lying on the table when the clown had attacked the Phantom. Her mind spun. If Todd had had a meeting downtown a few hours before the party, the timeline worked. He could have been the one in the loft apartment that night. "And you haven't seen him or talked to him since then?"

"No, but just wait 'til I do. The gutless wonder didn't have the nerve to show up at the café yesterday. I went by his house this morning, and he hadn't picked up the mail, which usually means he's out of town on business. I don't know where he went, though. The spineless jerk won't return my calls."

The puzzle pieces started to fall into place. "Sabrina, you didn't see Todd at the party. You saw Silas. He was dressed as the Phantom. He was the one all over Lizzie Montgomery."

Confusion followed by mortification crossed Sabrina's face. She sat ramrod straight on the couch. "Blake, are you sure?"

She nodded vigorously.

Sabrina opened her mouth then closed it again. She thought for a moment before she finally spoke. "That doesn't make sense. If that wasn't him, then that means he asked me to meet him at the party and didn't show up. Why would he do that? And why hasn't he returned any of my calls?" The woman frowned, obviously trying to work things out in her head.

Blake closed her eyes briefly. She could tell Sabrina what she suspected, but she really didn't want to upset the woman more if she was wrong. "Sabrina, I have to go."

Sabrina stood up. "But—"

"I'm sorry." She ran to her car as fast as she could. Once there, she rummaged through her purse, searching for her phone. When she couldn't find it, she dumped the entire contents of her purse out on the passenger seat. She plucked the phone out of the mess and called Kyle.

When her sister's voice mail picked up, Blake's words came out in a rush. "Kyle, I know you're in training, but you have to get back here. Call me as soon as you get this." She took a deep breath and blew it out as her eyes traveled back up to Sabrina's house.

"Kyle, I know who was murdered."

Chapter Eleven

The screech of her tires made Blake's fists clench tightly on the steering wheel when her car jerked to a stop. A teenage boy looking at his phone glanced up, obviously not realizing that he should be thankful she had such good reflexes. He made his way across the street, and she continued on her way at a slower speed.

When she took a right turn to drive in front of the café so she could circle around to the alley, she almost slammed on her brakes again. At least a hundred people were lined up down the block and around the corner. Several of them had a book tucked under their arm—Jax's book.

"Holy moly." The line of people looked like a combination of locals and tourists from what she could tell, searching the faces as she drove by. *Suspects galore. But is anyone in that line capable of murder?* The front of the line disappeared into Macabre Reads, making Blake smile. Sean's bookstore was doing better than it ever had under his aunt's patronage. This was the fourth book signing Sean had done with either a mystery or true-crime writer, and it looked to be his biggest crowd yet.

She searched the cars parked in front of Sliced and was disappointed to see that Micah hadn't made an appearance. So she zipped around and parked in her usual spot behind the café, got out of the car, and hurried inside. She really needed to start parking in front. The alley had made her nervous ever since she'd been attacked there last spring. Continuing to park back there had been her way of feeling self-empowered, like Batman. She liked to believe she wasn't scared of anything, but the truth was that she was scared of way too much.

She pulled the red bib apron over her head and tied it as she moved toward the café door. The notable buzz of people made it clear that Mystery Cup was crowded, which surprised her. Usually, when Sean had a book signing, the customers didn't head to Mystery Cup until after the signing was over, but when she pushed through the door, her eyes widened at the line that reached to the front entrance.

"Hey, guys, sorry I didn't get back before the rush." She punched buttons on the second register, signing in next to the one Rachel was already running. Work would keep her grounded while she figured out what she was going to do next. She needed a plan.

Her sister-in-law glanced up at her as she ran a person's credit card. "We got busy way early. I think a lot of people are heading over here beforehand this time."

"Too chilly to wait in line outside," said the middle-aged man stepping up to the register. "Seems better to warm up with a cup of coffee. Man next door said you have a caramel-pumpkin latte that's real good."

Blake smiled. "Yes, sir. What size would you like?"

"Well, a large, of course." The man patted his rotund belly then reached up to stroke his wiry beard. "And I'm awful hungry. Why dontcha throw in one of them there coffee brownies?"

Blake punched his order in on the register. "Absolutely. And I'll tell you what? How about a piece of chocolate-chip-pumpkin bread for the road? On the house. You can munch on it while you're waiting in line."

"Well, that's mighty nice of ya. Man next door sure was right about y'all over here. Kind of funny that a town famous for some scary murders has such nice people."

"Well, thank you, sir. We like to think so. Can I get a name for your order?"

"Name's Cat. Cat Schroder."

"Well, Mr. Schroder, welcome to Wilton. And to Mystery Cup."

"Hey, I can take over your register," Giselle said. "We really need a few more loaves of pumpkin bread, and I have trouble getting it out of the pan without ripping it. If you do that, I can cover out here." Her eyes flicked to the right, where Eli was pulling espresso shots and steaming milk with the speed of a Tasmanian devil.

Blake doubted that being helpful was the only reason Giselle wanted to take over out front. "Thanks, Giselle. I'll mix up some more cookies too. It looks like those are running low." She smiled at the woman who stepped up to the register as she headed back toward the kitchen.

"Aaron," she heard Eli call out as she swung the kitchen door open. "Aaron."

"That's mine. And my name's Eric," a man's voice countered.

She didn't know why it made her giggle every time Eli called the wrong name, but it did.

The rest of the afternoon went by in a blur. Blake had made four dozen chocolate-chunk-oatmeal cookies, five loaves of pumpkin bread, and three pans of espresso brownies.

When the last customer left the shop, she locked the door behind them and turned the closed sign before she plopped down on the couch where Rachel lay, looking like she was about half passed out. She pulled out her phone to see if her sister had called back, but it displayed no new calls. Todd Lang, the loft, the knife, the clown—it had all spun around in her head the whole day.

"That. Was. Crazy," her sister-in-law said. "As many customers as we had, that had to be the biggest book signing Sean's had by far."

"Not surprising," Eli said as he came over and set two iced coffees down on the table in front of them. "Jax's book hit the *New York*

Times bestseller list last week. Talk of the Red Rose Killer still draws in the crowds. Combine that with Halloween, and cha-ching."

The roses still sitting on top of the pastry case drew her attention. "I forgot to ask—was Jax right? Are the shop owners along Main really receiving anonymous roses?"

"Just the women, and not all of them shop owners." Eli plunked down across from her. "You, Sabrina, Mrs. Russell, I think, over at the museum, and Julie down at that new flower shop, Kabloom. I mean who sends roses to a flower shop? It's weird, man, but whatever."

The trepidation on her face must have shown. "Don't let it bug you. Someone's just playing a joke," Giselle said.

"If it's a joke, it's not funny."

"Blake, I can hear the wheels turning." Rachel swatted her arm. "Come on, just forget it. It wouldn't surprise me if it was some trick by Jax's publicist to draw attention to the book signing. You should ask him about it next time he comes in. Anyway, don't worry about it. Instead, why don't you tell me if you ever found out anything with Todd Lang."

If her theory was right, then Todd Lang was dead. She really wished Kyle were back. She hadn't had the chance to check her phone until late afternoon, and she'd missed three calls from Kyle. Of course, when she'd called her sister back, it had gone to voice mail again. Weapons training meant Kyle was in the field and nowhere near her phone, so her sister's lack of response shouldn't surprise her.

Blake knew she should call the police chief or the detective filling in for Kyle, but Chief Raimy wouldn't take her seriously. That much, she knew. No, to get anyone to take her seriously, she needed hard evidence.

"Uh, I didn't run into Todd Lang, but I did talk to Sabrina." She sat up straighter on the couch, tapping her fingers on the armrest as she tried to decide exactly how much she wanted to share. She was hesitant to start more gossip, but she knew she could trust Giselle and Eli.

"And?" Giselle sat across from them in the chair next to Eli. "Come on, Blake, spit it out. I know something happened. Something happens every time you see Sabrina."

She blew out a breath. "Sabrina said she hasn't seen Todd since Sunday. He hasn't returned her calls, and he hasn't been home."

Rachel looked at her with a confused expression as if she were waiting for Blake to say something more newsworthy. "Yeah. He's a photojournalist. He travels a lot. Why is that a big deal?"

Her fingers ran along the seam of the couch until she realized her hand was shaking. "That's not all. Do you remember how upset she was the night of the party? She said it was because Todd was flirting with some girls?"

"Yeah?" Rachel made a hurry-up motion with her hand. "*Mija*, you're going to have to give me more here."

"Todd was dressed as the Phantom of the Opera," she said in a rush.

For a moment, it seemed like everyone stopped breathing. Eli leaned forward in his chair and rested his elbows on his knees. "Say again."

She took a shaky breath. "Todd was dressed as the Phantom for the Halloween party. When Sabrina came in and saw the Phantom hitting on Red's granddaughter, she freaked out because she thought it was Todd."

"But... Silas was the one hitting on Lizzie," Eli said slowly. "I don't think he left her side all night." He shook his head. "There was nobody else dressed as the Phantom at the party, Blake. I was running up and down those stairs all night. I saw everyone there."

Giselle looked back and forth among them, her eyes wide as realization seemed to hit her. "So if the person Sabrina saw was actually Silas, then..."

Rachel reached over and squeezed Blake's hand. "Then the Phantom who Blake saw being stabbed… could have been Todd."

"Holy crap!" Giselle nearly shouted.

Eli hung his head. "Todd may be a jerk, but if what you say is true, even he doesn't deserve that."

Blake focused on her sister-in-law. "Rach, I need to get back up to that apartment. I need to look in that attic."

THAT PROVED TO BE EASIER said than done. The afternoon had passed in a busy blur, and Blake still hadn't had luck getting ahold of Micah to get a key to the loft. She also hadn't figured out how to get into the apartment without getting arrested for breaking and entering.

After the four of them had cleaned up and Blake had mixed up and chilled cookie dough to bake the next morning, Eli and Giselle headed out. Blake stood in the doorway between the kitchen and the café and stared out the front window. Even with the streetlights dotting the landscape, she could still make out a few twinkling stars in the dark night sky.

Her eyes searched for the North Star so she could make a wish. Except she didn't know what to wish for. *I could wish to be right, or I could wish to be completely nuts. That way, everyone is alive and safe.* Maybe that was what she should wish for—safety.

Her eyes drifted to the dark windows above Sliced. If only she had a way to get up there. The body had to be there…

"Don't do it." Rachel's voice behind her made Blake jolt.

She turned to see her sister-in-law shrugging into a lightweight red jacket and pulling her long black ponytail out of the collar.

She put both palms up in a gesture that said, "I don't know what you're talking about."

That brought a sigh from Rachel. "I know you're trying to figure out a way to get in there. Just wait 'til Kyle gets back, or—here's a revelation—call the police. But don't go up there by yourself."

Blake glanced out the window. "I couldn't even if I wanted to. I don't have a way to get in, and there are two deadbolts on that door. So I don't really have a choice."

"Good." Rachel leaned over to give her a one-armed hug. "You should go home and take a bubble bath. Forget all this for now. I'll see you in the morning." She zipped up her jacket. "And don't forget dinner at my house tomorrow. You promised to practice Emma's zombie makeup."

Blake chuckled at the thought of her zombie-princess niece. "I'll be there. Don't worry."

"I parked out front today," Rachel said as she walked to the door. "Lock the door behind me?"

Blake followed her. "'K. See you tomorrow."

She turned the lock on the front door behind Rachel. Then Blake's eyes drifted back up to the loft. Maybe she should at least call the police and try to get someone to listen to her. It wouldn't hurt to try.

As she started to turn, a car drove up and parked in front of her café. The driver's door opened, and a redheaded mop top popped out. Micah.

A grin pulled at her lips as she unlocked the door when Micah walked up to the café. "Hey, did you get my message?" she asked, ushering him inside.

Her smile faded when she saw her friend's red-rimmed eyes. "Yeah. I just got back in town. I didn't feel like going home and being by myself, so I thought I'd just come see you in person."

Micah was a sweet man. Seeing him in pain made her heart ache. She leaned forward to give him a big hug, and he squeezed her back tightly. She wanted to ask how his visit at the prison had gone, but she didn't want to pour salt into wounds that looked to be raw.

"Where's Bree?" Maybe his girlfriend could give Micah some much-needed comfort.

He backed away and ran a hand through his messy hair. "Council meeting tonight. It's supposed to be a big one. I guess Mr. Hamilton is proposing a budget increase for next year.

She nodded, glad she wasn't planning to go to the meeting. Mr. Hamilton could be long-winded for sure. Plus, she didn't think there was any way she could focus enough to listen to the council go over numbers for two hours.

"Uh, so, I got a message from Silas." Micah dug in his pocket and pulled out a large key ring. "He said you wanted to get back up in the loft."

Her breath caught as the key swung in front of her face. "The key..." She considered telling him her theory, but when she looked at his troubled expression, she decided she really didn't want to upset him more. She also didn't know if Micah would just be one more person to try to talk her out of her plan. "Yeah. I thought I looked at everything, but I didn't realize there was an attic until someone mentioned it."

Micah nodded, slipping a key off the key ring. "Yeah, in the closet. It's a pull-down. Great for storage."

He handed her the key. "Anyway, if you want to look around, just make sure you do it soon. I know the new tenant moves in next week, then I won't have access anymore."

Her hand closed around the key in a tight grip. Although she was anxious to get over there, she didn't feel like she could kick Micah out the door. "Thanks. Do you want to come in?" She motioned toward the kitchen. "Have some coffee?"

Red curls bobbled as he shook his head. "Nah, I think I'll go wait on Bree. Maybe she'll finish early."

"Okay. Oh! Just a second. I have something I want you to try."
She hustled back into the kitchen and grabbed a pastry bag then
filled it with a dozen cookies. She came back out and handed the bag
to Micah. "I'm trying a new recipe for next month. I wanted to get
your opinion."

He opened the bag and breathed deeply. "Mmm, chocolate and
marshmallow." Then he did crack a smile. "Thanks. These smell deli-
cious."

She smiled back. "Well, enjoy. You can give me a critique tomorrow." She reached over to give Micah one more hug before he walked
out the door.

Before she shut the door, he turned and looked at her. "Blake,
one more thing. I... uh..." His eyes welled, and Blake held up a hand
to stop his words.

After every visit with his sister, he felt the need to take on the
guilt that she didn't seem to feel. "If you are about to apologize one
more time for Molly, I'll take your cookies away."

When his eyes widened, she said, "I mean it, Micah. You're not
her. You're a good man. A kind man. Whatever she did is not on
you. You don't have to apologize to me every month, okay? You're
my friend, and I love you. I sure as heck don't hold you responsible
for anything she did." When he looked like he was tearing up again,
she continued. "Just like you don't hold me responsible for the choic-
es Kyle makes, which is a good thing because I really wouldn't want
to be held accountable for the music she listens to." She grimaced. "I
mean, honestly, who's ever heard of country rap?"

He chuckled and dabbed at his eyes. With a quick nod, he leaned
in and embraced her quickly but firmly. Then without a word, he
continued to his car and waved at Blake as she locked the door behind him.

Once he'd driven away, Blake looked down at the key in her
palm. She leaned her back against the front door as she flipped the

key over again and again, thinking. She wanted to go by the book. Taking things in her own hands before had not gone well, and she really didn't want to make the same mistake twice. She refused to put herself in danger again, if for no other reason than Rachel would kick her ass.

"Maybe I could actually get the police to listen this time." The key rested heavily in her hand as she walked back toward the kitchen. A cordless phone lay on her desk, next to her computer. It wouldn't hurt to call and ask someone to look at the apartment.

Blake dialed with one hand as she fiddled with the key in her other hand, tracing its ridges with her thumb.

"Wilton Police Department," a male voice answered.

"Um, hi. This is Blake Harper. I was wondering if I could—"

"Blake? Hey, this is Officer Thornhill." When she didn't respond, he said, "Cary Thornhill."

A light bulb went on in her head. "Cary! I didn't know you were back in Wilton. I thought you were working in Kansas City now." Cary had been in her class in high school. Not only that, but he'd been best friends with Jeremy, her boyfriend at the time. Even though Jeremy had turned out to be a world-class jerk, Cary had always seemed pleasant enough.

"I just moved back a couple months ago. You know, to be closer to family. Look, if you're trying to find Kyle, she's actually out until Thursday."

"Yeah. No, I know. Uh, look, Cary, I was actually wondering if I could get someone to come down here to the café and check something out for me."

"At Mystery Cup? Is everything okay there?"

"Yeah, but I need someone to look through the apartment across the street. The one above Sliced. I think there might be... someone inside." No way would the cops come if she said, *Hey, I know you already think I'm nuts, but I'm pretty sure there's a body in the attic.*

There was a long pause. "Does this have something to do with the alleged murder you witnessed the other night?" he finally asked. "I thought officers already went through that place."

Her fingers clenched around the key at the word "alleged." If her name had been Hercule Poirot, people would have believed her. They wouldn't question her then. "They did, but I have some new information."

"Okay. Um, can I put you on hold a second?"

"Sure. Thanks, Cary."

Generic hold music blasted in her ear, complete with a deep voice that periodically announced her estimated wait time.

After a couple of minutes, a new voice came on the line. "This is Chief Raimy."

Crap, crap, double crap! She tried to sound as pleasant as she could possibly muster. "This is Blake Harper."

"What can I do for you? Officer Thornhill said you have new information for me about the loft above Sliced."

"Yes, sir, I do." She took a deep breath. *Here goes.* "Sir, I have reason to believe the person who was murdered is still in the apartment. You see, there's an attic—"

"Miss Harper, detectives already searched that apartment, did they not?" His annoyed voice was clipped, which set her on edge.

"They did, but—"

"But nothing." The chief's voice was firm. "My detectives conducted a thorough search. If there was a body there, they would have found it. There was no evidence that a murder had occurred, and there was most definitely no body."

Her hand clenched the edge of the counter in a death grip as frustration cut through her. "Chief, I do understand that, but if you could just listen. I know I'm right about this. I found out that—"

"Young lady, your sister might be willing to humor you, but I am not. If this is some sort of post-traumatic stress from last spring, then

I'm sorry. But you need to call a shrink, not send my department on wild goose chases. We're too short-staffed to waste our manpower like that."

Young lady? Of all the male chauvinist... Indignation sizzled through her. "Chief Raimy, look, if you could just—"

"No. Go home, Miss Harper. And stop watching so many crime movies."

Her phone beeped three times, indicating the person on the other end had hung up.

A growl rumbled out of Blake's throat and turned into a near yell as she punched the Off button on the phone. Once again, she wished for a landline so she could have had the satisfaction of slamming down the receiver.

The chief didn't like her, but she was really annoyed that he didn't take her seriously. She knew what she was talking about, which he would have known if he had shut up for two seconds and actually listened to her.

Blake had squeezed the key so hard that the indentations from it had made an impression on her palm. "I do know what I'm talking about."

With determination, she swung through the kitchen door and headed to the front. "I know what I'm talking about, and I'll show him."

Chapter Twelve

She locked the front door of Mystery Cup behind her and headed next door to Macabre Reads. She was determined to get up to that apartment, but she wasn't necessarily crazy about going by herself—especially if she was right about what was up there. Bringing Sean and his muscles for backup seemed like a much better option.

That idea was quickly dashed when she stepped up to the front window of the bookstore. People filled the place. There wasn't a line out the door anymore, but about thirty people were milling around inside. Jax stood in the corner, chatting animatedly to a group of about half a dozen people who surrounded him. Sean stood behind the counter, looking breathtaking in a dark-gray Henley.

As if he felt her eyes on him, his head jerked up, and he met her gaze. A grin spread across his handsome face, making Blake's heart skip a beat. He gestured to all the people around the shop and shrugged as if to say, "I had no idea it would be so busy." Then he stretched out his thumb and pinky, mimicking a phone, and held it to his ear, mouthing the words, "I'll call you."

She nodded and gave him a little wave as his attention returned to the people at the register.

So much for that idea. She could call Adam for backup, but she knew how he felt about her extracurricular investigations, so that probably wouldn't have gone well.

She looked directly across the street at the loft. "Suck it up, Blake. Let's just get this over with."

With a deep breath, she quickened her steps and hurried across the street. Even though night had fallen, Main Street and the sidewalks were well lit. But when she walked around to the stairs on the side of Sliced, she stepped into the shadows.

She looked up the dark stairwell and started second-guessing herself. Although she and Giselle had been watching the stairway the night of the party, she asked herself if there was any way the killer had managed to get out without them seeing him. It was dark back here. It wasn't out of the realm of possibility that the killer could have slipped away unnoticed.

As quickly as the thought came, she shook it away. Even if that were true—and she doubted it because a clown would be hard to miss—there was no way a person could have ambled down these stairs carrying or dragging a body without them seeing.

Gripping the handrail, she began her ascent. About halfway up the stairs, she looked out onto the street, trying to put herself in the killer's shoes, looking at what would have been his view that night on the stairs. The empty street was illuminated by street lamps lining the sidewalk. It would have been easy for the killer to slip in unnoticed.

Anxious to get this over with, she took quick steps and reached the top landing. The key in her palm had become sweaty because she'd gripped it so hard, and it slipped in her shaky hand as she tried to slide it into the lock. On the second try, the key slid home. She turned it and gathered her courage before pushing the door open.

For a moment, she wondered if she should use the flashlight on her phone instead of turning on the light, but she quickly realized how silly that was. She had a key and permission to be there. Plus, the situation was eerie enough—she didn't need to up the creep factor by finding a body with nothing more than a flashlight.

She flicked the switch, and bright light flooded the room, forcing her to squint for a moment. The apartment looked exactly the same as it had when she and Sean had been there the day before. Same couch, table, desk. Nothing was out of place because there really wasn't anything there to *be* out of place. But what she was looking for wouldn't have been in the living room.

Her eyes drifted to the doorway that led to the dark bedroom. She swallowed hard, wishing the butterflies in her stomach would take a freaking rest. The floor creaked under her feet when she walked slowly across the hardwood floor, and her heart beat a little faster. The noise seemed almost jarring in the quiet apartment.

When she reached the bedroom door, she paused, readying herself to go inside, when a loud scream made her jump. She rushed to the window to see what had happened and immediately saw Mr. Jeffries's open-air bus stopped in the middle of the street. He was standing at the front of the bus, pointing to Sliced and making a beating motion as though he was bludgeoning someone. One woman screamed again, apparently sensitive to his description of the real-life murder.

Blake rolled her eyes, half-tempted to yank the window up and yell at him. Ghost tours were one thing, but a star tour of the town's grisly murders was another.

She turned her back to the window and pressed her hand to her chest in hopes of stemming the rapid beat of her heart. If nothing else, that had really broken the tension. But she really needed to talk to Mr. Jeffries about his tour. Maybe it gave her business a boost, but she drew the line at him actually acting out the murders. Before she knew it, he was going to incorporate props or worse.

"On second thought, maybe I shouldn't say anything. All that'll do is give him ideas."

With a shake of her head, Blake walked brusquely to the bedroom and flipped on the light. She turned to face the closet door, which was tightly shut. Furrowing her brow, she tried to remember if she and Sean had shut the door or left it open when they'd been there, but for the life of her, she couldn't remember.

"We should have left the dang thing open." She marched forward, trying to forget the trepidation she'd felt the first time they'd had the big closet reveal.

With her hand on the doorknob, she took a deep breath. "I can do this. I'm a strong, independent woman, and I can do this." She jerked open the door and peeked inside. Empty. Except...

She leaned forward and crinkled her nose at the awkward odor. It smelled almost like someone had left their garbage out to rot, but no one lived there. "What on earth could—" With a gasp, she looked up. "Oh God," she whispered.

Two rope strings hung in front of her, and she reached up to pull one, turning on the light.

When she looked at the ceiling, it became perfectly clear why she, Sean, and the police had missed the fact that there was an attic in the closet. When she'd heard there was an attic, she thought maybe they'd missed it because the entrance was so small. But the opposite was true. There was a seam around nearly the entire rectangle of the ceiling, indicating that the whole thing folded down. If she hadn't known there was an attic there, she totally would have missed it. Without the light on, it would have been near impossible to notice.

The pull-down rope to the attic hung right next to the light string—again, something that could be easily missed. If someone wasn't looking close enough, the pull ropes could have easily been mistaken for one string instead of two.

Blake reached up and fingered the rope string, and she would swear the weird smell got stronger. She had a feeling she knew what it was, and she wished as hard as she could that she were wrong.

She fisted her hand around the pull-down rope. "Here goes." She counted to three and pulled down firmly. The ceiling gave way, folding back, and the narrow stairs unfolded slowly. The rotten odor that hit her was so strong, it knocked her back a step.

She closed her eyes, which started watering. He was there. She knew he was there. Even though she'd never smelled a decomposing body before, she couldn't imagine anything that could smell so horrible.

Leave. You should turn around and leave right now. Call the police back.

But if I do that, what am I supposed to say? No, Chief, I didn't see a dead body, but I'm pretty sure I smelled one. No, she didn't have a choice. She looked up into the dark attic. She had to go up there.

She took the first step. "I can't believe I talked myself into this." Two more steps. "I really need to move to a less murdery town." Three more steps. "Maybe I could buy an island. Open a coffee shop on the beach." Two more steps, and her upper body was in the attic opening.

"Oh lord." Blake clamped her hand over her mouth. The smell was overwhelming. Light. She needed light.

She patted her jeans pockets then delved inside and pulled out her phone, fumbling with the new case that looked like it was covered in coffee beans with the phrase, "Coffee is my spirit animal."

With shaking hands, she turned on the flashlight app and raised it to the level of her eyes. She shined it to the left but saw nothing but empty space. Slowly, she moved her phone in front of her. Nothing. Then she moved the phone to the right.

A blood-curdling scream sounded in the quiet attic. This time, the scream came from her. Not even a foot from her was the face of Todd Lang. Even through the shower curtain he was wrapped in, Blake could see that his open eyes were fixed and lifeless, his face a pale gray.

She barely had time to take it in before she stumbled backward, instinctively wanting to get away from the sight before her. Completely forgetting she was on stairs, she missed the step beneath her when she stepped back, lost her footing, and tumbled backward, dropping her phone. She hit the carpeted floor of the closet, landing flat on her back, the impact knocking an "oof" out of her.

The adrenaline had taken over her body, so if Blake felt any pain, her brain didn't even take the time to register it before she was scrambling up. She snatched her phone and ran for the door then flung it open. She took the steps two at a time, desperately needing to erase the horrible image from her head. She didn't realize she was running until she reached the deserted sidewalk in front of Sliced.

Her stomach clenched, a wave of nausea surging through her body. Bending over, she grabbed her knees and took breath after breath, trying hard not to toss her cookies.

Police. She had to call the police. Standing up straight, she covered her mouth with one hand and realized she still had a death grip on the phone with the other. Her hand shook so badly that she didn't think she could dial.

"Blake!" The rich-chocolate voice made her jerk her head up and look across the street. Adam stood on the sidewalk in front of Mystery Cup, waving at her. But as soon as his eyes met hers, the smile died on his lips.

She nearly went weak with relief, starting across the street so she could feel the safety of Adam's arms around her. She'd walked about halfway across, when the loud roar of an engine and the screech of tires made her look up. Headlights blinded her as a truck barreled down. At least, she thought it was a truck. The lights glared so brightly that she couldn't make the vehicle out.

Fear paralyzed her. She couldn't move. She couldn't look away. This was it. This was how she was going to die. A woman screamed, and she heard someone yell her name. Before she could react, she felt a body slam into hers, knocking her sideways a second before the truck sped over the spot where she'd been standing.

Arms curled around her as she fell—one arm holding her body close to his, and the other protecting her head, tucking it into his shoulder as he rolled, cushioning her so she didn't land on the hard ground but on him instead.

Voices around them rose in panic as footsteps pounded their way. When Blake raised her head, it took her a moment to realize that she rested on Adam.

His blue eyes searched her face as he sat up, shifting Blake to his lap. "Are you okay, sugar?" His hands ran over her body, searching for injuries. "Someone call an ambulance."

She shook her head, tears welling up in her eyes. "Don't call an ambulance," she said as the tears spilled over and streamed down her cheeks. "Call the police. There's been a murder. Todd Lang is dead."

Chapter Thirteen

"It's not like I go looking for trouble. It just seems to... I don't know... find me," Blake said as Sean sat next to her on the big purple couch in Mystery Cup, squeezing her hand.

Adam sighed as he continued to run his fingers through her hair, prodding her scalp for lumps. "Sugar, trouble doesn't have to find you. It seems to have your address and cell phone number."

Sean snorted a laugh. Hopefully, that was a good sign. When Sean had walked in and seen Adam, the temperature in the room had dropped to an icy chill. It would be nice if the frigid undertone between the two men would begin to thaw.

She put her hand on Adam's and gently pulled it away from her head. "Adam, you've checked me fifteen times in the last two hours. I'm fine. Sit down. I'll make coffee."

When she started to get up, Sean and Adam both put a hand on her arm. "No, you don't. You stay put. I'll make coffee," Sean said.

Adam, who looked as if he was going to have an aneurysm anytime she moved, shot a harsh glare at Sean. "Don't you think you've done enough?"

Oh no. It really wasn't the best time for everything to come to a head between Sean and Adam.

But Sean wasn't about to let a comment like that slide. His entire body stiffened next to her. "Excuse me?" His voice had gone low, and if Blake didn't know what an amazing heart he had, she would have been a little scared.

Adam stood up to his full height, and in an instant, Sean was off the couch and right in his face. "If you have something to say, Doc, just say it."

"Okay." Adam jabbed his finger at Sean. "From the get-go, you have been the one encouraging her to pursue this thing. She almost got killed tonight."

Her mouth popped open. "Adam, that's not—"

"And you think that's my fault?" Sean asked incredulously. "That I would ever put her in danger or want her hurt? You are living in your own flipping world, Doc."

"Am I?" This time, he shoved his finger into Sean's chest. "The last time she was up in that apartment, you were right there alongside her."

Blake's head was spinning. *What has gotten into him? And how did he even know Sean was with me?* She certainly hoped Rachel wasn't spewing her business to everyone.

As she assessed the situation between the two men, dread hit her square in the gut. The muscles in Sean's arms bunched as he brought his hand up in a controlled movement and gave Adam a good hard shove. "You touch me again, and you'll regret it," he said through gritted teeth.

Adam took a step forward. His usually warm blue eyes could have given her frostbite. "Is that a threat?"

"That's it!" She jumped up and inserted herself in between the two men, putting a hand on each of their chests. "Would you two stop? I don't need a brawl in my café. The evening's been eventful enough."

Adam's body was still tense, but his eyes softened as he took her in. "Sugar..."

"Don't 'sugar' me, Adam Bryant. You're acting like I need a chaperone now? Like I'm not smart enough to assess danger and make decisions on my own?"

When she turned to Sean, the smirk on his face infuriated her. "And you! Your jealousy is more than I can handle."

His jaw dropped. "I... what?"

"You have been giving me the cold shoulder because I got roses. You react, but you don't talk to me." She huffed. "I don't know what's going on with you two, but you'd better figure it out, because I am really tired of all of this. I would think two intelligent, professional, ex-military men would know how to freaking act like they weren't in junior high."

Surprise crossed Sean's face as he looked over her head at Adam. "You were in the military?"

The doc's chin jerked up in a nod. "Naval flight surgeon."

Sean grinned. "Well, I'll be damned." He jerked a thumb at his chest. "Sealift Command."

Blake swiveled her head back and forth as something unspoken passed between the two men—some sort of navy brotherhood thing that she didn't quite understand. But whatever it was, it seemed to make both of them relax a notch, and for that she was grateful.

She lowered her hands and took a deep breath. When Adam turned and motioned for her to sit back down, she saw a raw patch at his temple. "Jeez, Adam, you're the one that needs to be checked out. Look at your head! I landed on you, and you took the brunt of the fall."

A grin stretched across his angular face. "I'm fine, sugar. Military training and all. I know how to take a fall."

Sean's guided her to sit down and motioned for Adam to take a seat. "Blake, you stay here with the doc. I'll go make some coffee."

She started to get up again. "But you don't know how to work the—"

"Sweetheart," he said in a calming tone, "I'm just going to make it on the little coffeepot you have in the kitchen. I'm not going to attempt to control espresso hub central. It's fine." When she didn't look convinced, he chuckled, his dimple flashing beneath his beard. "I *do* know how to make coffee... Goddess," he added with a wink.

When he walked away, Adam plopped down next to Blake on the couch. The purple cushion sank beneath his weight, and he turned so he could lean his back against the armrest and see her as well as look out the window behind her. The blue and red lights of the police cars parked outside swirled across his face.

He held her gaze for a moment, and guilt filled his expression. "I'm sorry about that." He motioned toward the kitchen, where Sean had gone. "I just... the thought of something happening to you..." He shook his head. "If you had just waited ten minutes, I would have been here, I would have—"

"I know." She blew out a breath. "I didn't know you were coming. And you couldn't have known I was going to go over there tonight. I really didn't plan to do this on my own, you know. I called the police. I told you they wouldn't listen. And I am fully capable of making my own decisions, you know. No chaperone needed."

"I know." The corner of his mouth tipped up. "I thought we were going to have to bail out Sean. The way he got in Chief Raimy's face when the cops finally showed up..."

Her lips twitched as she thought of Sean laying into the ruddy-faced chief of police for ignoring her phone call. "Right? It's a good thing you were here to pull him back. He wasn't listening to me. I think you got him right before he was about to throw a punch." She shook her head. She'd never seen Sean so angry as when he'd found out the police had completely disregarded her concerns. It had meant a lot that he'd stood up for her and defended her.

"I think our biggest worry right now, aside from finding out who killed Lang, is figuring out who tried to run you down, because that was very obviously deliberate." He looked outside again. "When are the police supposed to be in here to question you about that, anyway?"

She turned to look out the window. In addition to the three police cars and a handful of officers, she saw two men carrying a body bag out to the weird coroner's car that looked like a cross between a hearse and a van. A shiver went through her. Just then, a car pulled up on the street out front, and her brother slammed out of his minivan. He did not look happy.

"Uh-oh." Ryan's buckle-up-because-you're-about-to-get-a-lecture look was one she'd been familiar with since her teen years. She turned back to Adam and could hear the whine in her voice. "You called my brother?"

He held his hands up as if in surrender. "Don't look at me, sugar. It must have been one of the cops."

Ryan hadn't even taken two steps inside the café door before his normally calm demeanor cracked. As soon as he spotted her, he started yelling, his blue eyes wild behind his wire-rimmed glasses. "What the actual crap, Blake? A body? You found *another* body—by yourself? What were you doing up there by yourself?" He waved his hands around as he spoke, which made him look a little bit crazed. "And then you were almost hit by a car!" He shoved both hands into his dark-blond hair. "I didn't think at thirty-whatever years old that you needed a freaking babysitter, but maybe you do."

"Now wait a second," Adam began at the same time Sean came out of the kitchen with a silver carafe of coffee.

"Watch how you talk to her, Harper," Sean said.

Ryan looked from one man to the other. "Great, the pseudo boyfriends are here now. Where were the two of you a couple of hours ago?"

"I don't need a babysitter." Blake jumped up, so frustrated with her older brother's attitude that she shoved him in the shoulder. "And it's not like I try to go out and find bodies." Well, okay, so maybe she kind of did this time, but that totally wasn't the point. "And you should be thanking Adam. He saved my life tonight."

Her brother's eyes were spitting fire. "My point exactly. You shouldn't be doing anything that requires somebody to save your life."

"It's not her fault, man," Adam said to his colleague and friend. "She tried to call the police. They wouldn't listen."

Ryan took a few calming breaths as Sean set the tray down that held the carafe and three red ceramic mugs. "Kyle said you called them. Did Raimy really hang up on you?"

"Yeah, he did." Blake shoved her hands onto her hips. She hadn't tried to call Kyle since before she'd gone across the street to the apartment. "Wait, how did Kyle know that? When did you talk to her?"

"She called me. She and Jason are on their way back from St. Louis right now. They should be here"—Ryan looked at the Timex on his left wrist—"anytime, really."

Blake's brows furrowed. "But that's a two-and-a-half-hour drive. There's no way they could make it in..."

Sirens sounded in the distance, getting louder as they turned down her street. A moment later, a Wilton police car screeched to a stop in the middle of the street with sirens and lights blazing. Jason cut the siren as the passenger door swung open and Kyle emerged with a dangerous look on her face. Blake could practically feel the fire coming off her from where she stood as Kyle stomped up to her boss.

Chief Raimy, who was standing across the street in front of Sliced with two other officers literally backed up two steps when he saw her coming.

Kyle stepped up on the curb and immediately invaded the man's personal space. Blake watched with Ryan, Adam, and Sean as her sister jabbed her finger in the chief's chest as she yelled. They couldn't hear what she was saying, but her face was red as she gestured up at the loft and then pointed across the street at Mystery Cup. With each second, the chief's face became paler and paler. The officers that had been standing next to him had retreated a good couple of feet, not wanting to be caught in Kyle's crosshairs.

The chief looked as though he were attempting to offer answers to her questions until Kyle put her hand in his face and shook her head. She pointed to one of the other officers and yelled something at him then waved toward the coffee shop. Then she stomped away from the men and headed in the direction of Mystery Cup.

Aw crap, don't tell me she's going to yell at me too.

Ryan opened the door for her as she steamrolled through. She rushed right toward Blake and almost knocked her over with her strong bear hug. The sisters embraced each other for a full minute before Kyle pulled back and looked at her sister, her hands running along Blake's shoulders and head, much the way Adam's had done when he'd been searching for injuries. As soon as Kyle seemed convinced Blake was fine, she raised her hand and flicked her right in the middle of the forehead.

"Ow!" Blake rubbed the sore spot between her eyes. "What was that for?"

"I know you couldn't get my asshat of a boss to listen to you, but that does *not* mean you go in search of a dead body on your own." She whirled on Sean. "And where were you? You're right next door. You couldn't talk her out of something like that? Or at the very least go with her?"

Sean paled, his face awash with guilt. But Blake jumped in before he could speak. "Oh my God! If one more person acts like I need someone else to make decisions for me, I am going to scream! It's not his fault!" Blake grabbed her sister's arm and yanked her around. "I had a key and permission to be up there. I have a brain of my own, you know."

"Really?" Kyle seethed. "Because sometimes I'm not too sure you use it."

Blake saw red and had a desperate urge to yank her sister's dark ponytail.

Luckily for her, Ryan saw that coming and stepped in between them. "Whoa, I know what comes next, you two. And before we resort to hair-pulling, I really think everyone should calm down."

Blake stuck her head out to look around her brother and address her sister. "You may be a cop, but you're not the boss of me!"

"Listen to yourself!" Kyle jabbed a finger at her and unsuccessfully tried to shove Ryan out of the way. "You sound like you're five. You need someone to be the boss of you!"

"Ladies, can we please calm down?" Adam stepped forward to put his hands on Blake's shoulders, and Sean stepped closer to Kyle, looking as though he was afraid to touch her but, at the same time, seemed ready to grab her if she decided to lunge at her sibling. "Blake, you know your sister loves you and just wants to see you safe."

Blake huffed. She knew she should appreciate that, and she did, but she was really annoyed her sister was treating her like an idiot who couldn't make her own decisions.

The bell jingled above the door, causing all of them to turn their heads in that direction. Officer Cary Thornhill stood in the doorway, taking in the situation. "Uh... Detective Harper, you wanted me to come question your sister?" he asked hesitantly. "Is this a bad time?"

Kyle took several calming breaths. "No, this is a perfect time." She jerkily motioned for everyone to have a seat.

Blake was just happy that Cary was the one questioning her and not the chief. He would have only turned up the heat on a situation that was already boiling over.

When Ryan was convinced his sisters weren't going to go all WWE in the middle of the café, he said, "I'm going to go get a few more coffee mugs. I'll be right back."

Blake took her previous position on the center of the purple couch, and Adam and Sean sat on either side of her. Their presence calmed her.

Cary sat in a chair across from them, still glancing tentatively at Kyle, who stood with her arms crossed, shifting her weight from one foot to the other.

Before the officer could ask a question, she said, "Let's start with the car that tried to run her down first. I'm anxious to get an APB out on that if we have enough information." She looked out the window. "Not that it'll do much good two hours after the fact. I can't believe Raimy—" She rubbed a hand across her mouth. "Never mind. Go ahead, officer."

"Uh, right." He opened the minitablet he carried and tapped on it, clearing his throat. "So, from my understanding, you were coming across the street from there"—he pointed out the window at Sliced—"to here. And a truck almost hit you?"

"Yeah." Blake rubbed her sweaty palms on the thighs of her faded jeans. "I was in shock because I'd just found the bo—I'd just found Todd. When I came outside, I thought I was going to be sick. And then I heard Adam calling my name." She blindly reached to her right, and Adam's hand found hers and gave it a squeeze.

"So you crossed the street," the officer said. "In your state, it's understandable that you may not have looked before crossing. Someone obviously wasn't paying attention."

"It was more than that," Adam said sternly, his words so firm that his slight Southern drawl was barely noticeable. "The truck came out of nowhere, almost like it was waiting for her. As soon as she stepped off the curb, it revved its engine and gunned for her. This was no accident. He didn't even try to stop, before or after."

Kyle stepped forward. "So someone purposely tried to..." She rubbed her eyes with her fingertips. "Christ."

Blake didn't want to believe someone was trying to kill her, but Adam was right. This was no accident. Dread filled her stomach, and she let go of the men's hands to wrap her arms around her middle.

"Do you think maybe someone knew she found the body?" Sean asked. "Maybe someone who didn't want her to alert people?"

Kyle paced back and forth in front of them. "If that's the case, then why did he even let her get that far? Why didn't he try to take her out beforehand?"

"So maybe it wasn't related at all," Officer Thornhill offered.

"Well, if that's true, then I most likely have more than one person who wants me dead." Blake rubbed her stomach. "Yep, just another day here at the Mystery Cup." Her flippant attitude did nothing to conceal her unease.

Kyle bit her lip and continued pacing. "I have an inkling that says one thing had to do with the other. I just have no idea how."

Blake looked up at her brother when he cleared his throat. "Her instincts are usually spot on." His mouth tightened into a thin line as he clenched and unclenched his teeth. "Not sure that's really a good thing in this case. I don't like the thought that someone out there wants you out of the way, Blake."

Kyle finally sat in a chair next to Cary as Ryan poured coffee and set cups on the large coffee table in front of them.

Kyle splayed her hands on the coffee table. "Let's lay this all out. What do we know so far?"

Sean put his arm on the back of the couch and toyed with a piece of Blake's hair that she'd long since stopped trying to control. The way he wound it around his finger gave her goose bumps.

Adam turned and noticed Sean's hand. A muscle began working in his jaw, but he said nothing. Thank God. She didn't need round two.

Sean cleared his throat. "We know that Blake saw Todd murdered the night of the party—stabbed—by a clown. I think everyone can quit trying to pretend she made that up now."

She had to stop herself from leaning into Sean. The way he defended her made her want to take up shelter in his arms.

"Todd was dressed like the Phantom, wasn't he?" Blake asked. At least that one little thing would confirm that she wasn't completely crazy.

"Yes, ma'am," Cary said. "The mask and hat were tossed in the attic next to the body."

In the current situation, being right really didn't make Blake feel any better.

Kyle made a fist then splayed her fingers out on her leg as she thought. Blake could almost hear the wheels turning in her head. "So who had motive to kill Todd?" She turned her attention to Sean. "He was a friend of yours, right? Can you tell me anything about who would have had something against him?"

Blake scoffed. Todd certainly hadn't been a super likable person. "It might be easier to ask who didn't."

"We weren't close friends," Sean said, addressing Kyle. "Money and women were Todd's biggest interests. He made some enemies."

"Sabrina?" Kyle asked.

Sean rolled his lip into his mouth as he thought. "I know she's upset they split up, but she loves him. I don't think she's a killer."

"What about Pepper?" Blake asked.

All eyes turned to her.

"I'm just saying. She's the one that rented the place. Maybe she was involved with Todd." She shrugged. "I mean, she's young, pretty, big boobs. Definitely his type. And she's tall. The height definitely fits for the clown." Pepper made sense.

"Okay, we will definitely talk to Pepper," Officer Thornhill said as he continued writing. "Would she be able to get a body up in the attic? We know the clown hid the body there before the police arrived that night."

"Right, it wouldn't have taken long to get the body in the attic, especially if the perp was in shape. She seems to be pretty fit. But I want to cast the net wide. Find out who Todd had business dealings with. Did he double-cross anyone? Was he sleeping with someone's wife? We have a lot of different avenues to check out here." Kyle leaned back in her chair and scrubbed a hand across her face. "I can't believe we didn't see the attic. How did we miss that? Since you guys never saw anyone leave, there's a chance the killer was there the whole time. He—or she—could have just waited in the attic until later that night when they were sure no one was watching." She uttered an expletive as she clenched her fist. "We could have had 'em."

Sean's hand clenched in Blake's hair. "If the killer was there, then he heard everything you and Jason said when you were in that apartment. Please tell me you didn't mention Blake's name."

Kyle drew her hands away from her face, which seemed to go pale. "Oh God. We did. We talked about what you saw and where you saw the people."

"So if he heard that, he knows Blake's onto him," Adam said.

"That explains why he showed up at the party." Blake thought back. "Remember, Kyle, I told you I saw a clown at the party. He came up the stairs and stood there, staring at me, but he was gone before I could make it over to him. He knew. He knew I saw him." She'd thought at the time that maybe the clown had heard her scream, but this made more sense. He'd known immediately that she had seen him when the police had mentioned her name.

"We're not doing this again," Ryan said firmly. "You need protection. I'm not going to have another killer after you. Kyle, we need—"

"Wait a second," Blake interrupted. "He knows I saw a clown kill the Phantom in that apartment. Everything I know, you know. There's no reason for him to have it in for me. Maybe the truck...

maybe he was trying to keep me from telling anyone I found the body, but everyone knows now. There's no reason for him to be after me. I don't have any more information."

Ryan didn't look convinced. "You've been going out of your way to investigate this murder on your own. And everyone knows how instrumental you were in catching a killer last spring. He probably sees you as a big threat. I'd rather you stay with Rachel and me until this is done. I'm not taking any chances."

Blake rolled her eyes. "I'll think about it."

"Wait a second, back to the truck," Kyle said. "You're sure it was a truck?"

"I... uh..." The only thing she remembered was the glare of lights as the truck sped toward her. "I just remember headlights."

"It was a truck," Adam confirmed. "I was standing to the side. It was a black F-150. I'm sure of it because I used to drive one. I just wish I could have made out the driver. I was so focused on her, I wasn't looking."

Blake clenched Adam's hand with both of hers. She didn't want to think what would have happened if Adam hadn't been there to push her out of the way.

Everyone was silent for a moment, most likely pondering the same thing. Kyle was the one who finally broke the silence. "Can you guys think of anyone who drives a truck like that?" She sighed when they all shook their heads. "Without a license plate number, it might take some time tracking down the truck." She mashed her lips together, thinking. "Let's switch gears. We know Pepper rented the place, but who else had access to the apartment?"

Blake told them about Micah's key and about the conversation she'd had with Bree regarding the holding companies. That was all information Kyle knew already, but everyone else listened with rapt attention. Then she told them all what Sabrina had said about Todd having a meeting with someone the night of the party.

"So we don't even know who technically owns the place, or who at the holding company even has access to it?" Sean blew out a breath as he leaned back and crossed his ankle over his knee. "Crap."

"Yeah, that's putting it mildly," Ryan said.

Kyle stood up. "I'll put in a call to Bree and the council members to see if they can shed any more light on the holding company. While I'm doing that, maybe Jason can go talk to Sabrina, and maybe we can get a lead on who would have wanted Todd dead. Jason will probably be able to get more out of her than I would."

Ryan set his coffee cup down on the table. "So we're back to square one?"

Kyle let out a very unladylike snort. "Big brother, we were never at square two."

Chapter Fourteen

Pumping her arms, Blake tried not to gasp for breath as she kept up with Rachel. She wondered what on earth had made her think power walking was a good idea. Looking down, she was quickly reminded of the five pounds that had been added to her waistline since she'd added chocolate-chip-pumpkin bread to the menu.

"I wish you'd consider staying with us like Ryan said." Rachel glanced back at her and slowed her pace to give Blake a chance to catch up.

The fall foliage in Wilton City Park was a colorful backdrop for their morning walk. Too bad Blake was too hyperfocused on attempting to breathe to appreciate the beauty as she wound around the mile-long walking path with Rachel.

"Oh, please," Blake said between gasps. "Everything was fine last night when I went home. No calls or anonymous threats, no boogeymen hiding in dark corners." She thought of Ninja curled up in the middle of the latte-colored quilt on her bed. "I'm pretty sure that whoever the bad guy is, he's afraid of my attack cat."

"You could have taken Adam or Sean up on their offers to sleep on your couch. Personally, I would have loved to see what would have happened if you'd let both of them sleep over." She gave Blake an exaggerated wink, making her huff out a laugh.

"They would have started smacking each other around in my living room is probably what would have happened."

Rachel grinned, walking at Blake's pace as she lifted the hand weights she held. "Come on. Two guys fighting over you? That is totally hot!" When Blake rolled her eyes, she laughed. "I'm just teasing.

I know you're stronger than the guys give you credit for, my husband included. They're just worried about you." She bobbled her head. "I have a feeling that Ryan thinks if you're staying in our guestroom, maybe I can talk my mother out of coming for a visit."

Blake felt herself light up. "Mama Bustos is coming to stay?" Even though Rachel's mom only lived an hour away, she liked to come to stay for an extended period every few months to spend time with the kids. Blake nearly started salivating at the thought of her homemade enchiladas.

"Send your mama over my way," Blake encouraged. "She can stay with me anytime if Ryan doesn't want her at your house."

"It's not that he doesn't want her." Rachel slowed as they approached her house. "He loves her. He just doesn't get why she likes to come to stay when she doesn't live that far away. And you know, she's pretty high-energy."

Blake laughed as her sister-in-law jogged in place, punching the weights above her head. "Yeah, I wouldn't know what that's like at all."

Rachel made a silly face and giggled.

When a car passed them and parked across the street, Blake's smile faded. Rachel turned, and they watched an older woman wearing black exit the Buick Lucerne and make her way up to Sabrina's house. At least eight cars were parked in front of the home—four in the drive and several more lined up on the street. Sabrina and Todd's family, no doubt.

"Do you know who told her the news?" Rachel asked as they made their way up her front steps.

"Kyle said Chief Raimy was going over there after he left the crime scene." Blake cast a glance back at Sabrina's before they went inside Rachel's house. "I can't imagine what she's going through. It was obvious when I talked to her that she's still in love with the jerk." Blake gasped and clasped a hand over her mouth. "Ugh, what's wrong with me. That's so disrespectful."

"It's okay." Rachel handed Blake a bottle of water, and they both sat down at the kitchen island. "Just because he's dead doesn't mean he wasn't a jerk. He was sleeping with half the women in town under the age of thirty." She shook her head slowly. "If you ask me, Sabrina was way better off without him."

Blake gulped her water and wiggled her legs, which felt like jelly after their power walk. "That makes me wonder... Kyle was asking about anyone who would have the motive to kill Todd. I should go talk to Pepper again and see if I can find out anything."

Water spewed out of Rachel's nose as she coughed, lowering the bottle to set it on the counter. Blake slapped her sister-in-law's back as she coughed and gasped for breath. When she could finally speak, she glared at Blake as if she'd just sprouted horns. "Have you lost your ever-loving mind?"

"I want to find out if she was capable of something like this. I mean she's a bit—a not very nice person," she corrected. "But is she a murderer?" Todd's face encased in plastic had floated through her mind every time she'd closed her eyes the night before. She knew she would never in her life be able to forget that image. "What if they were sleeping together and he tried to dump her?"

Rachel got up from her chair and got a box of steel-cut oatmeal out of the cabinet. "You said she was kissing Whit. She must have rebounded pretty fast. But you need to focus on keeping your own butt safe." She held up the box. "Breakfast?"

She crinkled her nose. *Oatmeal? Only if it's in cookies.* "Nah, I'd better get to the café. I have Giselle and Eli working this morning, and you never know what their dynamic's going to be at any given moment."

Rachel smirked as she ripped open a packet of oatmeal and poured it in a bowl. "Wasn't Eli's double date last night? That should give you some drama to deal with this morning."

A groan escaped Blake. "Next time I hire anyone, I need to make sure they're not attracted to anyone on my staff. I just want Eli and Giselle to be happy, but jeez, I've seen enough googly eyes and furtive glances in the last month to last me a lifetime."

She headed for the door as Rachel smirked. "Welcome to my world. Now you know what it's like for me every time Sean or Adam walk into Mystery Cup. Payback's a bitch."

When Blake's jaw dropped in an expression of righteous indignation, Rachel couldn't hold back her laughter. "Okay, well, have fun with your lovestruck staff. I'll be in around noon. Oh, and Blake, don't forget dinner. Tamales!"

She almost started drooling at the thought. "Don't worry, I'll be here!"

"That'll be incentive to get through the self-defense class," Rachel said as she walked to her coffeepot and started to measure spoonfuls of coffee grounds into the basket.

"The self-defense class." Blake smacked her forehead with her palm. "Crap. I completely forgot that was today." She looked up at her sister-in-law. "Maybe we can skip it, you know, since we have plans for me to come over and do the twins' makeup."

"Nice try." Rachel shook her head as she shoved the basket back into place and pulled the carafe off the burner to fill it with water. "Ryan specifically told me to make sure both you and I went. With your lead-footed admirer from last night, your brother wants to be absolutely certain you know how to defend yourself. Me too." A smile twitched her lips. "In fact, he's so determined that we both go, he's volunteered to be the bad guy at the class."

"The bad guy?"

After pouring the water, Rachel shoved the carafe back under the basket and hit the switch on the front of the coffee maker. "Yeah, the bad guy." She turned to Blake. "You know, the one who pretends to be the attacker, and we get to try to flip him to the ground."

"Seriously?" Blake's face lit up. "Okay, I might be wrong about this class. Now, I'm thinking it sounds super fun." And she did need to learn some self-defense moves. She'd always told herself she was going to take a self-defense class, but she'd never gotten around to it.

Rachel laughed. "All I ask is that you don't hit my husband anywhere that will harm his ability to have future children."

They both giggled as Blake thought of flipping Ryan to the ground. "So is the class for guys, too, or just ladies?"

Rachel wiggled her eyebrows. "Why? Are you thinking of inviting one of your two hot men?"

Blake gave her a droll look. "Two ex-military guys? I'm thinking they're probably good on the self-defense. Besides, both of them are crazy busy with work, I don't even know when I'm going to see either one of them."

"You might have to bite the bullet and—gasp—actually ask one of them out." Rachel waved her hands around her head as if that were the craziest thought in the world.

"You're quite the comedian today, aren't you?" Blake hiked her purse over her shoulder, not ready to evaluate her love life quite yet. "Okay, I really have to get going. See you in a little bit, Rach." She waved goodbye to her sister-in-law, ready to tackle her to-do list. And the first thing on that list was to figure out a reason to go to Crossbones and question Pepper that wouldn't make her look super obvious.

AS SOON AS SHE TURNED down the alley behind Mystery Cup, Blake saw Derek's delivery truck blocking her way. Dang it, she'd completely forgotten it was delivery day.

She put her Civic in reverse and backed out of the alley, continuing on to Main Street, where she turned in front of Mystery Cup... and immediately slammed on her brakes. People. So many people were everywhere. Blake was quickly reminded of the increase in foot traffic after her barista had been murdered in the café last spring. People certainly did seem to have a yearning for the macabre around here. The second there was a hint of crime, especially a murder, the crowds came en masse. She wasn't quite sure how she felt about that. Half of her brain rolled its eyes, while the other half just kept hearing "cha-ching."

It looked as though Micah was getting the brunt of it today. She knew the cops had the apartment above Sliced taped off, but that didn't seem to be stopping people from heading inside and, most likely, searching for gossip. At least Micah would get the financial boost from it all.

The Civic crept slowly down the street as Blake looked for a parking spot. Finally, she saw reverse lights go on. What luck! She was able to snatch the spot right in front of Mystery Cup. When she got out and looked in the front window, she saw that Micah wasn't the only one who seemed to be experiencing an increase in business. From her vantage point, she could see that most of the tables in the café were filled, and the line of people stretched from the register almost to the front door. *Whoa!* If that kind of traffic kept up, she was going to have to think about hiring more staff.

When Blake was about to go inside, she heard someone calling her name. "Blake! Miss Harper!" Orlando was running down the sidewalk, his hand outstretched and holding something.

"Orlando." She smiled as he caught up with her.

His black muscle shirt was stretched tight across his broad chest and had the word Buttkick printed across the front. For a brief moment, she wondered if the man owned any shirts with sleeves.

"I'm surprised to see you here this morning. I thought you'd be home resting. Are you sure you're okay?" Orlando asked.

It didn't surprise her at all that he knew about the events of the night before. She would give anything to be able to follow the chain of gossip just once to see how it spread so fast. "I'm fine, Orlando. But thank you for asking."

"Good. Good. Hey, I wanted to ask if you've seen Mr. Hamilton this morning?"

Blake furrowed her brow. "Uh, no, I just got here, but he usually comes in after he opens up the chamber of commerce every morning."

Orlando gave her a confused expression then smiled. "Oh no, no. Wrong Mr. Hamilton. I mean young Mr. Hamilton. Whitley."

"Oh! I haven't seen him unless he's inside." She motioned to the café. "Why are you looking for him?"

Orlando held up the black wallet. "He dropped this on the floor of the locker room after his workout. We're improving his quads," he said with a proud grin.

Blake raised her eyebrows. "Quads. Great."

"I have innovative quad exercises. You really should come by. Maybe when you come to the self-defense class, I could show you our new weight-lifting machine."

"Thanks, Orlando, but I haven't really been dying to work my quad muscles. My arms are fine. See?" She made a fist and flexed her bicep, a little confused when Orlando laughed.

"Quads, Miss Harper"—he bent at the waist and patted his thigh—"are in the legs."

Oops. Wait a second, is he saying my legs need work?

"Blake, my dear. There you are! We've been waiting to ask you some questions." Ruby Cross stood in the doorway to Mystery Cup, frantically motioning her inside. "Come in, come in."

"We?" Crap, it was book-club day. And the day after a dead body had been found... by her. There was no doubt in Blake's mind that she was about to experience an inquisition. She supposed she could try to beg off, but that would only delay the inevitable.

"Come on, Orlando, you can look for Whit while I entertain Ms. Cross."

Orlando followed her inside and headed directly to Giselle at the counter, who was helping a customer.

Eli lifted his head from where he was pulling an espresso shot and nodded in Blake's direction, his lips twitching as he noticed that Ruby had tucked Blake's arm into both of hers and was leading her to where the book-club ladies had a table reserved in the corner.

"Here she is!" Ruby all but pushed Blake into a chair at the table. She was surprisingly strong for a tiny woman.

As Blake sat, she looked at Ruby's normally white hair, unsure if she should say anything. Ruby had obviously been to her weekly salon appointment already that morning, and the aqua tint to her hair was evidence that she'd tried that "fandangled rinse" she'd been considering.

Ruby took her seat in between Red Montgomery and Penny Driver, who looked at Blake with enthusiastic expressions. Penny's eager violet eyes were lit with excitement, and Blake wondered if her new gig as Jax's assistant had gotten her more interested in true crime.

Elaine Page sat across from her and rolled her brown eyes, tossing her dark-auburn hair as she let her head flop back on her chair. "I don't know what you all are so excited about. She's not going to tell us anything."

"Oh, hush it," Red told her. "You're just in a bad mood 'cause that boy dumped you. I'm telling you, Elaine. You're better off without him." The woman's fiery red hair didn't move as she swung her gaze back and forth between Elaine and Blake.

Blake arched a brow in Elaine's direction and watched the divorcée's face redden. It looked as though she and Whit were history. Probably a good thing by Blake's estimation. Elaine seemed to be happier when she was with a man she could control, and that was not Whit Hamilton.

"He did not dump me, Red," Elaine said emphatically. "I told you—I didn't want to see him anymore. It was *my* decision."

Penny piped up, "But you said he was sleepin' with that pink-haired girl. If he was sleepin' with the pink-haired girl, that means he was pretty much done with you first, right?"

Blake pressed her lips together, not wanting to be anywhere near that conversation.

A sound that was a cross between a groan and a growl came out of Elaine, and she stood up so fast that she nearly knocked her chair over behind her. "I don't know why I hang out with you all. I'm getting a brownie." She stomped off in her high heels and just about mowed down Jax Talon, who was rushing to their table.

"Ooh, what did I miss?" He took the seat Elaine had just vacated and looked at Blake with the same hungry expression as the rest of the ladies. "We have Angela Lansbury in our midst, I see. Do tell, Blake. We want all the details."

"Uh, I don't know, guys. We're awfully busy. I might have to help out behind the counter."

They all looked behind the counter, where Blake's staff had a streamlined system that was moving with quick precision.

"Nope." Jax turned his attention back to her. "Looks like they've got it under control. So dish."

Her sister would kill her if she gave out details of the investigation—not that she really wanted to. The book club was the one singular way to guarantee gossip was spread all over town. She decided to take a different tactic. "Well"—she leaned in closer and looked around—"I was in such shock last night that it's all kind of a blur really." She massaged her temple. "I can only imagine what you all must have heard."

Red patted her arm. "Oh, you poor dear. I'm sure it was such a shock."

"If you ask me, that Todd Lang got what he deserved." Ruby sniffed and lifted her head. "You can't go diddlin' around with that many women and not expect for it to catch up with you in the end."

Penny's eyes widened. "Do you think that's what happened? He got on the bad side of one of 'em, and she came at him with a knife?"

"Uh, well..." Todd was a big guy, but a woman in shape could have definitely dragged his body up in the attic. Oh, how she desperately wanted to talk to Pepper and see if she could find out if the two were involved. But she needed a reason to go over there and a way to get Pepper to open up.

"Well, I wouldn't doubt it." Red looked at Blake for confirmation. "You said the killer was wearing a clown mask, right? So you don't know that it was a man. See, that's the problem. You'd think after last spring, everyone would have learned their lesson. Just 'cause someone's a killer doesn't mean they have to be a man. In fact, I think that's pretty chauvinist, if you ask me."

Blake almost laughed at the vibrant seventy-year-old woman.

"What's that look for? I'm all about equal opportunity. A woman can do anything a man can do. Even be a killer. Why, look at that one actress with the blond hair, got herself an award for playing that one serial killer."

Ruby bent forward slightly to put in her two cents. "I'll tell you what I think. I think there's more women killers out there than men. The difference is that the men get caught." She shook her finger at the group. "Not the women. No sirree. The women are smarter." She tapped a bony finger against her temple. "We have the brains."

Blake turned her amused expression on Jax. "That's not a bad theory. Jax, maybe you should look into that. The Red Rose Killer was never caught. Maybe that's because it was a woman. Maybe she was too smart. You should totally look into that."

Divert attention—that had been Blake's strategy. And it was working. But Jax wasn't stupid. He knew exactly what she was doing. The older women excitedly shot questions at him about the Red Rose Killer, and he tipped an imaginary hat to Blake. She used that opportunity to slide her chair back and make her escape. She gave him a little wink before she hustled behind the counter.

"Hey, Boss Lady." Eli put a lid on a to-go cup and set it on the bar. "Ellen!" he called out.

Elaine Page snatched it up. "Elaine, you moron!" she grumbled before she tromped off.

Eli turned to Blake as if he hadn't heard anything, and she bit her lip to control a laugh. "Busy morning, but we're rocking it. No worries. It's a good thing you made extra brownies last night, but I think we're going to need some more cookies."

"No problem. I have batter in the freezer. I'll go bake some up so they're ready by lunch."

"Great." Eli's cheerful expression darkened as he spotted something over her shoulder.

Blake turned her head to see Orlando with his ever-present smile. "No luck." He held up the wallet.

"Why don't you just call Whit?" she asked as Eli went back to busying himself with making coffee.

"I don't have his number. I suppose I can head to Crossbones later to give it to him after I'm done with my training sessions. Or maybe I can catch his dad. I think he has a workout scheduled today or tomorrow sometime."

Surprise caused Blake's eyebrows to shoot up. "His dad? Mr. Hamilton has a workout scheduled?" The most intense exercise she'd ever seen Mr. Hamilton do was walk from the commerce building to Mystery Cup. She wondered if Whit was pushing his dad to exercise more.

"Oh yes, he's been working with one of our personal trainers. I just have to check the books and see when he's scheduled."

Light bulbs began flashing in Blake's head. Kyle had said she was headed over to Crossbones that morning to question Pepper. So if Blake went over there later, she most certainly wouldn't run into her sister. Besides, no one could fault her for going over there when she had a legitimate reason like returning a wallet. And if she happened to ask a few questions to see if Pepper had been involved with Todd Lang, well, there wasn't anything wrong with that. She had to stop herself from pumping her fist. The wallet had to be a sign that she was supposed to go to Crossbones. "You know, I have to run over to Crossbones at lunch. I could just bring it to Whit then. So you won't have to worry about it."

Eli shot her a glance. "Since when do you have to run over to Crossbones?"

"Since now," she said through clenched teeth.

Orlando breathed a sigh of relief. "Great, thanks, Blake." He slid the wallet to her across the counter. "I'm sure he'll appreciate it."

"No problem!" She smiled as he turned and walked out, then turned to Eli, who was narrowing his eyes at her. "I'm just going to return Whit's wallet and get a burger."

"But didn't your sister tell you not to—"

"Well, what my sister doesn't know won't hurt her, right?"

Eli smirked and shook his head in amusement. "Right."

AFTER SHE'D MADE SIX dozen cookies and three loaves of chocolate-chip-pumpkin bread, Blake raised her arms above her head and stretched to the side. The morning had flown by. She'd been so busy with her new recipes that she'd barely had time to think about the new case. Luckily, Eli and Giselle had kept things running smoothly, so she was able to keep the baked goods coming out on schedule.

It wasn't until Rachel came through the back door that she realized it was already noon. "Sorry I'm late! Aiden forgot his lunch, so I had to run it by the school. Did you see how busy they are over at Sliced? It's really popping, Batman. You should get a cut of that profit."

Blake walked to her desk and sat, bending to touch her toes. "If discovering dead bodies is the best way to pick up extra business, count me out. I don't want the credit for that. I'm more worried about how Micah's doing." She picked up the wallet Orlando had brought by, which she'd tossed on the desk by her purse.

"Yeah, Sliced seems to be the center for everything murdery, doesn't it? Maybe we can take him out for drinks or something." Rachel glanced up as she slipped her apron over her head. "What's that? You stealing men's wallets now too? Adding that to your repertoire?"

"Very funny." She fingered the wallet as she thought about what the book-club ladies had said earlier. Killers didn't always have to be men. They were right about that. She visualized the pink-haired beauty at Crossbones and tried to guesstimate if she was tall enough to pull off the clown costume. The billowy outfit had made it impossible to make out any sort of body type, so she really only had height to go on.

Grabbing her purse, Blake stood up. "I'm heading to Crossbones for lunch."

"Wait, what?" Rachel looked at her as if she'd sprouted tentacles. "What do you mean you're going to Crossbones?"

"I need to return Whit's wallet."

Rachel stepped in front of her as she headed for the door. "Whoa, there, Miss Marple. You know your sister is going to Crossbones to question people. She's going to flip a gasket if you go over there."

"There's no need for gasket-flipping. Kyle will be done with talking to Pepper anyway because she was going to go this morning. So she won't even know. Besides, I have to return Whit's wallet. That's like a real reason and everything. She can't argue with that."

Rachel scoffed. "Wanna bet?"

"Since when are you the voice of reason?"

Rachel crossed her arms. "Take that back. I just don't want anything to happen to you. I have way too much invested in my matchmaking efforts."

"Oh God." Blake's eyes rolled heavenward. "Who did you invite to dinner tonight?"

"What? I said nothing." Rachel waggled her eyebrows. "But don't get yourself into too much trouble. As soon as the self-defense class is over, I'm heading home to make tamales. And I don't want you to be late."

She started to argue as Rachel walked into the café but realized she wasn't quite sure what she was arguing about. If she had to dodge one more blind date, she might have to smack her sister-in-law, but Rachel had been so focused on shoving her at Adam that Blake would have been surprised if she brought someone new into the picture. But she would think about that after she went to Crossbones.

The crowd in the café had died down, but there were still quite a few people both inside and on the sidewalk as she made her way out. As she made a beeline to her car, Blake was stopped by a voice calling her name. Sean was jogging out of Macabre Reads, coming her direction. She couldn't help but smile as her eyes fell to the tattoos that roamed upward on his arm. *He should really wear short-sleeve shirts more often. I miss summer.*

"Hey, Coffee Goddess, I was just going to come see if you wanted to get lunch." He eyed the purse on her shoulder. "Where ya headed?"

Before she was even finished explaining about Whit's wallet, Sean was climbing into the passenger side of her car. "Wait a second. Sean?"

But he was already slamming his door shut. With a sigh, she slid into the driver's side next to him. "What are you doing?"

His eyes raked over her, smiling as he took her in. "What do you think I'm doing? I'm going with you. I've long since learned it's near impossible to try to talk you out of anything, so…" He reached for his seat belt and stretched it across his muscular torso. "I'm hungry. Crossbones serves lunch." The seat belt clicked shut. "I'm good with that."

"But—" Her mouth opened and shut like a fish out of water. "I was just going to return Whit's wallet."

He arched an eyebrow at her. "Right. You're not going to track Pink Hair down and ask her any questions at all."

She huffed and crossed her arms over her chest. "Getting info out of Kyle can be like pulling teeth. I never know how much she's going to tell me. If I knew she would let me in on any information, I wouldn't have to do my own investigation."

"Blake." Sean shoved a hand through his hair and fisted it. "Look, Kyle's job is not to—you know what?" He held his hand up. "Never mind. Let's just go."

Realizing he wasn't going to get out of her car, Blake started the engine. Fine, if he wanted to come with her, then he could help her ask some questions. But if he started arguing with her, she was totally kicking him out the next time they slowed down.

Chapter Fifteen

When they pulled into the parking lot at Crossbones, Blake saw no police cars. She put the car in park and let it idle as she leaned back in her seat and gave a little sigh of relief. At least she didn't have to worry about her sister being there.

Sean glanced from her to the door and back again. "We *are* actually going to go inside, right?"

"Of course we're going inside. I just want to wait a few minutes. The other day, Pepper was driving a Camry, and I don't see her car anywhere. Maybe she's on break or something." She glanced over at the man next to her and remembered what her major focus had been before this whole mess had started: her preoccupation—okay, *obsession*—that he hadn't kissed her yet.

Those thoughts still hadn't left her mind. They'd just gotten pushed back a little bit. Her eyes slid over his features as he studied the parking lot, and nerves trembled in her stomach. She'd known him over six months, and he still caused sparks to shoot across her skin. It didn't help that they were in close quarters or that he smelled of old books and coffee, which was about the biggest aphrodisiac in her wheelhouse.

The dimple in his cheek flashed a second before he turned his head and caught her gaze. Her cheeks heated as she jerked her head away, embarrassed to be caught staring.

But he wasn't having it. He reached over and cupped her cheek, gently turning her head back to face him. "What're you thinking, pretty lady?"

She should totally do it. She should just press her lips to his and make the first move, but the freight train of nerves clattering through her body wouldn't let her do it. "I was just, um..." She glanced down. "Wondering why you came with me," she finished lamely.

He leaned back, his smile fading a notch as he assessed her. He'd given her the opportunity, and she hadn't taken it. She knew she would kick herself later. Heck, she was already kicking herself.

"What I'm doing here is caring about you. Worrying about you."

When she started to open her mouth to protest, he reached up and pressed his fingertips to her lips. "And before you tell me you don't need a babysitter, trust me, I'm fully aware you can handle yourself. But at the same time, you've gotta understand that the thought of you stumbling across dead bodies with killer clowns running around makes me just a tad bit anxious. A lot of people love you, Blake. A lot of people would be really upset if you got hurt. And personally, I feel a little bit better serving as backup in case you stumble across Pennywise and he happens to be feeling a little bit stabby. So you're just going to have to deal with that."

She reached up and pulled his fingers away from her mouth, yet she couldn't help but lick her lips. "I wasn't going to argue with you. I was just going to say thank you for being here."

He leaned in, sending a cascade of shivers down her spine as he reached up to tuck a strand of dark-blond hair behind her ear. "Baby, I'm always here for you." He leaned in a bit more, and her eyes started to drift shut, when Sean's grasp tightened. "There she is!"

Blake's eyes shot open. "What! Who?" For a moment, Blake had forgotten where the two of them even were.

Sean gently turned her head in the direction of the door to Crossbones. Pepper had parked her Camry right in front and was swaying her pointy hips as she walked inside.

She looked at Sean. "You ready?"

Disappointment crossed his face, but then he grinned. "Hey, I'm just Robin on this mission. Lead the way, Batman."

They walked across the lot, and Sean opened the door for her, letting her indeed lead the way.

The lunch crowd at Crossbones didn't seem too busy, but several booths were filled with patrons—mostly an older crowd from what she could see. A bearded man looked up when she entered and waved from his booth. Cat Schroder. She remembered him from his stop by Mystery Cup. She raised her hand to wave, when she heard a snippy voice at her back.

"Oh lord, it's you. I should have known that after the cop sister comes the nosy sister."

Blake turned and came eye to eye with Pepper. Her pinched face narrowed as she stared down her nose, and Blake had the strong urge to tell her that if someone slapped her on the back, her features might stick that way. The woman didn't look as though she'd settled in for her workday since she still had her bedazzled pink duffel purse slung over her shoulder. *Do they even sell Bedazzlers anymore?*

Sean slid onto a barstool and patted the one next to him. "Actually, Blake came to return something, and we thought we'd stay for lunch."

She took the barstool next to Sean as Pepper's eyes flicked back and forth between them. "Return something? Return what?"

Blake dug the wallet out of her purse. "Whit left his wallet when he was at Buttkick this morning. Orlando asked me to return it. Is he around?"

"My wallet?" Whit stuck his head out from behind the wall of liquor that lined the back of the bar. "Oh, thank God! I was about to call and cancel my credit cards."

He glanced up at Pepper as he walked out from behind the liquor wall, and his expression became stern. "Miss Wright, good to see you're back from lunch." His eyes snapped to the clock, leading

Blake to believe that Pepper had taken more than her allotted hour. The young woman's cheeks turned the same shade of pink as her hair as she stomped behind the bar. The chill in Whit's attitude surprised Blake. It was a far cry from how friendly the two had been last time she was in.

Whit turned his attention back to Blake as she slid the wallet across the counter to him. "No worries, I didn't take any of your credit cards. No online shopping or anything."

Sean winked. "She says that, but if an Amazon order of horror movies and chocolate-covered coffee beans shows up on your statement, you know where to turn."

Whit laughed as she playfully smacked Sean on the arm.

Pepper, who seemed forever opposed to cracking a smile, rolled her eyes and turned away from them. Blake watched her as Sean and Whit made small talk. She vaguely heard Sean order cheeseburgers for them both as she tried to think of a good way to casually ask, "Were you sleeping with Todd Lang, and oh, by the way, did you murder him and drag his body into an attic?"

Pepper walked over to the edge of the bar and looped her beaded keychain over a hook on a panel next to three other sets of keys before she stuffed her purse in a cubby underneath it. The little area at the edge of the bar seemed like a good hiding place for personal effects, and she wondered if Pepper kept her personal belongings there all the time.

When Pepper turned back her way, she kept her eyes on Whit as she gathered her pink hair up in a ponytail and secured it with an elastic band.

"Is that really a safe place?" Blake asked, interrupting a conversation that she hadn't been at all paying attention to.

"Huh?" Whit looked at her with a confused expression. "Is what a safe place for what?"

"Oh, sorry." She gave her head a little shake, trying to remember that people couldn't see exactly what was going on inside her brain, which was most definitely a good thing. She pointed to the panel behind the bar. "The keys. I noticed a lot of keys hanging there. I was just wondering if that's where everyone keeps their keys. That just doesn't seem like a safe place. I mean anyone could grab them, right? Wouldn't it make more sense to keep them in your pocket or purse or something?"

Sean's eyes followed hers to the panel along the wall, where the sets of keys hung, and Blake wondered if he saw what she did. As soon as Pepper had looped her keys around the hook, Blake's eyes had zeroed in on the triangular key that she was quite familiar with because it looked just like the one Micah had given her to get into the apartment above Sliced.

"Oh that." Whit waved it off. "The managers keep their keys there because we all have keys on our key rings to different spots in the building—storage, back doors, cabinets, whatever. It just makes sense to keep the keys there in case someone needs to get into something."

Alarm bells were going off in Blake's head. "But doesn't that seem kind of dangerous? I mean, anyone could come up and snatch the keys." She could almost smack herself for not realizing that the first time she'd been in to talk to Pepper. But she really wanted to know just how methodical a person Pepper was. If she were the killer, she could throw up the defense that anyone could have gotten to her keys since everyone knew she hung them right by the bar. Heck, she could even claim they'd gone missing, when in reality she could just be covering her skinny behind.

Whit chuckled. "No one's getting behind the bar unless they're supposed to be back here."

Blake could see that the way the bar was set up, it would be difficult for a person to get back there. They would have to lift up a section of the bar to be able to walk through. That wasn't something that could really be done without someone behind the bar noticing. The place was so busy, with employees coming and going behind the bar, that one person slipping in and out didn't catch anyone's attention. Maybe that had been exactly what Pepper was counting on.

The girl sidled up to Whit and crossed her thin arms over her ample breasts. "You don't owe her an explanation, Whit." She jerked her chin at Blake. "Why are you so concerned about our keys, anyway?"

"No reason," she lied. "Just an observation. At the café, everyone is leery about leaving anything personal out front where a customer could get to it. Have any of your keys ever gone missing?"

Pepper ignored the question. "Of course the omnipotent Blake Harper"—she waved her hands around to prove her sarcastic point—"knows how to do everything right."

"Pepper!" Whit snapped. "What has gotten into you? We're making conversation. Blake was nice enough to bring my wallet back. What right do you have to be rude to her?"

The pink-haired woman shrank back a bit, still seething. "I'm rude to her because she seems intent on screwing up my life!"

That seemed a bit melodramatic. She'd come down a couple of times to ask some questions, but she wasn't quite sure how that had ruined Pepper's life. "Uh, what are you talking about?"

Pepper jabbed a finger at her. "Bad luck surrounds you. Death surrounds you. Because of you, I have to wait another two weeks before I can even get into my new apartment. Apparently, it's going to take the cleaning service that long to get the smell out. I'm homeless! And it's your fault!"

Sean put a protective hand on Blake's arm. "Are you serious right now? Blake didn't kill anyone. If she hadn't found the body, *you* would have found it, and guess what? You still wouldn't have gotten to move in."

"He's right," Whit agreed. "You can't blame that on her, Pepper."

The woman's furious brown eyes pinged from one of them to the other. "But I can blame her for the rumors that have been started about me. I can tell some of the things you must have been sharing with everyone just from the questions your sister asked me this morning. She actually asked me if I had a clown suit! People think I'm a killer! And not only that, they think I was involved with that slimy Todd Lang because that's what you're probably telling everyone!"

"I..." Okay, so that was her theory, but she hadn't shared it with... Okay, so she'd shared it with a few people. But even if she hadn't, Pepper was talking loudly enough that the people in the next town were probably getting an earful of the situation. In Blake's opinion, the louder Pepper's protests got, the more suspicion around her grew. *The lady doth protest too much.*

"Okay, I never spread any rumors about you, Pepper." Blake kept her voice calm. "I never said you were dressed as a clown. As far as Todd Lang..." She bobbled her head. "Well, he did like to date younger women, so... sorry, but that wouldn't be much of a stretch for anyone to come up with. Are you saying you weren't involved with him?"

"Oh my God!" Pepper growled, lunging in Blake's direction. Thank goodness for Whit's quick reflexes, or Pepper would have come over the bar at her. He had an arm firmly around Pepper's waist as she continued to seethe. "I'm a black belt, Blake Harper. Come here and let me show you how I take care of nosy busybodies."

"Uh, Whit." Sean moved a protective arm around Blake. "Maybe you should box our lunch up to go."

"Yeah." He cast a stern look at the woman struggling in his arms. "I think that might be best."

Whit put his face close to Pepper's ear, and Blake couldn't hear what he said, but as pale as Pepper got, it couldn't have been good.

After he finally let her go, Pepper quickly retreated to the back and out of sight, while the other patrons turned back to their own conversations.

Whit proceeded to make small talk with Sean until their lunch was delivered moments later. By then, Blake was more than ready to make a quick exit.

"You okay?" Sean asked as they left the building.

"I'm fine," she said dejectedly.

Sean stopped and turned to her. "What is it? If it's Pepper, don't listen to her. Don't let her upset you."

"It's not that." Blake blew out a breath and raked a hand through her hair. "I'm just irked that the visit was a total bust. And what about that apartment key hanging in plain sight? Anyone could have figured out a way to grab it, or maybe that's what Pepper wants everyone to think. I keep trying to narrow things down, and all I end up doing is casting the net wider."

"Well, come on back to the bookstore. We can discuss it over lunch," he said, lifting up the sack of food he held. "Double cheeseburgers. I'll even let you have my pickles."

Blake grinned and started across the lot to her car. But when she noticed the police car parked next to hers, she stopped dead in her tracks. "Oh, sweet holy crapballs."

Kyle slid out of the passenger seat as Jason climbed out of the driver's seat and stood next to the car, looking as though he would rather be anywhere else. *What on earth are they doing back here if they already questioned Pepper?*

Blake stood her ground as her younger sister walked up to stand directly in front of her.

Kyle crossed her arms over her chest and firmed her lips. Her eyes tensed before she finally spoke. "That's the last straw, Blake Harper. You're under arrest for obstructing an investigation."

Chapter Sixteen

"Okay, you really didn't have to drive me downtown in the back of a police cruiser. Don't you think that part was overkill?" Blake sulked with her arms crossed over her chest as she sat in the hard-plastic chair in front of her sister's desk at the police station. She looked out Kyle's office window but didn't see Sean. Jason had probably sent him on his merry way. It was probably a good thing too. He'd been way too amused over the whole situation. She turned her attention back to her sister. "I wasn't even doing anything. I went to return Whit's wallet."

Kyle took off her lightweight jacket, revealing her holster and weapon, and hung it on the back of her spinny chair.

Blake eyed the gun at her sister's waist. "If you're pissed at me, can you take that off before we start talking?"

Kyle glanced down at the gun then rolled her eyes before she stalked over and shut the door. She didn't say a word until she had walked behind her desk and plopped down in her chair. She steepled her fingers as she assessed Blake.

Unimpressed with her sister's dramatics, Blake just sighed and raised her eyebrows. "Yes? Say it. Go on!"

Kyle propped her elbows on the desk and leaned forward. "Okay, I'm willing to give you the benefit of the doubt. If you can honestly look at me and tell me you only went to Crossbones to return Whit's wallet and have lunch with Sean, I will apologize all over myself. If it really didn't have anything to do with investigating anything on your own, then I really will. Hell, I'll take out an ad in the *Wilton Daily*

News if I'm wrong." She looked Blake in the eyes, daring her to tell the truth.

With a lift of her chin, Blake was so tempted to lie... but she couldn't do it. Instead, she blew out a breath, her body deflating like a balloon. "Fine. I may have used that as an excuse so I could ask Pepper some questions."

To Kyle's credit, a self-satisfied smirk only crossed her face for a second.

"Who told you I was down there, anyway?" Blake still hadn't figured that out.

"I stopped by the café. Eli told me after he made my latte." She picked up a paper cup at the corner of her desk that said "Kelly" in black Sharpie on the side.

Despite herself, Blake couldn't help the chuckle that burst forth. "I shouldn't have tried to put anything past you, *Kelly*," she said with a giggle.

Kyle tried to stifle a grin and slipped a hand over her mouth when she couldn't, laughing along with Blake.

The tension in the room lessened, and Blake felt as though she was finally able to breathe. "You know," she finally said after a long pause, "I really don't do it to antagonize you. I just thought that last time we made a good team. I was able to find out some things that you didn't. So this time..." She shrugged a shoulder.

Kyle offered a brief smile. "We always did make a good team. But Blake, this is different. You're not a cop. Yeah, you're good at getting information out of people. I think working in a café is like being a bartender. People tend to just tell you stuff they'd never share with me. But that's not the point. You saw last spring how dangerous investigating things on your own can be, and you've already had someone try to run you down this week. I don't want you antagonizing Killer Bozo."

"I know. You're right. I promise I'll try not to take any more risks. I swear." She held up her hand in a pledge for emphasis.

When Kyle arched an eyebrow at her, she said, "No, seriously. You have all the information I do. The body was found. You know about the clown. You have the information from Bree. You know all about Pepper, and the fact that she's a black belt and could totally move a body, *and* the key thing at the club. You have everything I—"

"Wait. She's a black belt? And what key thing?" Kyle interrupted.

"You know." Blake mimed a rectangle with her hands. "That panel behind the bar where everyone hangs their keys. When I saw the apartment key on Pepper's key ring right out there in the open, it made me realize how easy it would be for somebody to get to. Or if she is the killer, that would be the perfect way to throw blame in another direction."

Kyle was suddenly pressing her fingertips against her temples again. "Crap! When I talked to Pepper, she was on her way out to lunch. I can't believe I've never noticed there's a panel of keys behind the bar!"

A smile tipped Blake's lips up, and she tilted her head, proud of herself. Her smile died when Kyle jabbed a finger at her. "No gloating!"

"I'm not gloating." Blake rubbed her hands on the thighs of her jeans. "Come on, it's not like that helps. That just opens the net to more people than we could count. If she didn't do it, anyone could have managed to sneak back there and get her key to get into the apartment. If that even happened at all. Heck, we still don't know if someone from the holding company was in the apartment. Maybe the killer works for the holding company. Who knows? My whole search for clues is really sucking right about now."

"But this at least gives me some people to look into." Kyle grabbed a notepad and a pen from her desk and began scribbling on it. "I can start by finding out who's allowed behind the counter so I can try to get a composite list of anyone who has a key.

"So I helped?"

Kyle paused her writing at Blake's question.

Blake clapped her hands together. "Oh, come on, I helped. Give me this one little victory."

Kyle rolled her eyes and sighed dramatically. "Fiiine, you helped a little."

"Awesome!" She bounced in her seat. "So, I tried to get information out of Pepper."

"Of course you did." Kyle tapped her pen on her notepad and raised her eyebrows.

"Not much luck. She claims she wasn't involved with Todd, but I don't know if I believe that. I mean, she says she wasn't, but she could be lying, and that would have given her a perfect—"

"She has an alibi," Kyle interrupted.

Blake felt herself deflate like a balloon. "She... Wait, what?

"We need to verify it, but she claims she was babysitting her nephew in Kansas City."

"Aha!" Blake held up a finger. "So you don't know for sure."

"Not yet, Columbo. But while we're verifying that, I don't want to just sit on my hands." Kyle started scribbling again. "So I can at least make a list of who else had access to those keys."

She didn't have time to offer any suggestions because the door opened behind her and Jason walked in. "You ready, Blake?"

"Ready?" Her eyes widened, and she jerked her head back to Kyle. "Oh God, you're not booking me, are you? You're really going to arrest me?" She pressed a hand to her chest. "Your own sister?"

Kyle stood up and pulled her handcuffs from her belt. "Turn around, sis."

Blake's stomach dropped. "Oh my God, Kyle, are you serious?"

Jason chuckled as Kyle burst out laughing. "The look on your face was priceless." She dabbed at her eyes, still giggling. "Oh, that was so worth it. I'm not going to arrest you. Jason will take you back to the café."

"I have to admit I'd love to see Raimy's face if you were raising hell down in holding," Jason said, laughing as he ushered her out.

"That was so not funny." Blake picked up her purse, taking a shaky breath as she turned to follow Jason. "I'll see you later at the self-defense class, you sadist." She started to walk out the door but then stopped and turned one last time. "Oh, and Kyle, you're welcome."

Blake didn't miss her sister sticking out her tongue as she closed the office door behind her.

AT FOUR O'CLOCK, BLAKE was hanging her apron over a hook in the kitchen as Giselle hopped back and forth from foot to foot. "Come on, Blake, we're going to be late."

"Whose idea exactly was a self-defense class anyway?" She turned to the small wall mirror and gave her outfit a once-over, thankful she'd had time to run home and change into leggings and a T-shirt that proclaimed, "I'm not addicted to coffee. We're just in a very committed relationship." Blake ran a hand over her hair, trying to smooth down the part that wasn't secured by her ponytail. "Oh, screw it," she muttered, grabbing her purse.

"Orlando's idea, I think, but he doesn't have much to do with it. It's all Jason and Kyle. Perfect timing too. After Todd's murder and someone trying to run you down, it sounds like there's going to be a good crowd of women, from what I've heard." Giselle continued talking about how smart it was for Orlando to come up with such a great idea, and Blake tried really hard not to roll her eyes as they made their way out front. No amount of self-defense would help her win a battle against a speeding truck.

"Eli, are you sure you can handle things by yourself until closing?"

"No problem, Boss Lady," he said as he wiped down the spigot on the espresso machine. "Watching the shop by myself will be my penance for telling Kyle you went to Crossbones. I still say she tricked me. Totally not my fault."

She laughed. "I have no doubt. See you later, Eli."

"Just be careful." He winked at them. "Don't break anyone's kneecaps, Janelle."

The muscle along the side of Giselle's jaw tensed as she gritted her teeth, but to her credit, she didn't respond as they walked out of the café and headed across the street.

When they walked into Buttkick, the smell of sweat and cologne wafted over Blake.

"Mmm." Giselle was practically purring. "It smells just like Orlando."

Blake resisted the urge to ask if that was a good thing. Considering the smile on Giselle's face when she spotted him and rushed in his direction, it was.

A huge red banner above the snack bar area contained a graphic of a woman kicking a masked man in the face and read, "Fight Like a Lady." And ladies, there were. At least thirty women occupied the center of the gym, where several mats were spread out across the wide-open area. Blake was so focused on the number of women gathered that she almost ran into Mr. Hamilton.

She had to blink a couple of times. "Mr. Hamilton, I don't think I've ever seen you without a suit on before." The older man wore a short-sleeved shirt, which showed off his surprisingly well-toned arms. *Mr. Hamilton has muscles?*

He chuckled as he blushed. "Yes, well, it's easier to lift weights without a suit. Whitley has me working out since he's been back in town. I'm not sure what that has to do with lowering my cholesterol, but the boy seems to think there's some sort of correlation."

"Oh, is Whit here too?" She looked around but didn't see anyone near the weight machines.

"No, he couldn't join me for today's workout. Apparently, they're shorthanded at Crossbones. Anyhow, I thought I should get out of the way before you all get started." He looked back at the group of women—and at Ruby Cross in particular, who wore a bright-yellow leotard and matching headband. She winked at him. Mr. Hamilton turned around, looking alarmed. "Ms. Cross seems very animated tonight."

Blake cleared her throat in an effort to hide her laugh. "Nothing new there."

The tapping of a microphone got Blake's attention, and Jason walked to the center of the mats as the women quieted. "Ladies, if everyone is about ready, we'll start here in just a couple of minutes."

"I'm going to get out of the line of fire. Enjoy yourself," Mr. Hamilton said as he headed for the door.

Blake made her way over to the group and headed to where Giselle and Rachel had saved her a spot. "Where's Ryan? I thought he was going to be our bad guy," she said as she sat criss-cross applesauce between the two of them. They were three of about thirty women who sat in a giant circle around the large blue mat in the center of the gym. Kyle and Jason stood in the middle of the circle, talking in low tones.

Rachel shook her head. "Your sister nixed that plan. She was afraid there was too high a risk that he could hurt a hand, and she didn't want to be responsible for him having to reschedule surgeries."

Blake pouted. "I suppose that makes sense, but crud, I was all ready to flip him."

"You'll have to flip Jason instead. Did you get a load of his protective gear?" Rachel inclined her head as she took in the rubber-looking pad covering Jason's groin. "I wonder what he thinks we're going to do to him."

Before she could answer Rachel, she nearly jumped out of her skin at Kyle's yell.

"Are you following me?" her sister practically screamed at Jason. When he lunged for her, she shouted, "No, no, no, no!" as she brought the heel of her hand up against his nose and kicked him so hard in his padded groin that it made Blake wince.

If their goal had been to quiet the group, they'd succeeded. All the women sat in stunned silence... except Rachel. "Nice!" She cupped her hands to her mouth to amplify her voice. "Kick him again!"

Red Montgomery cleared her throat. The older woman had on a neon-pink leotard that somehow worked on her even though it clashed garishly with her bright-red hair. "Kyle, dear, if you ever plan to have children with that boy, I would avoid kicking him in the jewels that hard, even if he is wearing padding."

Her comment sent several women, including Blake and Rachel, erupting into a fit of giggles, but they quieted at Kyle's sharp glare.

"Thank you, Red." Kyle patted Jason on the back. "I can assure you that Jason came well-protected."

He grinned and winked at Kyle, making her lips twitch. "Ladies." Jason stepped forward, seeming no worse for wear, except for his tousled caramel-colored hair. "You see how Kyle's loud voice got your attention. We wanted to show you that an attack actually begins before there's any physical contact. An attacker is looking for a target. They don't want someone strong and loud who's going to fight back."

Kyle nodded. "We're throwing ladylike out the window. We want you to draw attention to yourself. You have permission to be loud, scream, fight back, do everything you can to get away from your attacker." She looked specifically at the older women in the group, although Blake was pretty sure Ruby Cross could take out an attacker without half trying. If being loud did the trick, all of the women in the book club were safe.

Penny Driver raised her hand, and Kyle pointed to her.

The older woman reached up to adjust her silver hair, which she had tied up in a messy bun atop her head. "I had a knee replacement last year, so it's harder for me to get my knees up to kick somebody in the balls. Do you have other tips?"

Rachel reached over to squeeze Blake's hand, and Blake bit her lip, not daring to look at her sister-in-law. It was all she could do to hold it together when Penny said the word "balls." If she looked at Rachel, they would both dissolve into laughter.

As Kyle explained that they were going to show moves that anyone could do, the swish of the front door caught Blake's attention. Her face dropped when she saw Sabrina Lang and Elaine Page walk in together. Both women were in designer athletic wear, and when they saw Blake, they both looked as if they could take her out with the daggers they were mentally shooting at her.

Blake winced. "Seriously?" Even though a part of her wanted to talk to Sabrina to see if she could zero in on exactly who Todd had been seeing since their divorce, she really didn't have the energy to be on defense.

"What is she doing here?" Rachel hiss-whispered. "Shouldn't she still be in mourning?"

Jason acknowledged the women and motioned for them to sit.

Blake leaned close to Rachel's ear. "Not only that, but since when are they friends?" she whispered.

"Maybe they met at 'how to be a royal bitch' class." Rachel mumbled. "I hear they both graduated with top honors."

Either that, or they were forming an anti-Blake club. Elaine still must not have been over her assumption that Blake had interfered in her relationship with Whit.

Blake averted her eyes when Sabrina caught her staring. She certainly didn't want to draw unwanted attention.

"Tonight, we want to show you a few simple moves that anyone can do to defend yourself." Kyle widened her stance. "What we're going for here is either incapacitating your attacker or stunning them long enough that you can get away."

Jason stepped up. "But the best way to protect yourself is to be aware and not put yourself in a volatile situation." He counted the items off on his fingers. "Always be aware of your surroundings. Do not walk alone at night. Always take well-lit paths. Be smart, ladies."

"And look both ways before crossing the street," Blake mumbled, thinking of the truck that tried to run her down.

"Exactly," Kyle said in response to Jason as she looked around the room. "Now we want to focus on simple moves you can remember. Your main goal should be to cause your attacker pain, and you don't need complicated moves to do that. Let's say an attacker comes at you from the front."

Jason reached up and gently wrapped his hands around Kyle's throat.

"Focus on the weakest parts of your attacker's body. If he's close enough, go right for his face." Kyle brought her hands up and mimicked hitting Jason in the eyes, nose, and ears with the palms of her hand. "Now if your attacker is a little farther away, you want to get their hands away from your throat."

Jason wrapped his hands around Kyle's throat again, and she brought her hands up between his arms, shoved them away, then went at his face again. Jason resumed his position, and Kyle continued. "If you can manage to get ahold of one of their fingers, you can really do some damage." She reached up where his hands were on her throat and managed to pry off his pinky finger. "Bend it back as hard as you can. You want to break it." When some of the women winced, Kyle said, "Pain. You want to cause your attacker pain so you can get away. Remember that. Now, who would like to try this for real? Volunteers?"

Several hands shot up, including Blake. When Kyle pointed to Ruby Cross, Blake let out a gasp. "What is Kyle thinking? Ruby could probably take both her and Jason out."

Jason turned on his full-wattage smile. "Come on up here, Ms. Cross."

Kyle positioned the petite woman in front of Jason. "This technique has nothing to do with how old or how big you are. Now remember, Ruby, I want you to try the move, but don't hit Jason with force. It'll be hard for him to teach the class if he's out cold."

"I'll try not to hurt him, dear, but I can't promise anything." Ruby got into position and clenched her bony fists.

When Jason reached up and put his hands around her throat, a growl came out of the older woman that was so primal, it caused Blake's jaw to drop. The flicker that went across Kyle's face said that her sister realized a moment too late that she'd picked the wrong volunteer. Before she could stop Ruby, the woman started swinging her hands like crazy, pummeling Jason with the heels of her palms. He immediately let go and dropped to the ground.

But Ruby didn't stop. With some sort of senior-citizen power yell, she leapt on him, her yellow leotard a blur as she punched and kicked the poor man as if she were Rocky Balboa.

"Ruby, stop!" Blake yelled, jumping up, but the little woman kept going as Jason curled into a ball, covering his hands with his face.

Red Montgomery casually stood and perched her hands on her thin hips. "Now Ruby, you stop hittin' that poor boy. You're gonna give him a black eye, and if you make him too mad, he'll arrest ya for all those parking tickets."

At that, Ruby stopped and paled a bit. "I'm so sorry," she said. "I just got carried away." She ambled off of Jason, looking as though she'd finally come to her senses. "I'm so sorry, Detective Harper." Ruby looked from Kyle to Jason, who was peeking through his fingers. "You're not going to arrest me for assaulting a police officer, are you?"

Kyle's expression looked as though it was somewhere between complete shock and total amusement. "No, no, of course not, Ruby. But why don't you sit down? I think we'll get another volunteer for this next round." She leaned over and whispered something to Jason, and he nodded then whispered back.

"He's okay, everyone," Kyle announced as Jason got up and brushed himself off.

The group of women applauded, either ignoring or not noticing that Jason's face was a bit red and his upper lip looked as though it was starting to swell.

"Jason's going to take a break, so can I get another volunteer to help me with this next demonstration?"

Absolutely no one raised their hand this time, all the woman looking a bit fearful as they eyed Ruby Cross. Blake sure didn't want to be used as a punching bag. Ruby plopped down next to her friends, smiling as if beating the crap out of a big, burly cop was an everyday occurrence for her.

Kyle sighed. "Blake, thanks for volunteering. Come on up."

"What?" Blake backed up. "But I-I..." She didn't want to get her ass kicked.

Rachel and Giselle pushed her forward. "Go on. She's dying out there," Rachel hiss-whispered.

Crap! "Okay, okay." Blake lumbered up, walked to the center of the mat, and stood next to Kyle. She would have protested more, but maybe helping out would get her back into Kyle's good graces.

Penny Cross's hand immediately shot up. "Detective Harper, can you show us the Sandra Bullock move?" When Kyle's brows drew together, perplexed, Penny said, "You know, S.I.N.G. *Miss Congeniality* is one of my favorite movies."

Understanding seemed to dawn on Kyle, and a slow grin spread across her face. "S.I.N.G. Of course. That's more of an elaborate move that I wanted to stay away from, but I will show you how to properly execute it so it can work."

Blake's shoulders relaxed a little. Sandra Bullock was a total badass. She was pretty sure she could rock that move.

"In this case, S.I.N.G. stands for solar plexus, instep, nose, and groin. And this is a move you can use if someone grabs you from behind. Blake, I want you to grab me from behind." She wrapped her arms around herself. "In a bear hug."

Strands of hair flew out of Blake's ponytail as she vigorously shook her head.

Kyle turned to look at her sister. "Blake," she said through gritted teeth as some of the women chuckled. "Come at me from behind."

She blew out a breath. "Okay, but do not give me a fat lip."

Kyle turned her back, and Blake grabbed her in a bear hug.

"Okay, ladies," Kyle said loudly. "Here you are going for weak parts on your attacker's body. "First, solar plexus." Kyle drew her arm back and lightly jabbed Blake in the stomach with her elbow. "And remember, you are not aiming *at* your target, you're hitting *through* them. In this case, you're trying to elbow right through their stomach. That's how hard I want you to do it. That will throw your attacker off, and then you shift your weight." She shifted to the side and shouted, "Instep," before she brought her foot down, mimicking a stomp on Blake's foot. "Then nose." She brought her fist up and lightly hit Blake in the nose. "And groin." The same fist came down, and she mimicked hitting Blake in the privates repeatedly. "Or the stomach, depending on the height of you and your attacker. Got it?"

Blake clapped her hands and bent her knees. "Oh, I am all over this." She was ready to go.

Elaine Page raised her hand. "Give her the foam pads and beat the hell out of her." A cruel smile twisted her lips. "Or don't give her the foam pads."

Sabrina laughed. *The witch.*

But Ruby turned an evil eye on Elaine. "Now you be nice, Elaine, or I'll do another demonstration on you."

The woman's smile faded, and she paled. "Sorry, Ruby." For some reason, Ruby, Red, and Penny could always put Elaine in her place. Blake didn't know how they did it, but after seeing Ruby in action, maybe a good dose of fear was involved.

Kyle bestowed a death glare on Elaine before she pursed her lips and turned back to Blake. She shook her head, and Blake could see that her sister was trying her hardest to control her frustration with the woman. "You ready to try it, Blake?"

Clapping her hands together, Blake blew out a breath, ready to blow off some steam. "Sure, I'll give it a shot."

"Okay, I'm going to grab you from behind."

Blake widened her stance as Kyle moved into position behind her. "Just don't confuse me with Elaine or Sabrina and take my head off," she whispered, causing Blake to giggle.

"Okay, here we go." Kyle's arms came around her in a bear hug. "Remember, solar plexus, instep, nose, groin."

With her sister's moves fresh in her mind, Blake made a motion of elbowing her in the stomach. "Solar plexus." Then she shifted her hips so she could bring her foot down lightly on Kyle's. "Instep."

"Good!" Kyle encouraged.

"Nose," Blake said as she brought her fist up and stopped an inch before Kyle's face. "And groin or stomach." She brought her fist down and pretended to punch Kyle repeatedly in the abdomen.

All the women in the circle clapped, and Rachel gave a shrill wolf whistle.

"All right, who's next? Blake can be our attacker. Who wants to be her victim?"

"I'll do it."

Blake turned at the sharp voice and was surprised when Sabrina popped up and stepped forward. Her long blond ponytail hung down her back, and her narrowed eyes were focused on Blake. They appeared sharp and deadly, not red-rimmed as they had the last time Blake had seen her.

Uh-oh. The woman obviously had some anger, and Blake was pretty sure she was about to be Sabrina's target.

Kyle's eyes flitted from Sabrina to Blake. "Uh, maybe we should get someone else."

She was about to take Kyle up on that offer and reclaim her seat by Rachel and Giselle, when a superior smirk tilted Sabrina's mouth. Then all of a sudden, whether it was a good decision or not, Blake was determined not to give her the satisfaction of backing down.

"No, that's okay." Blake jutted her chin out. "Let's do this."

"Uh, okay." Kyle sounded unsure. She moved toward Blake as Sabrina started to get in position. "You sure about this?" she whispered.

"I'm sure." Blake got behind Sabrina. "Just like before, right? Easy peasy."

Kyle's blue eyes studied her then turned to the other woman. "Remember, Sabrina, this is a simple demonstration. There is *no* actual contact. Got it?"

"Of course." Sabrina's voice was pleasant, which made it sound all the more eerie in Blake's opinion.

"Okaaay." Kyle backed up hesitantly. "Here we go."

Blake wrapped her arms around Sabrina, keeping the embrace light. For a moment, nothing happened, and she thought maybe Sabrina wasn't going to perform the demonstration at all. Just when she was about to let go, her nemesis went into action. And Sabrina moved fast. Her elbow went back, catching Blake in the stomach, hard enough to knock the wind out of her. Before she could catch her breath, Sabrina was bringing her foot down on top of Blake's firmly.

"Ow!" Blake started to move back, but Sabrina caught her in the face to the right of her nose. The blow knocked her back, and she stumbled, seeing stars. She braced herself for the punch to her stomach or groin she was sure would come, but when she managed to focus, she saw Sabrina's mouth form an O as she reeled back. Blake realized that Kyle had grabbed Sabrina and had her on the ground in a blur of movement.

"What the hell do you think you're doing to my sister?" Fury shook Kyle's voice.

"Oh, please." Venom filled Sabrina's voice. "She had that coming and more. The goody-goody Blake Harper can't keep her nose out of everyone's business, and now my husband's dead."

Blake rubbed her face. "Are you crazy? I didn't have anything to do with his death."

Sabrina looked up at her, her gaze giving off so much ice that Blake shivered. "Maybe you didn't drive the knife through his heart, but your name is all over this case. I'm sick of it. I'm sick and tired of you being everywhere every time I turn around." She glared at Kyle. "Now let me off of this mat. It smells like feet!"

The women were all standing by then, and Penny Driver crossed her arms. "Sabrina, you sound like a child. I'm sorry Todd's dead, but Blake doesn't have a thing to do with that, and you know it."

"Yeah." Giselle stepped closer. "You're just using that as an excuse to get some good punches in against her."

"You should arrest her for assault," Red offered, adjusting her pink headband.

"Assault?" Sabrina looked at Blake and then Kyle with mortification. "You wouldn't?"

Jason sauntered over calmly and put a hand on Kyle's tense shoulder. She still had Sabrina pinned to the mat.

"Blake?" he asked, not taking his eyes off Kyle. "Do you want to press charges?"

All eyes turned to Blake. It warmed her heart that so many of her friends would stand up for her like that. And throwing Sabrina in jail sure sounded appealing. But with Todd lying in a coffin across town, she just couldn't bring herself to do it, no matter how much Sabrina deserved it. Her mother's voice sounded in her head. *Take the high road, Blake Mildred.* "No, just let her go."

The room held their breath, watching Kyle, who didn't move. Finally, she let out a low growl and stood up.

Sabrina scrambled away and ran to Elaine, who had remained uncharacteristically silent during the whole ordeal. "Let's go," Sabrina bit out.

The two women made a beeline for the front door, leaving the rest of the group staring after them.

Blake let out a huge breath.

"Well." Jason clapped his hands together and smiled at them. "I think that was enough excitement for one night. Why don't we stop there? We can pick this up again next week."

The women erupted into grumbles and whispers as Orlando came rushing over to Blake with an ice pack. "I'm so sorry, Blake." He pressed the pack to her face. "I didn't know it would get so physical."

"I say we send Ruby after Sabrina to kick her surgically enhanced buttocks," Rachel said, walking up. *"Perra enojada."*

Blake's cheek was starting to throb beneath the ice. "Okay, I don't know what that means, and I'm not sure I want to."

"You okay?" Kyle walked up and moved the ice pack then made a face as she looked at Blake's cheek.

"That bad?" She started to look around for a mirror.

Orlando held up a finger as though a light bulb had just lit up in his head. "I have some arnica cream to put on it to help reduce swelling. I'll be right back."

"Great," she grumbled. "I hope I don't scare the kids." *Maybe I should bow out and just go home.*

Rachel glanced at the clock on the far wall. "I have to get home so I can start dinner." She jabbed a finger at Blake. "I know you. Don't you think about canceling." Then she pointed at Kyle. "You and Jason are still coming, right?"

"Oh, we'll be there." Jason tossed an arm around Kyle's shoulder. "Blake and I got our butts kicked. We have to go drown our sorrows in tamales and pie."

But Blake's mind was on more than food. "Does anyone find it curious that Sabrina found the time for a night out when she has a houseful of people and Todd's funeral coming up on Sunday?"

Kyle began nibbling on a nail. "I've stopped trying to figure that woman out."

"But you don't think it's suspicious?" Blake asked. Sabrina hadn't really landed on her suspect list, only because she would never in a million years have thought that Sabrina would hurt Todd. *Maybe I should look a little closer at my rival.*

Her sister studied her nails then crossed her arms. "Sabrina always acts suspicious. But I don't know if she really needs a reason. She's just that bizarre all on her own. Not to mention that grief makes people act weird sometimes. Anyway, I know what you're thinking, and it's a no-go. Sabrina was at Café Muerte at the time your clown was getting all stabby. Concrete alibi."

Rachel wrapped an arm around Blake in a side hug. "Forget her, sister. Forget about everybody. Tonight, just let your problems float away and focus on your family... and my ah-ma-zing cooking."

Blake didn't know if tamales existed that were good enough for her to do that.

Chapter Seventeen

When Blake drove up to her brother's house that evening, she couldn't help but take a moment to stare across the street at the Lang house before she got out of the car. One solitary light shone in an upstairs window of the brick Tudor, which was most likely a bedroom. The horde of cars that had been there was gone, and only one remained. It wasn't Sabrina's, so she must have still had a guest.

She'd heard Todd's funeral was scheduled for Sunday. Sean was planning to go, but Blake hadn't considered it because she knew her presence would not be appreciated. She'd naturally thought there would be family staying with Sabrina until after the funeral was over. Yet Sabrina had made time to go to Buttkick. Any sympathy Blake had had for Sabrina had vanished with that punch to the face. *What is with that woman?*

Maybe they'd all gone out to dinner and Sabrina wasn't home at all, or maybe she was with her new buddy, Elaine. Blake's gaze focused on the lit window, but before she could look away, someone stepped in front of the window, making her jolt.

"Crap." Adrenaline sped up her heartbeat, and she pressed a hand to her chest. She was scaring herself—as if her life weren't scary enough lately all on its own. She glanced back up and saw a silhouette at the window. With the backlighting, she couldn't see who it was, but most likely, Sabrina was wondering why the heck Blake was parked across the street, staring at her house.

Before Blake could turn to ring the doorbell, someone else— taller and bulkier than the first person—stepped in front of the window. Squinting, Blake tried to make out any detail, but that became impossible as the two pressed themselves together, faces included.

Blake's eyes widened in surprise. *Sabrina has male company? Was her big blowup over Todd just an act?* They moved away from the window, and Blake blinked a few times, her mind reeling. If Sabrina had been seeing anyone, she would have heard through the grapevine.

Her eyes dropped to the car sitting in Sabrina's driveway, and she looked at the beat-up Toyota more closely. "Wait a second," she said to herself. "I know that car." She'd seen it in front of Mr. Hamilton's house, in front of Buttkick, and in front of Crossbones. That car belonged to Whit Hamilton. Her mouth dropped open as reality hit her. *Whit and Sabrina? No way.*

Blake shook her head and grabbed the box of pastries she'd brought with her from the bakery. "This is ridiculous." If Sabrina caught her staring, she would be out here for round two. *But what is up with Whit and Sabrina? Is he jealous enough to take out Sabrina's ex? Or is she just one more woman on the list of Wilton women he seems to be going through?* She stepped out of the car and made her way up Ryan and Rachel's front steps.

After ringing the doorbell, she waited mere seconds before Rachel flung the door open. She let out a little gasp when she saw Blake's face but quickly covered with a smile.

"Crap, it's swelling, isn't it?"

"No, no, it's fine." Rachel didn't lie very convincingly. "Come on in. I have someone pouring a glass of wine for you."

"Someone?" *Ugh!* She had totally forgotten Rachel was inviting someone else for dinner. Her hand flew to her face. She was not looking forward to seeing anyone, especially Adam or Sean, when she looked like Quasimodo. Who did you—" Blake didn't get the rest of her words out before she was jumped by two rambunctious six-year-olds.

"Auntie B! Auntie B!" Emma came flying down the stairs in a sparkly pink dress, and Aiden closely followed in an oversized Royals jersey. Emma studied her bruised face. "I like your zombie makeup. Can you do mine like that? Except on both cheeks?"

"No. She's doing my makeup first," cried Aiden, jumping up and down in front of her, his black mop top springing around with his little body.

"No, she's doing mine first." Emma bounced up and down in a miniature copy of Rachel's signature move. "I'm a zombie princess. That's two things. I win!"

Aiden stomped his little sock-covered foot. "I'm two things too. And mine has fake blood. It takes longer. Mo-om, tell Emma I get to go first."

Rachel put a hand on each of her offsprings' heads. "Oh lord, you found the Halloween candy, didn't you?

They both stopped arguing and looked up at their mother with wide eyes.

"Nooo," Emma drew out, which wouldn't have been convincing even if she didn't have chocolate all around her mouth.

"Hey, she's here. How was Fight Club?" Ryan asking, coming into the room and taking the pastry box out of Blake's hand before he grabbed his sister in a hug. "Nice shiner."

"Don't be a smartass. She got in a lucky punch," Blake mumbled into Ryan's shoulder.

A gasp came out of Aiden. "Auntie B, you said a bad word. You have to put a quarter in the swear jar."

She nearly groaned. "Aw, crap, I forgot about the swear jar."

"That's two!" Emma started jumping up and down again. "She said the C word."

She stuck a hand on her hip and looked down at her niece then glanced up at Rachel. "Since when is crap a swear word? That totally should not count."

"You owe us one more quarter." Aiden clapped his hands. "That's three!"

Blake clamped a hand over her mouth before she said anything else. She didn't have that much money in her purse.

Rachel laughed and led Blake into the great room off the kitchen. "Just go with 'fudge.' You'll be safer."

On the way to the kitchen, Blake noticed the dining room table, which was decorated perfectly for fall. Pumpkin-colored candles adorned the middle of the table, with orange, brown, and yellow leaves strewn down the center of the coffee-colored tablecloth. The decorations coordinated perfectly with the napkins and Rachel's Fiestaware.

But what really got Blake's attention was the fact that there were eight place settings. She knew Kyle and Jason were coming, but that still only added up to seven people.

Her eyes jerked to her sister-in-law. "Rach, who did you…" As she entered the kitchen, she saw Adam twisting a corkscrew into a bottle of red wine. Her heart leapt into her throat as the handsome doctor pinned her with his steel-blue gaze.

"Right on time." A slow grin crept across his face, but his smile faltered when his gaze landed on her cheek.

"Adam." Lord, she hoped her voice didn't sound as breathy as she thought it did. As she studied Adam, her insides melted a little bit. He normally looked good, but the dark-blue sweater stretched across his muscular chest really accented his… eyes.

Rachel grabbed a jar off the top of the refrigerator and shoved it at her as Blake tossed her purse and jacket over one of the barstools at the kitchen island.

Blake looked at the big sign taped to the front of the jar: "Curse Jar 25 cents" was written in bright-red crayon.

Rolling her eyes, she opened her purse and pulled out her wallet. "Bloodsuckers," she grumbled, shoving a dollar in the jar.

Adam raised a brow at her. "A whole dollar? Haven't you only been here like sixty seconds?"

She tossed him a glance. "Don't start. Their curse words aren't curse words, and that includes one credit! Totally not my fault."

Adam continued to study her closely, his face tight.

She pointed to her cheek. "Yeah, it's been an interesting day."

"So I heard." He poured a glass half full of wine and slid it across the counter to Blake. "You look like you could use this."

Blake hadn't been thrilled that her sister-in-law had invited a "surprise guest," but she was surprised by how happy she was to see Adam.

Rachel took a sip of her own wine. "Before you get too tipsy, we do makeup. You promised me an easy way to do zombie makeup that wouldn't take me a year to put on Emma. In fact, we have about twenty minutes before the enchiladas come out of the oven, so why don't we do that first?"

Emma, who came into the room in time to catch the last part of the conversation, started jumping up and down again. "Yay!" she screeched, clapping her hands together. "I get to be zombified!"

Blake laughed then winced as the movement pulled her sore facial muscles. She picked up her wine glass and followed Rachel in the direction of the bathroom. "Come on, princess," she said, putting a hand on her niece's shoulder. Zombies usually aren't covered in chocolate, so step one is to wash your face."

Blake followed her niece to the bathroom and lifted her up on to the vanity so that her little cherub face was at eye level. Emma's hair was a skewed halo of black curls, and Blake stared into the little girl's blue eyes, a mirror of her own. They were the same eyes she shared not only with both twins but with both of her siblings as well.

"Auntie B, you're still coming trick-or-treating with us on Saturday, right?" her niece asked. "You promised!"

She pressed a kiss against Emma's forehead. "I wouldn't miss it, baby. Especially because you've promised me Tootsie Rolls. I can't pass that up."

Emma giggled. "I like the Reese's. Those are my favorite."

Rachel wiped the chocolate off her daughter's face with a damp washcloth as Blake discussed the pros and cons of M&M's versus Skittles with her niece. When Emma was clean, Blake picked up a tube of green cream makeup and began to lightly sponge it on her cheeks.

A loud grumble sounded, and Blake looked at the toilet, wondering if a monster lived inside.

"It's always doing that." Emma yawned, and Blake wondering if she was starting to come down from the sugar high. "Last time it made the noise, water came out of the potty and Mommy cursed so much that she had to put five dollars in the jar!"

That seemed to make Emma happy, but Rachel frowned. "If it overflows tonight, I'm going take a sledgehammer to that septic tank. I refuse to pay the plumber one more cent."

Blake starting sponging Emma's makeup on again. "Why don't you guys just get a new one? This one's been giving you problems forever."

"It's so expensive," Rachel nearly whined. "I was hoping we could wait until after Christmas. Unless that's what the twins would like on Christmas morning. What do you say, Em? How about a shiny new septic tank for Christmas?"

The little girl's mouth popped open. "Nuh-uh! Mommy, are you teasing, or are you serial?"

Blake chuckled as Rachel leaned over to tickle Emma's tummy.

Thirty minutes later, after two reapplications of green glitter lipstick and a break to do Aiden's makeup, the little boy was running around in his Royals jersey, his vampire teeth in, happy with the blood that looked like it was dripping from his mouth, and Blake was applying a dusting of glitter to Emma's finished look with a kabuki brush.

When she declared her niece finished, the little girl scrambled off the vanity. "Daddy! Adam! Look at my zombie sparkles!" she yelled as she ran into the kitchen.

"Think you can handle that?" Blake asked Rachel, who was on her second glass of wine.

"That didn't look too hard. But how did you get so good at Halloween makeup?"

Blake took a sip of wine. "YouTube and way too much free time."

A tiny smile pursed Rachel's lips as she began screwing the lids back on the makeup tubes. "So, you haven't said anything about Hot Doc in the kitchen. You're not mad I invited him?"

The heat in her cheeks told Blake she was blushing without even having to look in the mirror. "I'm not mad. I was actually hoping to spend some more time with him. He did save my life, and I haven't even had a chance to really thank him." She also hoped that spending time with him would help her cement her decision about which man was the best match for her.

After she was almost hit by the car, there had been such a crowd of people, from her family, to the police, to curious onlookers, to Sean—not to mention their whole altercation—that she'd had no time alone with Adam. She hadn't even had time to truly process the whole situation until she'd gotten home.

"Thank him, huh? How are you going to thank him?"

Before Blake could answer, Rachel puckered her lips and started making kissy noises.

Blake laughed and threw a towel at her. "Very funny."

Rachel put the last of the makeup back in the large plastic makeup divider on the counter. "So you're not mad at him for going at Sean like he did?"

She sighed. "The truth is, I kind of blame myself for that. It's my fault that I haven't made my feelings clear. How's he supposed to feel when I've left him up in the air?"

As they walked downstairs, Rachel said, "Well, no matter what you have in mind for Adam, I think I can easily make sure you guys have some alone time together tonight. But you better take advantage of it, or I'm just going to flat-out tell him he needs to kiss you."

"Don't you dare," she said as they rounded the corner into the great room. She wanted him to kiss her, but not because her sister-in-law told him to.

"Don't you dare what?" Adam asked, sitting on the couch in front of the fireplace with one ankle crossed over his other knee. Now that he was out from behind the kitchen counter, she noticed his faded jeans. She loved the faded jeans.

Emma rushed over to her. "Auntie B, Aiden said that zombies don't have glitter."

"'Course they dunt," Aiden said in a muffled voice as he spoke through his plastic teeth. "Everyone knoss dat!"

Blake reached over to give her nephew a side hug. "Well, normal zombies don't have glitter, but princess zombies are way sparkly."

Emma giggled. "Told you!"

The oven buzzer ended the conversation, and the twins started squealing for dinner. Blake started to follow them to see if she could help, but Rachel shooed her away. "You go sit. This has to cool, and Ryan and the twins will help me finish." She eyed her son. "Mijo, you have to take out the teeth to eat enchiladas and tamales."

"We're helping?" Ryan looked confused from his spot on the couch but seemed to come around when his wife cut him a glare. "I mean, of course we're helping." He set his wine glass down and popped up. "Helpful is my middle name." He looked at his watch as he wandered into the kitchen. "I wonder where Kyle and Jason are. They were supposed to be here twenty minutes ago."

"I thought your middle name was Francis," Emma said from the dining room, making Blake chuckle.

She took the seat on the couch Ryan had just vacated and smiled at Adam as she set her wine glass on the table in front of her. "Um, I'm glad you're here. I was hoping to talk to you."

"Oh yeah?" He moved closer to Blake, sitting so close that their thighs touched.

"Yeah." Her eyelashes fluttered as she glanced up at him. "You saved my life last night, and uh..." Her fingers traced the seam along her leggings. "I never got a chance to thank you."

After a moment of silence, Adam leaned forward to set his wine glass on the coffee table then covered her hand with his, their fingers intertwining. Electricity shot up her arm at his touch, and all of a sudden, the tingling in her chest made it hard to catch her breath.

He gave her hand a squeeze. "You're welcome. And I wanted to apologize again for flying off the handle last night. You just could have been... I was so scared. It came out wrong. I shouldn't have gone off on Sean like that." He let out a sigh as he rubbed the pad of his thumb over the backs of her knuckles. "You know, Blake, I think you underestimate just how much you mean to me."

She held his eyes for several seconds. "What exactly are you saying?"

"Sugar, we've been dancing around each other for months. I haven't tried to push you, especially because I know there's someone else that..." He took a deep breath as he reached up to brush a strand of hair from her face. "I know I'm not the only person interested in you. And I don't know how you feel. I thought the best plan of action was us getting to know each other. And I think that's gone pretty well. I know a lot about *you*, anyway."

She scrunched her nose. "Yeah, enough to be scared off. And you know my crazy family. I don't know if that's always a good thing." While she appreciated him giving her time, the fact that both Adam and Sean had backed off seemed to be having the opposite effect. She was beginning to think it was going to take someone making a big move for her to truly figure out what she wanted.

Adam didn't laugh as his blue eyes studied her face. Then he trailed one finger along her jaw, making her shiver. "I know *you*, Blake. I know your middle name is Mildred, but you tell everyone it's Mary. I know you bring pastries to the nursing home every week and stay all afternoon to visit with the residents. I know you love animals and that you went out in the middle of torrential rain and a tornado warning to rescue a stray dog in the street outside the café. I know you love horror movies and the color red. I know you'd do anything for your family and friends. I know you love fiercely and have a great big heart."

When she felt her eyes well up, she blinked back tears, willing herself not to cry in front of this amazing man.

He caressed her cheeks with his thumbs. "But most of all, I know that inside that big heart of yours, I hope there's a place for me."

He leaned in until their lips were just a breath away. Her eyes began to flutter closed just when the back door opened.

"Sorry we're late!" Kyle yelled.

Blake's entire body clenched in frustration. "You have got to be freaking kidding me!"

"Auntie B, that's another quarter," Aiden said, running into the room.

Her mouth dropped open. "I said freaking!"

But Aiden was already lunging himself at Kyle, wrapping his arms around her legs. "Aunt K! Aunt K!"

Blake narrowed her eyes at her sister, who seriously had the worst possible timing known to man. Kyle's eyes widened. "What? What did I do?"

Before she could answer, Adam pulled Blake in for a hug, pressing his lips to her ear. "Don't worry, sugar. We'll finish this later."

She was counting on it.

ALL THROUGH DINNER, Blake noticed her sister was quieter than usual. And it was most definitely unusual for Kyle not to talk a mile a minute. She knew exactly what that meant—there was something specific that Kyle was trying not to say.

Blake just knew her sister had found something out—something about the investigation—and she wasn't sharing. In an effort to push her into opening up, Blake shared that she had seen Whit Hamilton's car in Sabrina's driveway and that it looked as though the two had been embracing in the upstairs window.

That caused Rachel to jump up and run to the window. "Ooh, his car's totally still there. And all the lights are off."

Aiden scrunched up his little face. "What are they doing in the dark? It's too early for grown-ups to go to sleep."

"Uhh..." Blake looked at Adam, who was sitting across from her.

A grin stretched across his face. "What do you think they're doing, Auntie B?"

She narrowed her eyes at him. "They're, uh—"

"Duh, Aiden." Emma rolled her heavily made-up zombie eyes. "They're probably watching scary movies."

Rachel suppressed a laugh as she sat back down next to her son. "Good guess, Em. I'm sure that's what they're doing."

After the huge dinner of enchiladas and tamales, Blake was so stuffed that she thought she might have to roll herself to the car. Except she felt the need to hug her brother for marrying such an incredible cook. And Rachel was the best—well, second only to her mother.

When Rachel took the twins upstairs to get their pajamas on, the rest of the adults retired to the family room to have their coffee and coconut cake.

When Kyle ate half of her cake without uttering a word, Blake couldn't take it any longer. "All right, that's it. Spill it."

Her sister's eyes flitted around at the other faces in the room. "Spill what? I don't know what you're talking about."

Ryan chuckled and forked up a big bite of cake before leaning back in his recliner. "C'mon, Kyle, it's even noticeable to me that you've been uncharacteristically quiet tonight. Not that I'm complaining." He held up a hand and smiled. "God knows I usually can't shut you up."

Kyle balled up her napkin and threw it at her older brother as Jason laughed.

"You two are paranoid. There's nothing to spill." But the way Kyle's eyes were avoiding hers made Blake certain that her sister was hiding something.

After a long look, Blake knew she wasn't going to get anything out of her sister, so she did the next best thing. Her eyes shifted to the right. "Jason, what's she not saying?"

Alarm crossed his face, and he winced when Kyle kicked him in the shin. "What?" He focused on his girlfriend and partner. "I didn't say a thing about Whit Hamilton or his shady real-estate scheme."

Kyle smacked a palm to her forehead as Blake's eyes about popped out of her head.

"Aw, crap."

"What!" Everything inside of her body stood at attention. "What about Whit Hamilton? What shady real-estate scheme?"

Jason groaned as Kyle smacked him in the arm.

"I am never taking you to dinner again, Chatty Cathy." She shifted her attention to Adam and Blake. "I was going to talk to you guys about this. I need to ask you some questions. I just didn't think dinner was the right time."

Adam's brow furrowed. "About Whit Hamilton? I think I met him briefly the night of Blake's Halloween party, but that's the only time I've ever talked to the guy."

"What did he do?" Blake scooted to the edge of her seat. "What does Jason mean about a shady real-estate scheme?"

"Well, crap!" Kyle forked up the last third of her cake in one bite then put her empty plate on the coffee table.

Blake pointed at her. "You have to pay a quarter. If I had to pay for saying 'crap,' then you do too!" She slid a hand over her mouth. "Oh god, I'm losing it."

Adam chuckled and slid an arm around her shoulders. "Calm down, sugar." He leaned over to press a kiss against the side of her head.

Kyle quirked an eyebrow as she centered her attention on Adam's arm. Oh boy, she was surely going to have thoughts on that later. Apparently letting it go for the time being, Kyle leaned back against Jason, mimicking Blake's own position as Jason's arm fell around her.

"I spent the afternoon looking into the employees at Crossbones who might have access to the apartment key. I figured I would start at the top and check out the ladies' man across the street." She reached up to yank the elastic from her ponytail and run her fingers through her hair. "Whit's story seemed easy enough to check out. He was in real estate. Moved from Miami."

"But we quickly learned there's a lot more to Whitley Hamilton," Jason added, running his hand in circles on Kyle's back. "When we went back to the station after the self-defense class, we got the results of his background check. It showed he'd been arrested in relation to a real-estate scam, but he got off when there wasn't enough evidence to connect him to it."

Kyle cut her eyes to him, and he shrugged. "What? It's all public record."

"Whoa, whoa, whoa." Blake waved her hand. "Back up. What kind of a real-estate scam?" All she could think of was Todd Lang in the real-estate office. If the two men were connected somehow, maybe Whit had something to do with Todd's murder.

With a sigh, Kyle crossed her legs, seeming to realize that she might as well just talk. "Well, he was CFO for this big real-estate company in Miami, which was legit. Then the company started setting up these subsidiaries and partner companies. They weren't really companies at all—just names on paper. The real-estate company used them to launder money. They transferred money around and made it look clean."

"They're sure the money wasn't legitimate?" Adam asked.

"All I know is these nonexistent companies were making a lot of money. If the real-estate company was turning a legit profit, there would have been no reason for them to do that. And it looks like they weren't profiting nearly as much as the amount of money in their accounts would indicate." Kyle gathered her hair away from her face. "But I don't know where the money was coming from. It's still under investigation, so I couldn't get that information. They weren't sharing because they're still trying to nab everyone involved. They said I had to talk to the lead investigator to get more details, but of course he's out of town."

Blake blew out a breath. "If they're arresting people, they must be able to prove they're getting the money illegally. Do you think it's drugs?"

Ryan set his plate on the end table. "So, how, pray tell, is Whit *not* involved if he was CFO?"

Kyle's mouth quirked as she shook her head. "That was my question exactly. I haven't found anyone who can give me a straight answer, just that he was indeed cleared. As soon as he was, he took off for Missouri."

"Real estate..." Blake felt as though she had been punched as the pieces started to fall together in her mind. "There's no way it can be a coincidence that he moves here and we find out there are different holding companies buying up the downtown lofts. That is way too convenient."

"Well, we're going to find that out," Jason exclaimed.

Kyle nodded vigorously. "Bree is going to be in my office at nine a.m. with all the information she has on these companies, and we're going to get to the bottom of this. My instincts tell me that if we find out what's up with these companies, we'll find who killed Todd Lang. He was really good at finding trouble. Maybe he somehow found out who was behind the holding companies and what they were trying to do."

"And maybe someone wanted to shut him up." Blake sat back. "Poor Mr. Hamilton. He seems so proud of Whit. He'll be crushed if his son's involved in something like that."

Kyle pressed her lips together in a thin line. "I know. Poor guy."

Jason looked back and forth between them for a few seconds. "You've gotta tell her the rest, babe."

Blake felt her stomach clench. "What's the rest? Oh God, does Whit have a clown costume? The height matches."

Kyle blew out a breath. "No, it's not that. But I said I needed to talk to the two of you. I need you to think about the person in the truck. The one who tried to run you down. Can you remember any more details about that?"

But Blake was already shaking her head. "I told you, all I saw were headlights. I couldn't even see the color of the truck, much less the driver. I was blinded."

Kyle looked at Adam, whose eyes were somewhere else, remembering. He slowly shook his head. "I wasn't focused on the driver. I was only focused on Blake. I'm lucky I even noticed what make it was. I'm sorry, Kyle." His voice held a note of irritation, and Blake could tell he was frustrated with himself for not being able to provide more. "God, I wish I'd seen him. You don't know how much I wish that!"

Blake squeezed his knee, and his arm tightened around her. "Kyle, why are you asking us this? We went over this the other night. We told you everything we know." Dread bloomed in her gut as her sister pinched her lips together.

"We're going over this again because I found something else about Whit Hamilton today." Kyle clasped her hands tightly together and looked directly into Blake's eyes. "He owns a black Ford F-150."

Chapter Eighteen

Once Blake was able to pick up her jaw, she couldn't seem to connect the information fast enough in her head. "But... but... that's not what he drives. He drives that beat-up Toyota that's sitting in Sabrina's driveway. Are you sure?"

Jason nodded. "We're sure that truck's registered to him. Maybe he just keeps it in the garage. Or maybe he's letting someone else use it. Who knows? But we can't go over to his place and take a look without a search warrant, and we don't have that kind of evidence—not yet. Everything we have is circumstantial, and we can't get a warrant based on a hunch."

Maybe they needed a search warrant, but she didn't. *Now, where could he be hiding that truck?*

Kyle sighed. "That's why we were really hoping with a little prodding, you guys would be able to remember him."

Blake raked her mind, but she knew she hadn't seen anything but headlights. She thought back to the night of the party. Whit had come in late with his dad. Racking her brain, she tried to calculate whether he'd had enough time to make an appearance dressed in a clown costume and then go change before coming back to the party. Before she could respond again, text alerts sounded around the room, making her jump. Adam's phone buzzed at his waist, and Jason reached for his pocket.

Kyle shot to attention. "What? What's going on?"

Jason looked at his phone and uttered a curse. "Some party got out of control in Miller's Field just outside of town. There was a shooting."

Adam held up his phone. "I'll bet that's my shooting victim. I've gotta get to the ER."

Blake couldn't help the stab of disappointment that shot through her at his departure, and she immediately felt guilty. "I didn't know you were on call."

He headed to the front door, stopping at the coat closet for his jacket. The man didn't waste any time. "Ryan," he called to her brother, "please thank your wife for the incredible dinner." Then he motioned for Blake to come closer. When she reached him, he lowered his voice so only she could hear him. "I'm so sorry I have to run. I will check on you tomorrow. Please be careful, sugar." He leaned down and pressed a firm kiss to her lips, making tingles zip around her insides.

She only had a brief second to register the kiss, which left her breathless, before he was pulling away and opening the front door. Blake had to fight every urge she had not to yank him back inside.

"Good night, everyone," he called, and gave her a wink before he pulled the door closed.

It took her a moment before she was able to tune in to the voices behind her. "I know he's doing this just to spite me," Kyle was saying to Jason as she trailed him into the foyer and watched him grab his WPD jacket.

"Babe, you're reading too much into this. You work all the time. This is your night off. You knew that. I'm the one on call, not you. I'll handle the shooting."

Blake wandered back into the family room so Kyle and Jason could finish their argument and tossed herself down on the loveseat across from her brother.

He shot a glance at their sister. "She really can't handle being left out, can she?"

"Yeah, what's up with that? Isn't that a middle-child-syndrome thing? I should be the one that drives you all crazy with my personality disorders."

"Oh, little sister, you do. Have no worries." Ryan dodged, laughing as Blake chucked a throw pillow right at his head.

The front door closed behind Jason, and Kyle looked to be fuming when she came back into the room.

Ryan pushed his glasses up his nose. "Give the poor guy a break."

"Oh, I'm not mad at him." Kyle kicked the corner of the sofa in frustration before she plopped down. "It's my idiot boss. Raimy's so pissed I yelled at him in front of his men, so he leaves me out of things like this just to spite me. Pansy ass."

Blake raised a finger. "That's another quar—" But she stopped abruptly when Kyle shot her a death glare. "Fine," she laughed. "You get a freebie. And you should be happy about getting a chance to relax and enjoy your night off. It's good to spend time with you when you're not threatening to arrest me."

Music sounded from the kitchen, a loud rap beat followed by the lyrics, "Heeeeeeey, it's your mama!"

Ryan stood up. "That's Rachel's phone. I better grab it. I know she's been waiting on a call from her mom." Ryan retreated to the kitchen as Blake turned her attention back to Kyle.

"I'm sorry about that," Blake said earnestly. "It's my fault Raimy's upset with you."

Kyle scrubbed a hand over her face. "No, it's really not. He should have listened to you when you called. He may not like you, but when you call about a murder for chrissakes, he can't blow you off. And he knows that. I think he's mad at himself, but me being your sister definitely doesn't help matters."

"Wait a second. He doesn't like me? But I bring cookies to the station!" She really wasn't used to people not liking her.

Kyle cracked a smile. "Yeah, he's allergic to tree nuts."

She didn't understand the connection until she thought about the cookies she'd brought in a couple weeks ago. Then she let out a groan. "Oh no, chocolate-chip-pecan. I am so sorry."

A laugh escaped Kyle. "Hey, they were labeled. That's his own fault."

Blake was happy to see her sister smile. It seemed like there had been a lot of tension between them throughout the week, so the fact that they were back in sync made her feel as though things were as they should be.

"Hey, we should probably get out of their hair." Blake jerked her head toward the kitchen, where they could hear Ryan talking on the phone. "And you're without a car. Need a lift? We could swing by my place first. I was going to bring you a box of my new chocolate-marshmallow cookies, but I left them setting on my kitchen counter."

"Cookies and a ride?" A big grin stretched across Kyle's face. "That's the best offer I've had all night."

Rachel rushed into the room. "Sorry that took so long. It took me awhile to scrub off all the twins' makeup. I heard my ringtone upstairs. Please tell me Ryan didn't—" She stopped when she heard Ryan's voice. "Oh, *mierda*! Please tell me he's not talking to my mama."

"Yeah, he didn't want you to miss the call," Kyle said.

Ryan walked into the room and spotted his wife before he pushed the end button on the phone. He narrowed his eyes at Rachel, and some emotion Blake couldn't quite place crossed his face.

Rachel looked at him with wide eyes, holding her breath, and Blake and Kyle just sat back, looking between the two of them.

Finally, Ryan broke the silence. "A month? She's staying for a month?" He gripped the phone and looked at it as if the piece of technology had seriously offended him. "Rach, when were you going to tell me? A month!"

"Mama Bustos is coming for a month?" Blake clapped her hands together in glee. Rachel's mom was amazing. Ryan was clearly not in the mood for her enthusiasm. He shot her a glare as Kyle tried to suppress a smile.

Then Rachel broke out in rapid-fire Spanish. *"Iba a decírtelo. Pero parecía tonto molestarte antes de saberlo. Por favor, no te enojes."*

Blake had no idea what that meant, but it didn't sound good.

"Babe, English, please." Ryan ran a hand through his hair and just glared at his sisters.

Kyle stood up and looked at Blake, jerking her head in the direction of the door.

"What?" Blake didn't really want to leave quite yet. She was way too curious about how the argument was going to turn out. But with the three people in the room glaring at her, she figured staying put probably wasn't the best decision. "Right. Okay, well, thank you for dinner," she said, getting up.

She and Kyle gave both Ryan and Rachel hugs, and Blake didn't like the fact that she could feel the tension rolling off both of them. She didn't even bother to ask for leftovers as she and her sister grabbed their jackets and made a quick getaway.

"I DON'T SEE WHY RYAN has such an issue with Mama Bustos visiting. Where else is she supposed to stay when she's having her house painted?" Blake turned onto her street. "I love that woman." She warmed at the thought of the pudgy little woman who had a giant smile and always smelled like cinnamon.

Kyle clapped. "I am so freaking excited to have her here over the holidays. That Christmas candy she always sends us? She's going to be here to make it fresh! Oh, this is going to be amazing!"

As Blake slowed in front of her house, Kyle gave her the side-eye. "So, this whole drive home, you haven't said a word about Hot Doc.

I saw the kiss he planted on you before he left. Did you guys get a chance to talk at all?"

"Yes," Blake said with annoyance. "And you, little sister, have the worst possible timing ever!"

Kyle made a face. "Sorry! I knew it looked like he was about to kiss you when we walked in. But that's good, right? You said he's been treating you like a sister. He sure didn't look like he was treating you very sisterly tonight."

The memory of Adam's words washed over Blake. *Inside that big heart of yours, I hope there's a place for me.*

Her hands shook a bit as she pushed the button to turn off her car engine. "He finally told me he has feelings for me."

Kyle gasped. "That's great!" She grabbed Blake's arm and shook it. "Why don't you seem excited? I thought that was what you want-ed!"

"It was! It is, I mean."

Kyle arched a brow. "But?" Blake shot her sister a glance, and Kyle sighed. "Sean. Right?"

She nodded. "Yeah. I mean, Adam's amazing. But before I start anything with him, I need to make sure that there's nothing there be-tween Sean and me. If there's any doubt, then that's not fair to Adam. I can't be with him unless I can give him my whole heart." It was past time for her to woman up and ask Sean straight out what was up. Maybe they would have some time together after Halloween.

Kyle leaned back in her seat, and her silence spoke volumes, caus-ing Blake to sigh. "You disagree." She could almost tell what her little sister was thinking.

"Blake," Kyle said gently, "I know that Rachel and I have joked over the last few months about being Team Adam or Team Sean, and maybe that's been putting too much pressure on you, I don't know. But it boils down to one thing. We want you to be happy." Kyle put a hand on her arm, making her look up. "You deserve someone who loves you more than the whole world. In the end, to me, that doesn't matter if it's Adam or Sean or someone else. I just want you to have the love in your life that you deserve." She dropped her hand in her lap. "That being said, is Sean still holding you at arm's length?"

She rolled her shoulders and squeezed the steering wheel in front of her, considering. "Well, with Todd's murder, it's not like we've had time to really socialize, so I don't know. But nothing's changed drastically over the last few months. I thought he was going to kiss me the other day, but we got interrupted."

"So ask him. Or grab him and lay one on him." When Blake looked at her sister in horror, Kyle shrugged. "What? Be direct. If you want to know how he feels about you, ask. Then you'll know. Remaining in limbo with those two is ridiculous. And it's dumb for you to wait around for Sean if there's nothing there. Hell, maybe he'll kiss you, and there'll be no spark whatsoever. That'll make your decision easier."

Kyle reached for the door handle. "I'm assuming there are sparks when you kiss Adam."

"Oh yeah," Blake said breathlessly, getting out of the car.

Kyle giggled—downright giggled—when she came around the car. "Yeah, I can tell. You should see how flushed your face gets when he touches you."

Blake couldn't help but roll her eyes as she nudged her sister's arm when they walked together up the front sidewalk. "That was totally the wine."

"Oh, bull," Kyle laughed.

Blake's wavy hair ruffled in the cool night air, and she shoved it out of her eyes. "So there's probably no chance you're going to let me manage my love life without all the external help, is there?"

"Heck no. What fun would that be?" Kyle draped an arm around her sister's shoulders. "Just remember not to let Rachel pressure you. We're Team Whoever-Makes-You-Happy. I like both Sean and

Adam. Or maybe you won't choose either one. Whit Hamilton's pretty cute, you know. If he turns out not to be Pennywise, you could turn to page three and go for him."

"Very funny." Whit Hamilton was such a player, the thought of dating him made her throw up in her mouth a little bit. "Besides, Whit is sleeping with Pepper Wright. And that was after he slept with Elaine Page. That's three big strikes in my book."

"Actually, that's only two strikes."

Blake turned to Kyle as they reached the front steps and shoved her hands on her hips. "You've met Pepper. She totally counts as two strikes all on her own."

Kyle started to laugh, when the sound of a breaking stick at the side of the house caught their attention.

The adrenaline rush was almost like a drug, causing every hair on Blake's body to go on high alert. "What was that?"

The neighborhood was quiet in the dark night. No one was out in the yard, no one was walking their dog, and a stray cat wasn't big enough to break a stick by stepping on it. Straining her ears in the direction the sound had come from, she distinctly heard the crunch of leaves as slow footfalls retreated. She took a step toward the side of the house when Kyle's hand landed on her arm.

"Whoa!" her sister whispered. "Where are you going?"

"There's someone back there," she whispered back.

"I know that. I will check it out." Kyle reached in her purse and pulled out her sidearm that she kept in an easy-to-get-to Velcro pouch. "Stay here."

"Kyle, be careful!" she hiss-whispered before her sister walked quickly away.

Blake watched as her sister made her way around the side of the house. She felt so helpless. She hoped the intruder hadn't gone inside her house. A shiver went through her at the thought.

Blake shuffled her feet on the sidewalk as she strained to listen. *Kyle should have made her way around the house by now. What if whoever it is attacks her? But I would have heard that, right? Yes, I definitely would have heard something.* The need to protect her baby sister overcame every other emotion in her body, and that was all she needed to man up.

Then she scoffed at the thought. "Man up, my ass. I'm going to woman up!" *Fight like a lady.* Her footsteps were strong and sure as she walked around the side of the house in the direction her sister had gone. A grunting noise and the sound of someone or something crashing to the ground came from the backyard. Before Blake could react, Kyle's voice yelped, and the sounds of a struggle started.

The drumbeat of Blake's heart echoed her pounding footsteps as she ran as fast as she could through the leaves and the grass to reach the back of the house. In the dim light of the lamppost in her backyard, she was able to make out Kyle lying on her back with a dark figure kneeling over her, his hand up holding something, ready to strike.

"Hey!" Blake ran straight for them, startling the intruder, who jumped up and began running.

Going after him was only a fleeting thought because the only thing in her mind was making sure her little sister was okay. "Kyle!" She fell to her knees beside her sister, who was breathing heavily as her hand searched the ground for her gun.

"Blake, I can't let him get away!" Kyle's voice was tight with pain, and her forearm was bent at an odd angle as she slid it along the grass.

On the far side of the yard, the intruder hit the fence and began climbing. When Blake looked down, she spotted the gun just out of her sister's reach.

"I got it!" She lunged for the gun, and the training Kyle had given her at the gun range once upon a time came back to her in full force. She remembered that Kyle had mentioned law-enforcement weapons didn't have a safety to click on and off, so all Blake had to do was point and shoot. With a surprisingly steady hand, she lifted her arm and aimed at the fence.

"Blake, what are you doing!" Kyle's panicked voice was desperate.

But Blake's focus was on the figure who was heaving his body over the top of the fence. She aimed as best she could at the person, closed one eye, and gently squeezed the trigger like Kyle had taught her. The kick from the gun knocked her back, flat on her butt, as the branch in her next-door neighbor's yard exploded right before she heard the man land with an "oof" on the other side of the fence, followed by his rapidly retreating footsteps.

"Oh my God, give me the gun!" Kyle reached up and let out a wounded sound when she lifted her arm.

"Stay put!" Blake yelled at her. There was no need to be quiet anymore. The intruder was long gone, and people were emerging from their back doors. The glow of porch lights began lighting up the night. She began to fumble around in her pockets for her phone then realized it was in her purse, which she'd dropped somewhere between the car and the backyard.

"My tree!" she heard Mrs. Amos yell.

"Is everyone okay?" hollered Mr. Richards.

Kyle was pulling herself up to a sitting position when Blake yelled back. "No, someone call an—"

Kyle gasped and slapped her good hand over Blake's mouth. "No ambulance! Don't you dare! I will never hear the end of it."

Blake gestured to the arm Kyle was cradling close to her body. "What do you think you're going to do?" she hiss-whispered. "Hide that from everyone?"

"Just let me handle it. Get me my phone, and I will call this in."

"Someone, call the police!" Mrs. Amos screamed.

"Uh-oh." Blake scrambled to her feet, thinking the intruder had attacked the elderly woman next door. "Mrs. Amos, are you okay?"

"Yes, I'm okay," the woman yelled back in exasperation. "But I want someone to catch the vandal that shot at my tree. I want whoever did that to be locked up."

Blake winced then rolled her eyes, because even with a broken arm, her little sister was behind her, giggling.

Chapter Nineteen

“So you’re staying with Kyle now?” Giselle asked with wide eyes as Blake related the story from the previous night.

“Yeah, I’m protecting her.” She made a show of blowing on her nails and polishing them against the front of her pumpkin-colored top.

Kyle groaned as she leaned against the counter of Mystery Cup, resting her casted arm in front of her. “I am never going to live this down, am I?”

“Hey, you just remember all this the next time you tell me I can’t take care of myself. Who protected you, little sister?”

Kyle lowered her chin and gave Blake a droll look through her lashes. “You protected me by shooting the birdhouse out of Mrs. Amos’s tree.” Kyle shot her gaze to Giselle. “She’s really pissed about that, by the way.”

Giselle’s eyes danced with mirth. “You don’t want to get on her bad side. I’ve seen how angry she gets when we’re out of espresso brownies. She’s scary.”

“So the guy got away, but you’re okay, and that’s all that matters.” As much as she teased her kid sister, the fear she’d felt the night before—and still felt at the thought of what could have happened—was all too real. If Blake hadn’t come around the corner of the house when she did...

“I still don’t understand how he managed to break your arm,” Eli said from the end of the bar, where he was wiping down the coffee machine after the long day. The café had closed early to prepare for Trick or Treat Down the Street, so they were doing their normal closing prep in costume before the kids arrived for candy. Eli hung his bar rag on the towel rack behind the counter and began adjusting the miniature cereal boxes glued all over his shirt.

"The jerk ambushed me," Kyle said as she cradled her arm. "I had my—what are you doing?"

Everyone turned to look at Eli as he took a handful of plastic knives from a box on the counter and began jabbing them one by one into the cereal boxes. He looked up and grinned sheepishly. "I'm a cereal killer. Ruby gave me the idea. Awesome, right?"

Blake and Kyle couldn't help but laugh, but Giselle just rolled her eyes. Even so, the girl's lips twitched as she tried to hide her grin.

"And you are?" Kyle asked, eyeing Giselle's pink wig.

"Katy Perry. Isn't it obvious? Oh, wait!" Giselle dug a microphone headset out of the pocket of her apron and attached it to her ear. "There. How about now?"

Blake chuckled, and amusement lit Kyle's eyes. "That makes all the difference."

"We didn't mean to interrupt your story," Eli said as he continued plunging knives into the cereal boxes. "You were saying the guy ambushed you?"

"Yeah." Kyle's smile faded. "I had my gun out in front of me, and when I came around the side of the house, he brought a heavy branch down and whacked my arm." She made a chopping motion with her good arm to punctuate.

"The same branch he was going to smack you in the head with when I came to your rescue." Blake's attempt at levity fell short when she met her sister's eyes, and the seriousness of the situation passed between them.

"My hero," Kyle said softly as she reached to squeeze Blake's hand.

"So you didn't get a look at him?" Giselle asked. "You're no closer to figuring out who this guy is?"

"I have a better idea of his height, at least," Kyle said. "But I still couldn't tell if it was a man or woman. The height was tall, and the person was thin. I wish they hadn't been wearing gloves. At least if I'd seen hairy knuckles, I could have narrowed it down a little. And we don't even know for sure which direction he ran once he landed in Mrs. Amos's yard, so no clues there."

"Yeah, right now we have someone who is thin and tall." Blake pressed her lips together. "That casts a pretty big net." But that vague description matched Whit—and Pepper, for that matter.

"We'll find him... her... whatever," Kyle assured. "Don't worry. I really have a feeling we're closer than we think."

She hoped her sister was right. Even though Blake had proven her badassery the night before, she still didn't relish the thought of Mr. Arm Breaker returning to her house. She was about to ask Kyle what made her think they were close to finding the guy, when she noticed her sister's eyes shifting back and forth. Blake realized there was something else Kyle knew that she hadn't had a chance to share yet.

"Wait, what did you—"

The bell above the door jingled a moment before they heard very excited little voices squealing, "Trick or treat! Trick or treat! Auntie B, you're our first stop."

She turned to take in her precious niece and nephew and had to bite her tongue to hold in her laugh. Not only did Emma have on her perfectly crafted zombie makeup, complete with glitter, but she wore a billowy Cinderella dress, clear-plastic slippers, and a sparkly tiara.

Aiden followed closely behind, his trick-or-treat bucket in one hand and the other holding a baseball bat propped over his shoulder. "Rick or reat!" he exclaimed through his vampire teeth.

Ryan and Rachel trailed their children inside, their fingers entwined. Their big smiles told Blake they must have worked out the argument that had started the night before, and she let out a little sigh of relief. Maybe it was because her own father had been such a deadbeat, always picking fights with their mom until he took off. Anytime Ryan and Rachel squabbled, it made her gut clench, but she should have known by then that those two were stronger than ever.

"How's the arm?" Ryan asked, turning his attention to his sister. "I really wish you would have called me so I could have met you at the hospital."

"No need." Kyle rotated her sore shoulder. "Adam got me all fixed up."

"I'm so glad you're okay," Rachel said. "I was so worried when Ryan told me what happened."

"Worried?" Kyle made a "pish" sound. "I'm invincible, remember."

Blake flexed her biceps. "And I'm a badass."

Aiden's little gasp had her biting back a curse because she knew exactly what he was going to say. "Auntie B, you said ass! That's a quart—"

"You know what?" Blake fished a five-dollar bill out of her pocket. "Here. I should be good for the whole night."

Eli came out from behind the counter with a giant basket of Halloween candy as Aiden looked at the bill wide-eyed, as if Blake had just handed him a hundred dollars. "Hey, little dude! Those are some gnarly teeth. You sure you can eat candy with those?"

Aiden pocketed the cash and immediately spit the teeth into his trick-or-treat bucket. "I can now!" he said with drool hanging from the corner of his mouth.

Emma scrunched her little nose. "Ew! You're so gross!"

"Am not!" Aiden countered.

"Whoa, whoa!" Rachel stepped in between her children. *"Silencio, por favor!* Or this will go on until infinity."

Aiden looked around his mom and caught his sister's eye. "Am not, infinity plus one."

Emma's little mouth popped open in annoyance. "Mo-om!"

"Stop!" Ryan motioned both of his children over and bent down so he was on their level. Blake couldn't hear what he said, but whatever it was got a very respectful "yes, sir" from the twins.

Giselle reached over to grab a plate of colorfully decorated pumpkin and ghost sugar cookies. "Here. I'll bet I can distract them." She walked around the counter, and the twins' eyes lit up as they followed Giselle to a table.

Ryan stood and stretched then stepped behind Rachel and wrapped his arms around his wife. "I'm already tired."

Rachel giggled and squeezed his arms. "Yeah, but that's not from the kids." She turned her head back to reach up for his kiss.

"Oh God." Blake clamped a hand over her mouth.

Kyle grinned, and Blake was impressed because the PDA of their older brother never seemed to make her sister gag. When she saw her big brother getting all kissy-face with his wife, it just didn't compute in her brain.

"I'm glad you two seem to have made up," Kyle said with a wink.

Rachel leaned back against her husband. "Making up's the best part."

"Huk!" Blake waved them off. "I'm going to get more candy. You two really need to separate while I'm gone. Huk!" She rushed into the kitchen and took a few deep breaths. As much as she didn't like to see her brother doing the whole kissy-face thing, it gave her courage to come clean with Sean. The next night was Halloween. Her plan was to invite him to go trick-or-treating with them. After that, she was going to lay it all out. Maybe her night would end in a kiss too.

The kitchen door opened behind her, and she looked back to see Kyle walk in.

Blake was on her way to the kitchen island, where bags and bags of Halloween candy were strewn about. "Hey, what's up? I figured you'd be headed out soon. Isn't this prime vandalism time—the night before Halloween?"

"Yeah, in a minute." Kyle hesitated as she looked at Blake, who paused while trying to rip open a bag of fun-size Snickers.

"Do you ever wonder why they call those fun-size?" Kyle quipped. "I mean, look how tiny they are. To me, a fun-size candy bar would be this big." She positioned her hands about two feet apart.

"You're rambling"—Blake set the bag down and studied her sister's face—"which means there's something you want to say but can't, or there's something that you need to say but don't want to. Which is it? Do you have a lead on the guy from last night?"

Kyle uttered a curse and started to cross her arms until she seemed to realize that was a bit difficult to do with her cast, so she just let both arms dangle at her sides. "I probably shouldn't be telling you this, but it has to do with you, so…"

Nervousness bubbled in Blake's stomach. "What?"

Kyle cleared her throat and leaned against the stainless-steel island. "We've been delving into the properties around town, trying to find out who's buying the lofts."

"Yeah?" Blake motioned her hand for Kyle to keep going.

"They're not just trying to buy the lofts, Blake. They want the buildings. Someone is trying to buy up all the downtown buildings."

"What? Why? That doesn't even make sense. We would have heard about this. And the city owns the buildings. I've been at most of the chamber meetings. No one has said anything about selling.

"The city has brought in several investors to be able to afford the buildings, hence the holding companies. And you're a renter, as are the other business owners. All they have to do is wait 'til your lease is up and kick you out."

Blake felt her cheeks heat with anger. "B-but how could investors take over? I don't understand."

Kyle looked over her shoulder to make sure the kitchen door was closed before she continued. "Jason has a friend over at the Financial Crime and Fraud Unit in KC. The city's plan on paper is to keep control of the buildings by controlling the majority share. The city sells shares of the buildings off to investors, but as long as they keep the majority, they still have control. But here's the problem. The city owns forty percent, investor number one holds thirty percent, and investor number two holds thirty percent. You with me so far?"

Blake rolled her eyes. "Yes. Math may not be my strong suit, but I'm not a dummy. Still, though, the city owns more than each investor, so what's the problem?"

"The holding companies are the problem. If the same person is behind each holding company..."

Understanding set in, and Blake's eyes went wide. "Then that one person owns sixty percent and can do whatever they want."

Kyle snapped her fingers. "Bingo. Think about it. If you owned all of downtown, you could do anything with the buildings you wanted. Knock 'em down, build a mall, whatever. We're talking big bucks. Whoever is behind this is serious."

Blake gasped. "But that would destroy Wilton! As the city commissioner, Bree's in charge. How could she allow something like this to happen?"

Kyle shook her head. "She didn't, at least not at first as far as I can tell. It sounded like the buyer and the management company made the arrangements before they ever took it back to the city for approval."

"But no one's approved anything?"

"Not yet."

Blake exhaled a sigh of relief and reached for a bag of Twix to dump into the candy basket. "Now that this is all coming out, the city would never approve this... right?"

"It's not likely, but then again, anything's for sale if the price is right." She shook her head. "But whether they sell or not, the important thing is figuring out if this was the motivation behind Todd's murder. I'm still trying to figure out the ins and outs of all the real estate. But I wanted to tell you because…" Nervous blue eyes flitted up to meet hers. Kyle never got nervous.

Blake's hand stopped in midair as she reached for a bag of Nestle Crunch. "Tell me what?"

"Blake, one of the properties they were working the hardest to buy was this one, this building. Someone, for whatever reason, really wants Mystery Cup."

Her jaw dropped. "No way. Never. Not in a million. I will chain myself to the front door if I have to. They will have to rip the coffeepot out of my cold, dead fingers. I won't—"

"Calm down, Batman. Like I said, nothing's been approved. But something's not right about the whole situation. I'm determined to find out who wants these buildings and why." Kyle dug her phone out of her pocket and looked at it. "Considering it's six o'clock on a Friday night and Halloween's tomorrow, I don't want you holding your breath that we're going to find anything new out in the next forty-eight hours. But I wanted to give you a heads-up."

"Do you think it's Whit? Have you had any luck getting a search warrant to see if his truck was involved in the accident?"

Kyle shook her head. "I still don't know where the truck is. If I get a search warrant without knowing that, he could clean up any evidence before he ever produces the vehicle, so I want to find it first." She drummed her fingers on the island. "I want to get close enough to Mr. Hamilton's place to see if I can find out if the truck is in his garage. But doing that and staying within in the law are hard to juggle." Her eyes got wide as Blake raised her hand.

"I can totally—"

"No! If Whit Hamilton is a killer, I don't want you anywhere near him. I will figure this out."

But she would be trick-or-treating right by Mr. Hamilton's house. If she looked around then, it wasn't as though it would be trespassing or anything.

Kyle jumped when her phone buzzed in her hand. Her eyes scanned the text. "Jason's out front. I gotta go." She walked over and leaned in for a hug. "Just be careful."

"I guess it's starting to make more sense why Todd's involved, huh?" Blake grumbled.

Pulling back, Kyle looked at her with brows drawn in confusion. "What do you mean by that?"

"Well..." She poured the Nestle Crunch bars into a bowl. "It was no secret that money was at the top of his priority list. If someone came up with a way to make a lot of cash, even if it has to do with screwing over the downtown business owners, it doesn't surprise me that Todd Lang was all over it."

Kyle's mouth quirked as she tapped her fingers against the island in thought. "You know, you might have a point there. But then who killed him?"

Blake lifted a shoulder and let it drop. "Maybe he wasn't the only one involved. I wouldn't put it past him to screw someone over to get their share of the profit. Money's a big motivator."

Kyle's phone beeped three times in succession. "Jason's getting impatient. I'll let you know if I find out anything more that pertains to you." She pointed a finger at Blake. "No investigating on your own."

A laugh escaped Blake as she dumped a big bag of Kit Kats into her basket. "I'm dressed as a pumpkin latte, passing out candy. How much trouble can I get into?" She adjusted her white hat, which had a giant straw sticking out of the top.

Kyle pursed her lips. "I don't know, but you're really talented at surprising me. And not in a good way."

"Oh, shut it," Blake laughed, picking up the full basket of candy. "It's fine. Just promise you'll let me know if you hear anything else."

She followed Kyle out into the front of the café, where more kids were streaming in. Her sister waved goodbye as miniature Elsas, Harry Potters, Princess Leias, and Kylo Rens ran up to Eli, who had the most notable basket of candy. Her barista, who was basically still a kid himself, seemed to be loving it. He seemed thrilled to be getting so many compliments on his cereal-killer costume. And his grin stretched from ear to ear as he high-fived the little ones and commented on each costume.

Giselle, decked out as Katy Perry, kept shooting sideways glances at Eli as she laid out trays of pastry samples for the parents. Blake was enjoying watching the way Eli was flicking furtive glances Giselle's way. Each of them tried to pretend at the same time that they didn't notice the other. It was proving to be very entertaining.

After the initial stream of traffic had died down inside, Blake decided to set up a table outside with Eli so Giselle could finish prepping everything for the next morning.

The smell of the fall leaves and the chill in the air made her happy as she greeted the trick-or-treaters. Halloween was her favorite time of year. It seemed once November hit, the stress of the holidays started, but Halloween was pure joy.

"Trick or treat, Coffee Goddess." The voice that sounded like chocolate-covered sexy warmed her despite the chill in the air.

She looked up to see Sean standing over her and felt the grin spread across her face. The stubble on his jaw was trimmed short, making his dimple much more noticeable, but she was drawn to his green eyes, which seemed more prominent than usual, most likely due to the copious amount of black eyeliner he wore. His pirate hat and long, braided wig made her smile, and her eyes traveled down his body, taking in the pirate vest, black boots, and long sword at his hip. "Well, well, Cap'n Jack, what brings you by tonight?"

"I heard a rumor you have the best candy." He winked. "What do you say? Can you give me something sweet?"

Blake was pretty sure that she blushed clear down to her toes. "Uh, I... sure, can I offer... I mean..." She blew out a breath, annoyed that he could make her so flustered so easily. "Shouldn't you be manning your own trick-or-treat table?"

Sean looked as though he were controlling a smirk. He wasn't succeeding. *The big tease.*

He jerked his head in the direction of the store. "I think they've got it covered."

She glanced over to where Eli had moved next to Sean's assistant, Ashley, who was dressed as Minnie Mouse. She was giggling as the two handed out candy. Quickly, she shifted her gaze to Giselle, who seemed blissfully ignorant at the moment, as she was engrossed in a conversation with two little girls dressed as Elsa and Anna from *Frozen*.

"I'm glad," she said, turning her attention back to Sean. I was hoping to talk to you for a minute." *Invite him trick-or-treating. It's now or never.*

"Well, what do you know? I wanted to talk to you too."

Uh-oh. A thread of worry went through her. Surely he hadn't heard that Adam had voiced his desire to have more of a relationship with her. She didn't really want Sean to know the details of that until she knew for sure where her relationship with Sean was going.

He tipped his hat up and held her gaze. "Your cheek looks better." He nodded to her bruise, which she'd worked hard to conceal.

She gently touched her cheek. "Halloween makeup has great coverage." She smiled up at him. "Don't tell me you came over to talk about self-defense class. Or 'fight club,' as my brother puts it."

A smile lit his lips. "No, I was... uh... Well, why don't you go first? What did you want to talk about?"

"No, no. That's okay. You go first." *You are such a big chicken, Blake Mildred.*

"Okay." His voice shook, making him sound as nervous as she was. "I don't know if you've heard, but the Bishop family is having a big Halloween party out at the lake tomorrow night. I thought if you're not doing anything, maybe we could... well, maybe you'd like to be my date."

Her ears perked up at the word "date." Before, when he'd asked her to do something, the asking had always been very casual. She could say with one hundred percent certainty that he had never used the word "date" when asking her out. *This is a really good sign.* If it weren't for Adam's words, which had jumbled up her feelings, she might have leapt on Sean at that very moment.

She'd been wanting to know for absolute certain if there was something there with Sean, and it looked like Halloween was her chance to find out. With Adam working the ER on Halloween night, she could focus on completely on Sean and figure out what her feelings actually were. Except her plan for a date would include a little more adult time. She bit her lip in a grimace.

"Uh-oh, that doesn't look promising," he said with a smile that didn't reach his eyes. "What's the matter, Goddess? Hot date?" She didn't know if she was imagining it, but jealousy seemed to color his words.

"Trick or treat!" Little voices distracted her from answering, and she smiled as she handed out Kit Kats to a group of Avengers.

"No, no, not at all," she said, turning back to Sean. "It's just that Ryan's working tomorrow night, so I promised to go with Rachel to take the twins trick-or-treating. I was actually planning to ask you to come with me, and then afterward, maybe we could hit the party. What do you think?"

She didn't realize she was holding her breath until Sean's eyes lit up. "I think that's a great idea. Trick-or-treating sounds fun. I can help the kids protect their candy so you don't steal all the Tootsie Rolls."

Her mouth popped open. "I do not steal candy!" When he cocked a brow, she said, "Okay, fine, but I don't steal candy from children."

He chuckled and took a seat in the bistro chair next to her. When he smoothed his hands on the legs of his black pants, she noticed there was still a slight tremble in his long fingers.

She glanced up at his face. "Is everything okay?"

"It is now." When he looked in her eyes, there was none of the usual humor or mischievousness she was used to seeing there. She felt his warm hand reach over and cover her own.

"Trick or treat! Hey, your costume looks like mine."

They both turned to see a little boy dressed as Cap'n Jack Sparrow holding out a candy bag. Sean's dimples winked as he put some Twix bars in the little boy's basket. "Great costume, buddy. That is the best pirate hat I've ever seen."

The child grinned to reveal missing front teeth. "Thanks! My mom made it. Happy Halloween," he yelled as he ran over to Eli and Ashley for more candy.

Sean turned back to Blake and took her hand again, but his smile faded as he seemed to struggle with what to say.

Come on, Blake! Stop pussyfooting around! Her hand tightened on his for a brief moment before she blew out a breath. "So, this weekend, I want us to have some time together. I think we need to discuss, um, well..." Chewing on her lip, she tried to decide how to word what she wanted to say without scaring him away. "Wow, I'm really not good at this."

If her insides hadn't been jumping all over the place, Blake would have tried for some levity. But at the moment, she wasn't quite sure which way Sean's train of thought was going, and she was too afraid to guess.

But then he met her gaze, and it was a good thing she was sitting because his heart-stopping smile made her knees go weak. "You're right. We do have things to discuss. I'm glad we're on the same page."

Relief flared deep within, but she was afraid to get ahead of herself. "Wait. We need to discuss what exactly?" Maybe she was reading him wrong, and this was the part where he totally blew her off and told her she was like a sister to him. Maybe that was what he wanted to discuss. She ground her molars together. If he punched her in the shoulder again in friendship, she might have to sock him one.

"More," he said simply, lacing his fingers through hers.

She felt her forehead crinkle. "More?"

They paused as a gaggle of young girls dressed as Disney princesses walked by laughing. Blake greeted the parents as the girls made a beeline to Eli and Ashley, who had all the good candy.

When the group was out of earshot, Sean turned his attention back to her. "We've spent a lot of time getting to know each other over the last few months... as friends. And that's been great. I mean, I've really enjoyed our time together."

Okay, that much was good. "Me too," she agreed.

"But now, I think things are moving..." He moved his head from side to side. "Well, let me rephrase that. Now, I want things to move beyond that."

Blake was pretty sure she stopped breathing as he reached up to gently skim her cheek with the backs of his knuckles.

"I want more." He held her eyes in a hypnotic trance.

More! He wants more! With me! It was probably only a few seconds, but it seemed like minutes before she could find her voice. "More. Yes, I think we should talk about—"

"Auntie B!" Aiden yelled, blowing up the moment between her and Sean that seemed oddly intimate despite the number of people passing by.

"Hey, buddy." She really hoped her voice didn't sound as shaky as she thought it did.

Aiden jumped up and down. "Mr. Jeffries is giving out full-size candy bars! Look I got a whole Twix!"

Sean laughed at the child's enthusiasm. "Did you get one for me?"

"No, but I can sneak you Emma's if you want," Aiden said in all seriousness.

"Heeey!" Emma yelled as she walked up holding Rachel's hand. "I heard that."

Sean chuckled as Blake's niece looked at her carefully, turning her head from side to side. "Auntie B, why is your face all red?"

Her hands flew to her cheeks. "Is it?" They were warm against her palms, and she could only imagine what everyone who had walked by and looked at them thought. "I suppose it's because I've just had too much coffee."

Sean slid his hand to her knee and gave her a squeeze, and Blake was impressed with how he could cause sparks to shoot up her body while he bestowed an innocent grin on the children.

Rachel's discerning eyes zipped back and forth between Blake and Sean and back again before a slow smile crept across her face. "Yeah, I'm sure that's it," she said with a wink.

"Whit!" someone yelled, and they all looked up to see Bree coming out of Sliced, walking with purpose.

Blake followed her trajectory and saw Bree was headed right for Whit, who was dressed in athletic shorts and a T-shirt, standing on the sidewalk and talking to Orlando as he handed out bags of treats—which she really hoped didn't consist of carrots. Her eyes narrowed as she looked at the young Mr. Hamilton, trying to picture what his body would look like in a clown suit.

Whit looked up at the sound of his name, and his face dropped as Bree descended on him. As soon as she started talking, Orlando moved away from them, causing Bree to inch so close to Whit that he backed up. His hands went up in an almost-defensive motion as she spoke, and that was when Blake really looked at her.

Saying Bree was tense would have been an understatement. Her entire body seemed rigid. One hand was clenched in a tight fist around the strap of her purse, and with the other hand, she was jabbing her finger in Whit's chest, her face a mask of anger.

Rachel turned to take in the scene. "Whoa! What the holy crap is that about? She looks pissed."

"Good question," Blake mumbled, trying to make sense of Bree's hand gestures. Too bad she couldn't lip-read. Maybe she should have gone over there to see if he had any bruises from falling out of Mrs. Amos's tree.

She stood up. If she could get proof that that asshat had attacked her sister, he would be praying for mercy.

Before she could bolt across the street, Sean grabbed her hand firmly. "Whoa, Batman. I don't know what's going through that head of yours, but nothing good can come of that look on your face. You need to calm down, Coffee Goddess."

"But he—"

"Mommy, mommy!" Emma yanked on Rachel's hand. "I have to go potty."

Rachel turned back distractedly. "Okay, sure. Come on, *mariquita*." She started to lead the twins inside but motioned her head in the direction of Bree and Whit. "Not now," she mouthed silently.

Blake looked around, taking in all the little kids trick-or-treating. No, it wasn't the time for a public confrontation. But soon. Soon, she would get the evidence to prove Whit was her man. He'd messed with the wrong family.

Before she could fill Sean in on her thought process, Silas came bounding across the street. "Hey, man!" he said to Sean, holding up a sack. "The dinner you ordered."

"Oh, right." Sean started to pat his pockets. "Shoot, give me a second. I need to grab my wallet, okay?"

"Groovy." Silas started swaying from side to side in a rhythm to a beat only he could hear.

"You gonna be all right, Coffee Goddess?"

Blake nodded, her eyes trailing across the street.

"Blake"—there was a warning in that rich-whiskey voice—"stay put until I get back."

"I'm not going anywhere." She held up three fingers in a salute. "Scout's honor."

Sean leaned in and pressed a kiss to her forehead before he jogged away.

Blake cleared her throat. "Hey, Silas, I just saw Bree come out of Sliced a couple minutes ago."

"Huh?" He looked at Blake for a minute then nodded. "Oh, yeah. She came in to get dinner or something." He looked up as if in thought. "But I never really saw her eat anything. She was just in Micah's office for a long time. I don't know what they do in his office together for so long with the door closed."

Blake choked on a laugh then nodded to where Bree still stood on the street, talking to Whit. Drawn up to her full height, she was nearly as tall as Whit. She had her hands perched on her hips, and Whit was making big, dramatic motions with his arms as he talked. He didn't look happy. "Do you have any idea what's going on with those two?"

Silas followed her gaze. "Huh. Nope. I'm kinda surprised they're talking to each other." He grabbed a piece of candy off the table and started to unwrap it.

"Why do you say that?" Blake picked up the bag of Hershey's Kisses she'd brought out with her and poured it on the table.

He shrugged. "I just heard her talking to Micah about him one day. I guess they worked together in Miami. I didn't get the feeling she was really a big fan of his, though."

Blake's mouth dropped open as puzzle pieces started racing around in her head, trying to click together. "Miami? I thought Bree was from Georgia."

Silas shook his head, popping the chocolate in his mouth. "That's where she's from originally. But she lived in Miami before coming here."

"What exactly was she telling Micah about Whit?"

"Uh, I don't know. Just that she didn't trust him. I didn't know why at the time, but the dude has quite a rep around town. Now, I'm guessing he wasn't the most faithful. I don't blame her for dumping the guy. Micah's a much better dude, ya know."

"Here you go, man." Sean came over and handed Silas a few bills. "Keep the change."

The boy's face lit up. "Thanks, Mr. Larson." He waved to Blake. "See ya, Ms. Harper."

"See ya, Silas," she said absently.

Sean studied her face as he reclaimed his seat. "Everything okay?"

Her gaze shot back across the street in time to see Bree turn on her heel and stomp off to her car. Whit stood stock still, staring at her retreating back with a menacing look that almost made her shiver. He had always seemed so charming and friendly, but with that one look, Blake could see a ruthlessness in him she'd never seen before.

She was spinning the possibilities of his connection with Bree. Whit had lived in Miami and worked in real estate. Bree had lived in Miami and was heading up the downtown real-estate sales. Someone was trying to buy up all the buildings. No way that was a coincidence. *What is their connection? Are they working together? And what did Whit do to make Bree so angry? Most importantly, how does Todd Lang fit into their little scenario?* She couldn't wait to talk to Kyle about it.

Chapter Twenty

When Halloween night arrived, Blake was no closer to answers than she had been the night before. Kyle was at a standstill until she could get in touch with the lead investigator on Monday. Even Jax Talon hadn't been able to get her any more info, and he could usually find out anything. So Blake had turned to her go-to investigative source—sleuthbaby.com. Other than the public information available on the Miami case, there was nothing. She'd even scoured Bree's and Whit's Instagram and Facebook pages, but they didn't have so much as a photo of one another.

At least she'd managed to successfully cover her cheek bruise with stage makeup so she didn't look like a zombie latte. That was one thing in the plus column.

At the sound of the doorbell, she felt her insides jump around. Sean was early. He wasn't supposed to get there for another half hour. As soon as Sean arrived, they could head over to Ryan and Rachel's to take the kids trick-or-treating. Then afterward... Well, afterward, she was letting go of her inhibitions. As Rachel liked to say, she was going to find out what was up.

She ran to the hallway and stood in front of the mirror, straightening the coffee cup lid that was cocked on her head like a hat. One quick turn in front of the mirror convinced that her costume rocked. If that didn't make Sean sit up and take notice, then nothing would.

Ninja looked up at her with wide eyes, probably happy she was done flying around the house like a crazy person, trying to get ready in time. Her little black furball weaved through her legs as she turned and made her way to the front door. Propping a hand on her cocked hip, Blake did her best to strike an appealing pose. Then she took a deep breath and swung the door open, ready to greet Sean.

Her sister stood in the doorway, staring back at her, with Jason standing behind her. His eyes widened dramatically as he looked over Kyle's shoulder at Blake. "Whoa!" he exclaimed, then made an "oof" sound when Kyle lightly elbowed him in the stomach with her good arm.

Blake dropped her arm, her cheeks heating with embarrassment. Lovely. She'd struck a seductive pose for her sister. The mental groan echoed inside her head.

Kyle's eyes traveled up and down her sister, and her expression was somewhere between surprise and amusement. "First of all, never strike that pose again. Second of all, what happened to the coffee goddess?"

Blake crossed her arms over her chest and stepped back so the two could enter. "The crown kept falling off my head. I just thought this would be better for tonight."

"I love it!" Jason exclaimed. When Kyle rolled her eyes, he said, "What? It's supposed to be hot. It says so right on her dress!"

For the evening festivities, Blake had decided to go as a latte, easy enough. She had a caramel-colored dress that was the exact same color as the butterscotch-caramel latte she served at Mystery Cup. The dress was a little more formfitting than she had intended, most likely due to her excessive snacking of pumpkin bread and Halloween candy. And the dress said "HOT" all around the neck and all around the hem, just like the cups at Mystery Cup. To complete the ensemble, she had fashioned some cardboard to look like a Java Jacket and wrapped it around her waist. She'd even had the Mystery Cup logo stamped on it, so it matched perfectly. Topping it off was the coffee cup lid—complete with red splash guard—pinned in her hair. She'd been able to put the whole thing together herself with minimal cost. Pinterest freaking rocked.

She'd been hoping for sexy, and Jason's embarrassed reaction told her that she was right on the money.

Poor Jason was now trying to avert his eyes from her altogether. "What made you decide to go with that for trick-or-treating?"

Kyle smirked. "Haven't you heard? Sean is accompanying her trick-or-treating."

Jason grinned. "Lucky son of a—" He stopped and cleared his throat when Kyle shot him a death glare. "I mean you two are going to have a great time, I'm sure."

Ninja let out a soft meow and nuzzled against her leg. "Okay, enough with the teasing." Blake bent down and picked up her cat, cuddling him snugly to her chest. "You guys want to take off your jackets and stay for a while?"

Kyle shook her head. "We have to get back to the station. We just left for a dinner break. Halloween night, it's all hands on deck."

Blake turned to walk into the living room, and Kyle and Jason followed. "So that means you stopped by for a reason." She whirled around to her sister and let out a gasp. "You followed up on Bree, didn't you? On her and Whit? What did you find out? Tell me, tell me, tell me."

Jason smirked. "Told ya she'd be excited."

Kyle shook her head. "I'm not sure what you're thinking, Blake, but whatever it is, it's probably way more interesting than the truth."

She looked back and forth from Kyle to Jason. "What do you mean?"

"Well, we did talk to Bree. And yes, she did know Whit in Miami."

"I knew it!" Blake exclaimed, dancing from foot to foot. "That's it! That's the link. They're in this together. They—"

"Whoa, whoa, whoa." Kyle held up her hand. "Sister, you are seriously going to have to start writing crime fiction, the way you spin stories in your head."

She stopped dancing. "They're not in this together?"

"Sorry, there's nothing sinister going on between them." Jason craned his neck in the direction of the kitchen. "Hey, do you have any of those marshmallow-chocolate things?"

"Uh, yeah," she said absently. "In the blue Tupperware container on the counter."

A smile lit Jason's face. "Thanks!" he said, already halfway down the hall to the kitchen.

Blake turned her attention back to Kyle and grinned. "That boy is way too easy to bribe." She plopped on the couch next to where Ninja sat curled on the center cushion. "So if there's nothing sinister going on, then what's the connection? They obviously know each other."

"Oh, they know each other." Kyle plunked herself down on the other side of Ninja. His furry little head popped up, and he gave Kyle a once-over before leaning in to inspect her cast, his nose twitching with tentative little sniffs.

Blake crossed her arms and tried to resist the urge to tap her foot. Kyle really needed to figure out how to get faster at telling a story.

Her sister chuckled, noticing Blake's obvious impatience. "They're exes," she finally said.

"Exes?" She made a face. "Whit and Bree?" For some reason, that hadn't even crossed her mind. Bree seemed so sweet and fun—provided she wasn't using that as an act to hide something more ominous. And Whit, while incredibly charming, seemed like a player. "I don't see them as a good fit at all."

"Yeah, well, they weren't. Hence the harsh words yesterday." Kyle absently ran her fingers through Ninja's fur. "Apparently they dated in Miami, and Whit had Bree completely snowed, according to her."

"You mean with the real-estate scams?"

Kyle chuckled. "I mean that the reason he had to move to Missouri is because he's apparently bedded down with everyone east of St. Louis, many while he was dating Bree."

She scrunched her face. "Ew!"

Her sister lifted a shoulder as Ninja began purring and leapt onto her lap to make himself comfortable. "Yeah, well, he may be a himbo, but that's not illegal." When Blake frowned in confusion, Kyle explained, "Himbo. You know, male bimbo. Bree's word, not mine. Anyway, I guess all of the real-estate stuff went down in Miami last year, but Bree was oblivious to it until after the fact. That plus the cheating was enough for her to kick Whit to the curb."

"Even though it looks as though he didn't have anything to do with it?"

Kyle's ponytail fell forward as she bent her head to rub noses with Ninja. "Bree didn't sound like she was too sure about that. She didn't have any proof, but she said Whit's as slippery as an eel."

Blake blew out a breath and dropped into the club chair next to the couch. As soon as she did, Ninja abandoned Kyle to leap onto Blake's lap, where his purr revved up as he began marching on her thighs. "Just because he wasn't implicated doesn't mean he's innocent."

"That's Bree's thought. Apparently, that's what yesterday was about." Kyle looked up as Jason entered the room with a handful of cookies and handed her one. "Thanks, honey." She took a bite before finishing her thought. "Anyway, the more that comes out about the real-estate crap that someone seems to be trying to pull over on the downtown businesses, the more Bree thinks that Whit showing up at about the same time is more than just coincidence. When she saw him coming out of Buttkick yesterday, she got in his face."

Blake's shoulders slumped. "So what it boils down to is that she doesn't know any more than we do. Just lots of theories."

Jason's phone beeped as he shoved an entire cookie in his mouth. He unclipped it from his belt and swallowed as he looked at the screen. "Raimy. We'd better go."

"Are you guys going to question Whit?" Blake asked as Kyle rose. "Maybe if you bring him in, you can get something out of him."

"It doesn't work that way." Kyle and Jason headed to the door, while Blake picked up Ninja and followed them. "We have to have a reason to bring him in. We have to have some kind of proof. If I brought him in on a hunch, Raimy would flip a gasket. Besides, even if we can connect him to those holding companies, that doesn't implicate him in Todd's murder."

"But what if—"

A knock at the door interrupted Blake's thoughts.

"No what-ifs," Kyle said as she moved out of the way so Jason could open the door.

When Blake saw Sean standing there, all thoughts of Whit Hamilton fled.

A slow grin crept across Sean's face underneath the wide brim of his fedora. He wore a cream-colored button-down that was open at the collar, and a worn leather jacket that offered just the right amount of bad boy. But the kicker was the whip gathered in a circle and pinned on his belt loop. Indiana Jones had never looked so sexy, and Blake had to remind herself to breathe.

Kyle sighed and shook her head. "You know, normal people only have one Halloween costume."

"Huh?" Blake asked, tearing her eyes away from the man to look at her sister as Sean stepped inside.

"Never mind." Kyle turned to follow Jason out. "You guys have fun tonight." She closed the front door and looked at Sean. "And if you could keep her out of trouble tonight, that would be super helpful."

Sean gave her a little salute. "Don't worry, the birdhouses of the neighborhood are safe on my watch."

Kyle grinned as Blake stuck her tongue out at Sean.

"Happy Halloween," Jason called as he and Kyle made their way down the steps.

Blake closed the door behind them and turned to look at Sean in the light.

A Happy Halloween, indeed.

"YOU'RE TWISTED, BLAKE. How could you possibly think *The Exorcist* is funny?" Sean slid to a stop in front of Ryan and Rachel's house and put his car in Park.

Blake looked up at him through her lashes as he turned to study her. "Seriously? You've got a girl whose head is spinning around, and she's projectile-spitting pea soup and spider-crawling up the stairs. How is that *not* funny?"

A deep chuckle escaped Sean. "You worry me, Goddess. I think you've seen too many horror movies."

"Whatever." She reached for the door handle. "There's no such thing as too many horror movies."

"Hey, wait a second." Sean's warm hand landed on her arm, stopping her before she could open the door. He had such a serious expression that her heart stuttered for a moment. The amused glint in his eyes was gone, and the wide brim of his hat shadowed the hard set of his jaw.

Nerves set Blake's stomach aflutter. "What's wrong?"

He shook his head as his fingers trailed up her arm and played with a lock of her hair that she had taken the time to spiral curl in rivulets. "Nothing's wrong. I just wanted to talk to you. I was planning to at the end of the night, but I don't want to wait."

She swallowed hard and let out a shaky breath. Part of her was worried that her friend-zone status would be cemented as official, but if that were the case, he wouldn't be playing with her hair. He wouldn't be looking at her like he had a sweet tooth and she was a big fudge brownie... at least she didn't think he would.

The corner of his mouth tilted up enough that his dimple winked at her. "What's going through your head right now, Blake Harper?"

"I was just wondering if you..." Ugh, she needed to shut the heck up and just let the man say what he was going to.

He tilted his head. "You were wondering if I what?"

She pressed her lips together firmly as she thought about the past months, all the hope she'd had that Sean would ask her out on a real date, that when they had watched one of those many movies together, he might reach over and hold her hand... that he might kiss her. She'd asked herself over and over why she'd never inquired about his feelings, why she'd never laid it all out. But she suddenly knew without a doubt. She was afraid to hear what he might say. If she didn't know how he felt about her, she had hope that things might go the way she wanted. But if she asked him about it and found out that he looked at her like a sister or something, then every hope in her mind would be dashed. Then she would have to face the truth. She'd never wanted to... until that moment.

She took a deep breath, the only sound other than the whistling of the wind and the distant voices of children who dotted the street, trick-or-treating. "I was just wondering if I was being friend-zoned."

Sean's green eyes widened, and his mouth opened in what almost looked like disbelief. "I beg your pardon? Friend-zoned?"

His hand briefly tightened on hers, and her eyes drifted down to where their fingers were entwined. "We've spent a lot of time together over the past few months. I guess I just thought if you were interested in me, you would have..." She glanced up at him and saw his unreadable expression before she looked back down, focusing on their hands. "I don't know. Held my hand or"—thoughts of his lips on hers entered her mind, and she tried to shove them out"—or something." She shrugged a shoulder. "We've known each other for what? Six, seven months. At this point, the friend zone seems like—"

"Look at me, Blake." Sean's voice was stern yet gentle. "Please. Look at me."

Her tongue snaked out to lick her dry lips, and she raised her head slowly. She could smell the light cologne Sean always wore. The hint of his spicy scent was enough make the butterfly wings in her stomach flap a rapid beat.

"I've made a lot of mistakes in my life," Sean began. "A big one has been some of my past relationships. I have a tendency to rush into things."

She nearly laughed and had to bite the side of her cheek to stop herself. It seemed nearly impossible to believe that Mr. Friendly-Punch-in-the-Arm was someone who normally rushed things.

He let go of her hand and breathed out a long sigh. "I like you, Blake. I... really... like you."

Her head shot up. "You do?"

His incredulous look surprised her. "Of course I do. How could you not know that?"

"Um... well, it could be because I remember hoping for a good-night kiss and you punched me in the arm."

He winced. "Yeah, I really can't believe I did that." He removed his hat and raked a hand through his hair. "I liked being with you. I *like* being with you. I wanted more, but I was afraid of scaring you off. And not only that, but there's..."

"Adam." Her voice came out in a whisper.

"Exactly. I mean, Adam's a good guy, don't get me wrong. I just don't know where you stand. With him or with me. I guess I was afraid to ask. Afraid of hearing the wrong answer."

Oh my God. She couldn't believe it. All those months, she'd been so worried to press him about what was going on between them because she didn't want to be rejected. And that whole time, it turned out he was thinking the exact same thing. It was almost laughable. Almost.

She opened her mouth to respond but then realized she didn't know what to say. She had feelings for Sean. He made her laugh. He made her heart beat faster. When he wasn't with her, she found herself thinking about him and wanting to be with him.

And then there was Adam—sweet, kind Adam, who sent tingles shooting through her at the lightest touch. Her heart had gone back and forth over who was going to claim that top spot. It seemed as though she was the one who needed to make a decision. But aside from her feelings for Adam, she could be completely honest about one thing. "I like you, too, Sean." Her cheeks heated up. "I really like you too."

A grin split his handsome face. He leaned forward, reaching up to cup her face. His lips were a breath from hers.

Blake's eyes drifted shut.

Knock. Knock. Knock. "Auntie B! Ewww! What are you doing?"

She and Sean jumped apart as Emma continued to rap her little fist against the passenger window.

Blake turned back and saw that Sean's face was tight with disappointment. He winked before flashing that dimple. "Soon, Coffee Goddess." With that, he planted a kiss firmly on her cheek before turning to open his door. The moment was gone. And he'd been so close to kissing her. But in all honesty, the flutter in her chest surprised her, as did the lingering warmth on her cheek.

With a sigh, Blake opened the door and got out. Rachel was standing behind Emma, smirking and holding Aiden's hand. "Karma," she said with a little laugh, and then made "huk" noises like Blake so often did when her brother and sister-in-law were kissing.

She opened her mouth to offer a smart-aleck response, but Aiden was yanking at her dress. "Auntie B, look how much candy we already got!"

"Candy?" Sean came around the car and put a hand on Blake's lower back. "I thought you were going to wait for us to go trick-or-treating."

Rachel seemed to be trying hard—and unsuccessfully—to suppress her grin as she looked back and forth from Blake to Sean. "We just thought we'd get a head start and do this block. Mary and Joe down the block give out homemade doughnuts. You gotta get 'em while they're hot."

"Mommy, I have to pee!" Emma was dancing from foot to foot, her blue gown ruffling around her.

"I know. Come on, *mija*." Rachel ushered them up the front steps and punched in the code to unlock the front door.

Blake glanced at the house across the street. Sabrina's windows were dark. Blake wondered if she was even home. At least her porch light was off, so Blake didn't have to go through the awkwardness of taking the kids trick-or-treating at her door.

As she started to turn to follow the kids into the house, a second-story window in Sabrina's house lit up, making her jump in surprise. As she watched, someone came to stop in front of the window, and the curtain moved aside as if that someone was looking out, then fell back into place. An uneasy feeling settled in the pit of her stomach. *Well, that's not creepy at all. Is Sabrina always watching?*

"Blake, come on." Sean held the door open, waiting for her to follow the rest of them inside.

She was going to have to get a grip. If she let herself get spooked so easily, it was going to be a long night.

THE FALL LEAVES CRUNCHED underfoot as Aiden and Emma tromped through the grass. Even though Rachel had bought the two of them extra-large pumpkin buckets, they were nearly filled to the brim with candy. Ryan had already presented the kids with his master plan. They could keep a few pieces for themselves, and he would give them five dollars per pound of candy they collected and turned in to him. Then they planned to send all the candy to troops fighting in Afghanistan. The kids loved the idea. Even at their young age, they had good hearts. And it didn't hurt that they were each saving up for an iPad. It seemed like a win-win to Blake, but the way Rachel's wide eyes were surveying the candy buckets, she was no doubt wondering exactly how much this was going to cost her.

They had covered one side of the street and were on their way back home down the other side. "I am so glad you guys came along," Rachel said as they followed behind the kids, who were looking in each other's buckets, debating over whose was the fullest.

"Yeah, I didn't expect them to go running off in separate directions." Rather than going house to house, Emma seemed to run around in a zigzag pattern, wanting to go to the houses on each block with the best decorations first. As soon as Aiden had spotted his best friend, Wyatt, he had begged to go trick-or-treating with him. Blake had been following him, and Rachel had stayed with her daughter until their groups converged.

"Usually, I have a good handle on keeping an eye on both of them even though I'm outnumbered."

Sean tipped his hat up and looked around at all of the kids going up and down the street. "Better to be safe than sorry with so many people."

"Exactly." Rachel smiled at him. "Stranger danger, you know. Especially with a kill—" She clamped a hand over her mouth.

Especially with a killer on the loose. She didn't have to finish her sentence for Blake to see the concern in her eyes. But that was why they were in a group for just a few blocks of trick-or-treating before going right back home. Nervousness still bubbled in Blake's stomach, even though she knew they were safe.

"Luckily, we have Indy to keep us safe," she said, trying to lighten the mood.

Sean responded by going into a wide stance and grabbing the whip from his belt, looking ready to take on the enemy. "That's right, I'm ready to wave this at anything that slithers."

Emma and Aiden giggled. Rachel cracked up at his dead-on Harrison Ford impression, and Blake wondered if her sister-in-law was starting to shift from Team Adam to Team Sean—or maybe she just wanted to know that she wasn't the only one straddling that line between the two. The fact that Sean was so amazing with children was sure to win her over.

As they started walking again, Sean laced his fingers with hers and squeezed her hand, making her smile. As they started on the path to the next house, Emma stopped in front of her so suddenly that Blake nearly tripped over the little girl. "Em, what's wrong?" Blake put a hand on her back as Emma clutched her stomach.

"I don't feel so good."

Blake crouched down to look into her niece's face, which was a notable shade of green, and she was pretty sure it wasn't from the zombie makeup.

"Oh, Emma Bemma, you didn't." Rachel took Emma's candy bucket and began to paw through it. From what Blake could see, it was mostly wrappers.

"Whoa." The look on Sean's face was downright awestruck. "How did she manage to eat that much candy without us noticing? That is impressive." He started to raise his hand, but Blake swatted it back down.

"Do not high-five her. I'll be surprised if she doesn't hurl in the—" She was interrupted by Emma bending over and letting loose the contents of her stomach onto Mr. Hamilton's front lawn.

"Oh, baby." Rachel crouched down and rubbed her hand up and down Emma's back until the little girl took a shaky breath and stood back up, wiping the back of her hand across her mouth.

Aiden surveyed the mess on the lawn then looked at his sister. "I told you not to eat all the Skittles."

Sean stifled a laugh and put a hand on Aiden's shoulder as Rachel stood. "Come on, it's time to go home before your sister starts heaving up chocolate."

"What? Nooo!" Aiden whined. "We have two more blocks. We can't skip all those houses. Do you know how much candy that is, Mama?"

"Aiden"—Rachel shoved a hand on her hip as she cuddled Emma to her side—"your sister is sick. I need to go apologize to Mr. Hamilton for what she did to his front lawn, and then we need to get her home."

"But Mama—"

"Hey." Blake stepped in between them. Getting into Mr. Hamilton's place to snoop—er, look for evidence—was one of her main goals for the evening. This was the perfect opportunity. "I have an idea. Rach, why don't you take Emma home? I'll go apologize to Mr. Hamilton." She glanced at his two-story house with attached garage. If she could get a look in that garage, she could see if Whit's truck was in there. And if it was, the police could get a search warrant.

"And I'll taken Aiden trick-or-treating," Sean finished. "Divide and conquer, right?"

"Mommy..." Emma's voice was shaky.

"Crap, we gotta go." Rachel nudged Emma in the direction of home. "Thank you, thank you, thank you. You guys are lifesavers.

And tell Mr. Hamilton"—she gestured at the lawn—"well, tell him I'm sorry."

She hauled Emma into her arms then hurried down the street.

"And she says I'm gross." Aiden had the most satisfied smile Blake had ever seen on a six-year-old. "Ha!"

Sean rested his hand on Aiden's shoulder. "Come on, little man. What do you say we do the next few houses then wait for your Auntie B?"

"Hey, there's Wyatt!" Aiden started to run ahead, but Sean grabbed his arm.

"Hang on a sec, buddy."

"Go ahead." Blake waved down the street. "I'll just catch up with you after... No. You know what? I'll just meet you guys back at the house. You know how long-winded Mr. Hamilton can get."

Aiden tugged on Sean's hand with what looked like all his strength. "Sean, come on!"

Sean gave in and let Aiden pull him along the sidewalk. He winked at Blake. "Later, Auntie B."

Warmth filled her as she watched Sean walk away, holding Aiden's hand. He really was great with the kids.

"Trick or treat!" Children's voices startled her out of her thoughts, and she turned back to Mr. Hamilton's house. She really hoped he didn't want to take the opportunity to talk about how tight the city's budget was. Although she really wanted to get his thoughts on who was trying to buy up the downtown businesses, she wasn't sure how much Mr. Hamilton knew or how much she could share without Kyle knocking her upside the head.

Mr. Hamilton had told her Whit was staying with him. If he still was, then Blake could not only look in the garage, but she could try to poke around a little bit. No one could fault her for that. Well, Kyle probably could, but her sister would thank her if she managed to come up with some useful evidence.

Of course, Whit probably didn't keep a clown suit hanging in the front hall closet, but maybe she could find something.

A group of little girls dressed in My Little Pony costumes passed her on the curved walkway leading up to Mr. Hamilton's traditional white colonial. It was getting late enough that kids were thinning out, but she was really hoping a few more would head in her direction. Trick-or-treaters could distract Mr. Hamilton enough that maybe she could look around. It could also interrupt him if he started on his diatribe about not approving Mr. Jeffries's money request for the museum renovation.

She rang the doorbell, waited until the heavy wooden door swung open, then smiled. "Trick or treat!"

Chapter Twenty-one

A big smile lit Mr. Hamilton's face as he clutched a giant plastic orange bowl in both arms, filled with Heath Bars, Snickers, M&M's, Milky Ways, and Hershey bars.

Blake eyed the candy and started salivating. "Whoa, you've got the good stuff."

"Blake, my dear! What a nice surprise. Are you trick-or-treating with the twins?" He looked behind her for the children.

She winced as she thought of the news she had to break to him. He was easygoing, but he had an award-winning front lawn. Maybe she could spin it that candy-induced vomit provided good fertilizer. She nearly laughed at the thought. "Well, I was, but uh... about that..."

"Come in, come in!" He ushered her inside.

"Thanks." She stepped in behind him, twisting her fingers as she nervously looked around, hoping that Whit wasn't there. Low light from the tiered chandelier gave warmth to the grand foyer. A formal living room was to Blake's right, tastefully decorated in amber hues. "Are you here by yourself?"

"Oh yes." He shut the Revere red door behind them. "Whit had a date or something. I can't keep up with that boy's social life. He seems to be quite the ladies' man even though he's only been in town a short time." Mr. Hamilton said this with pride, but thinking about Whit's reputation as a player gave her the heebie-jeebies.

"You might catch Bree, though. She's supposed to come by with some papers for me."

Really? Hmm, maybe I can see if I can get any more information out of her. Even though Kyle had shared what Bree had told her, Blake was curious to get a firsthand account.

"Mr. Hamilton, I was trick-or-treating with Rachel and the twins, and it seems Emma ate too much candy. I'm so sorry, but she got sick on your lawn. If you just point me in the direction of your garden hose, I'm happy to clean it off."

"Oh, the poor girl." He turned to walk down the hall. "Here, before I forget, I got some of your mail by accident. Let me get you that, and then we'll get that hose.

Blake followed him down the long hall. She could see a big chef's kitchen at the back of the house, but Mr. Hamilton turned to his left before he reached the kitchen. Blake walked through the doorway into his office behind him.

"I feel for Emma," Mr. Hamilton continued. "It's hard when faced with temptation." He set the bowl of candy on an end table and walked around his large mahogany desk, which took up the center of the room. Bookshelves lined the wall to her left, and closet doors lined the opposite wall, making Blake wonder if the room had once been a bedroom. Her eyes took in the two buttery leather chairs that sat in front of the desk on a large oriental rug that tied the whole room together. Either Mr. Hamilton had an interior decorator, or he was very talented.

A cigarette lying in an ashtray on the desk was still smoking. Mr. Hamilton picked it up and took one long drag before crushing it out. "Some people don't do well with willpower when they're faced with something they want so badly."

"I can see. I thought you quit smoking."

"Not as easy as you might think." In an exaggerated whisper, Mr. Hamilton said, "But don't tell my son. When he ran across my cigarettes, he lost it."

"My lips are sealed." She reached up to her mouth then mimed zipping it shut. So far, she hadn't seen any evidence of Whit even living there, but she would really like to get a look in that closet. "So, uh, is your garden hose out back? Or maybe in the garage?" *Fingers crossed.* "If it doesn't stretch around to the front, I can move it. Or I can go get Rachel's and—" If she couldn't get into the garage, that would be the perfect opportunity for her to look in the window.

He waved her off. "We'll worry about that in a minute. First, I really wanted to get your thoughts on some new ideas for the museum." He opened the top drawer of his desk and pulled out a white, pocketed folder. "Have a seat," he said, stretching across the desk to hand her the folder.

Well, crap. She'd known she was going to get caught talking. Mr. Jeffries was adamant that he needed more funding for the museum. Tourism was really picking up in Wilton, and the museum was a big hot spot for people to learn about the Red Rose Murders.

Blake held in a sigh. Maybe instead of sending Sean and Aiden home, she should have had them meet her there. It would have given her a chance to look around and then an excuse to cut out rather than having to discuss business on Halloween night. She just needed to get outside to look for the hose so she could sneak a peek into the garage.

She sat in one of the two leather chairs in front of Mr. Hamilton's desk and opened the folder.

"Here's that envelope in there addressed to you," he said when she fingered the white envelope with her name on it. "It came to the chamber office."

That wasn't anything unusual. The chamber of commerce office was just down the street from Mystery Cup, and she was a chamber member, so sometimes people sent mail to her there. She glanced at the envelope before sliding the papers out to take a closer look at Mr. Hamilton's plans.

She furrowed her brow when she noticed the addresses on the two buildings listed. *Wait a second*—he'd said these were buildings he wanted to convert. *Convert into what?* The museum didn't need to be converted into anything. It just needed to be renovated. She opened her mouth to ask just what it all meant, when the front doorbell interrupted her.

"Ah, more trick-or-treaters." He walked over to the bowl of candy. "You take a look at that, Blake. I'll be right back."

She scanned the document in front of her as Mr. Hamilton went to answer his door. The two buildings listed were the buildings directly to the north of Mystery Cup—the museum and Fatal Shot Gifts. Those buildings weren't for sale. He knew that. As she turned the page, she let out a gasp. He didn't want to renovate the buildings. These were plans to tear them down. The two buildings took up a lot of square footage, and Mr. Hamilton was proposing they be torn down to build a mall. "Converted, my eye. Tearing down a museum and building a mall isn't converting anything, not when you're destroying a business."

Thoughts of the real-estate scam in Florida rushed to the forefront of her mind. Maybe it was Whit Hamilton's doing. Maybe he'd convinced his father to make the buildings downtown into a mall. But for what possible purpose, she had no idea. They couldn't tear down the museum. They were talking about destroying the town's history. And Fatal Shot Gifts was a huge moneymaker with all of the memorabilia and spooky-themed merchandise they sold.

"What do you think, Blake?" Mr. Hamilton's voice made her jump as he entered the room behind her. "Did you look at the page that goes over the numbers? The profit the city could make from these changes is astounding!"

She turned to him and saw the excitement on his face. "Mr. Hamilton, these aren't just changes. You're talking about tearing down two buildings, one of which is a historical landmark. Those businesses aren't even for sale."

His face tensed, and a muscle worked in his jaw. "Everything's for sale if the price is right, my dear. And the businesses can relocate. They only rent the buildings. Read over the proposed financing. You'll see that there's no way we could say no to that type of income."

Before he could set his bowl of candy down, the front doorbell rang again. He let out a sigh. "The traffic has ebbed and flowed all night. I guess it's safe to say it's flowing."

Before Blake could overcome her surprise at what he was proposing, he was walking back out of the room. She sat back in her chair and blinked. The city was making plenty of money. They weren't rolling in the dough or anything like that. But the tourism was enough that almost all of the downtown businesses maintained healthy profits. It completely floored her that Mr. Hamilton would want to change the heart of the town so radically. She couldn't imagine that the other business owners would be on board.

Her fingers tapped the sealed envelope in her lap as her mind went into overdrive. She definitely didn't think it was the time to go over whatever moneymaking scheme Mr. Hamilton—or his son—had come up with. It was going to take a while to wrap her brain around the new plan. She needed to talk to Sean. He owned Macabre Reads, so she knew he would have a strong opinion on the matter too.

Blake picked up the oddly taped envelope and saw that it was from Spirits and Brushes, the new business opening up at the other end of Main Street. The advertising for their upcoming grand opening had really picked up in the last couple of weeks. Turning the envelope over and over in her hand, she wondered how she was supposed to get into it. The thing was taped up on all sides, and she'd chewed her fingernails down to nubs, so they wouldn't be of any help.

The children's voices at the front door faded, when new, louder voices yelled "Trick or treat!"

Blake set the envelope on the desk, and her eyes drifted to the closet. She probably only had a few seconds. *It's now or never.* She bolted out of her seat and quickly padded over to the sliding closet door. With a deep breath, she slid the door open... and saw office supplies. "You have got to be kidding." Disappointment weighed her down. There was no clown suit hanging in the closet, no bloody dagger, no flashing neon sign that shouted, "Whit's the killer!" Okay, so she didn't know what exactly she'd been expecting, but it was more than reams of paper and a plastic filing cabinet that looked like it contained an array of pens, paper clips, and Post-it Notes.

She started to slide the closet door shut when it bumped something. She reached into the semidark closet to push back a pair of shoes so she could close the door. The overhead light from the room shined into the closet, and when she pushed back the shoes, her hand stilled in surprise. The red-leather dress shoes shined brightly even in the dark closet. *Red shoes. The clown wore red dress shoes.*

Her heart pounded against her ribs. "Calm down, Blake." Red dress shoes weren't concrete proof of anything. But they were a damn good start. She needed more, and she was close. She was so close, she could feel it.

Blake spun around and rushed back over to the desk, noticing Mr. Hamilton was very organized. A laptop sat in the center of the big desk, and a few office supplies lay to the right of that next to a mug of what looked like coffee. She saw a cup of pens and pencils, Post-it Notes, a box of paper clips, and a stapler.

"Nothing suspicious there." Biting her lip, Blake looked back at the door. She should just take it and go. She heard Mr. Hamilton's voice commenting on various costumes, so she walked around the big desk and pushed back his chair. If he caught her rummaging through his desk, she could just say she was looking for a letter opener.

The desk looked fairly standard with a shallow top drawer, a deep drawer on the left, and three smaller drawers on the right. She opened the top center drawer but only saw more pens, a calculator, and a staple remover. The large drawer on the left was packed full of file folders, so she opened the top drawer on the right.

The world fell away as Blake sucked in a breath. Her heart sped up, adding to the ringing in her ears as her mind whirled. A blade stuck out from beneath a few papers, but it looked too sharp to be a letter opener. With a shaking hand, she pulled the object out from beneath the papers and picked it up. Resting in her palms was a large ornate dagger.

"Oh my God."

There was no mistaking that dagger. At first glance, it resembled an arrow. The blade was triple-sided, making it look as though it could have been used as a stake. Hysterical laughter bubbled up as Blake remembered her mom taking her, Ryan, and Kyle camping as kids. It sure would have been something if they'd used ornamental silver daggers to stake the tent. Her mind was rambling. Her head popped up, and she listened as she heard Mr. Hamilton in the distance asking a child if he would rather have a candy bar or Skittles.

She studied the carved silver handle that formed intricate faces that almost looked as though they were in pain. The gold and turquoise jewels stood out in the silver, and she found it odd that an object could be so beautiful and so terrifying at the same time.

It was much heavier than it looked, but the weight in her hand was anything but a comfort. The powerful weapon sent chills down her spine. The last time she'd seen that dagger, it was in the hand of a clown, dripping with blood. No way were there two such distinct daggers in the world.

That could only mean one thing. Whit Hamilton had killed Todd Lang. He'd taken the dagger then slipped it back in the drawer in his father's office when he was finished. Poor Mr. Hamilton. Blake wondered if he knew. Maybe he was covering for his son. She didn't have time to evaluate the possibilities. She had to call her sister.

"A Tibetan silver dagger." Mr. Hamilton's voice made her jump, and she looked up to see an almost pleasant expression on his face as he slowly set the candy bowl down. Yet his smile didn't reach his eyes. "Used in rituals and tethering. It's such a beautiful piece." He nodded toward it. "The triple blade represents the three spirit worlds. The point is the axis that brings all three worlds together. This dagger specifically symbolizes the slaying of foes or obstructions." He looked up at her with eyes so cold they made her shiver. "I'd say it's working pretty well so far."

Blake swallowed thickly against the metallic taste in her mouth and realized she was gripping the dagger so tightly that her knuckles were white. "I... I... uh, I'm so sorry. I didn't mean to get into your desk. I was looking for a letter opener."

She dropped it back in the drawer as though it had burned her and slammed the drawer shut. "I should go. It's getting late, and Sean is waiting for me." Her words were coming out fast, and her breath was coming out faster. She felt as though she was almost panting at the surge of adrenaline.

As she took a step toward Mr. Hamilton, he slid the pocket door to the office shut.

Her movements slowed as he turned to look at her, tilting his head as he studied her with an unreadable expression. "I really wish you hadn't found that."

Chapter Twenty-two

Her teeth clenched tightly as her mind spun. Maybe if she just pretended she didn't understand the significance of the dagger, she could slip out. "I-I should really go, Mr. Hamilton. Sean is waiting for me. If I don't hurry, he'll come looking for me."

A harsh smile twisted Mr. Hamilton's lips. "Nice try, dear. I saw Sean headed down the street with Aiden, going toward your brother's house." He took another step closer. "It looks like you're all by yourself."

"Well, either way, I should..." She tried to walk around him to get to the door, but he sidestepped until he was right in front of her.

"You're not leaving, Blake."

She swallowed, and her lungs burned. Panic began to overtake her as he loomed over her. An image of him at the gym popped into her head, of how surprised she'd been when she'd seen how muscular he was. He lifted weights with ease, according to Orlando. Acid burned Blake's throat as she spoke. "M-Mr. Hamilton, I don't, uh, I don't know what—"

"Let's drop the games, shall we?" He took a step toward her, and she backed up on instinct. "It's not very becoming of you to play dumb. We both know you're too smart for your own good, don't we?"

Her hands clenched at her sides. "I don't know what you mean."

He smirked. "Rachel told me exactly what you saw. In fact, she described Todd's murder to me in detail, including the dagger."

Oh crap. Her eyes closed as she thought about how many people she and Rachel had related the information to. He knew everything.

Because of Rachel and her big mouth. And as the puzzle pieces fell into place in her head, Blake realized how completely dense she'd been the whole time.

"There's probably no chance you're trying to cover for Whit, is there?"

A laugh of disbelief escaped Mr. Hamilton. "Whitley? Are you kidding? He may enjoy the ladies, but you'd be surprised how much his morality gets in the way on a regular basis. I suppose that shouldn't surprise me. He's so much like his mother."

"But his experience with real estate... He didn't have anything to do with—"

"With what? Buying the downtown properties?" Mr. Hamilton pursed his lips together. "With his experience, I thought he would be helpful, but it turns out, his conscience is too great." He ran a hand through his thinning hair. "Did you know when he lived in Florida, he worked with people who were involved in a real-estate scam?"

Blake continued to take small steps backward as he was talking, just to make sure he stayed out of her personal space. "Yeah, I heard he was cleared of that." If she could get back around the desk, she could grab the dagger to defend herself. Out of her peripheral vision, she tried to gauge how close she was to the door, the only exit in the room. Ten steps, maybe. The problem was that she would have had to shove past Mr. Hamilton to get there.

"Yes. Not only was he cleared of it, but he's the person who turned the people in. He was working with the police." Mr. Hamilton shook his head as if he were disappointed that his son had been responsible. "So you see why I couldn't trust him with my plan."

She needed to keep him talking. Surely, Sean would come looking for her. *Mr. Hamilton is a killer.* Acid burned her throat as the realization hit her. He wasn't going to let her walk out of there. She needed more of a plan. She needed to think. If she could just keep him talking...

"And your plan is to buy out the buildings downtown? Why?"

"Don't look at me like that, Blake. I'm thinking of the city. If we convert the seven buildings at the north end of Main Street into an upscale shopping plaza with a winery, tourism will explode. The money that would pour into the economy of Wilton would benefit every citizen. Don't you understand?"

One of those seven buildings was Mystery Cup. The fear that had threatened to overcome Blake began to give away to anger. "What is wrong with you? You're talking about erasing the town's history! Getting rid of the museum. You can't do that. Not to mention that one of those seven buildings you're talking about is Mystery Cup. If you think I'm agreeing to this, you have seriously got a screw loose."

He chuckled then continued to move closer as she backed up. "You act like I'm greedy, like I'm pocketing this money. Don't you understand what adding millions of dollars to Wilton's economy could do for this town?"

On her next step backward, she hit the desk, and Mr. Hamilton advanced closer. She had nowhere to go. *Keep him talking.*

"Then why did you hire the different holding companies? I'm guessing your name is the one on the final deed. You say it's for the city, but if that's true, then you wouldn't be making a healthy profit. So, excuse me for saying so, but you're full of crap, Mr. Hamilton. If what you say is true, you would have let everyone in on your grand plan. I think this was about the money that you wanted."

His eyes flashed. "No!" He stepped next to her and slammed a hand down on the desk, making her jump. "I am not like that snake Todd Lang. Greed is not what drives me."

Blake swallowed as Todd's face, encased in plastic, flitted through her mind. "Is that why you killed him? How did you even get into the loft above Sliced?"

A cold smile slashed across his face. "That was pretty ingenious, I thought. I'm at Crossbones most days, having lunch. Did you know that some of the bartenders leave their keys on a hook behind the bar? Including Pepper? Once I knew she had picked up the key to the loft, it was easy to snatch it, make a copy, and have it back before she even missed it."

"So this was way premeditated. You lured Todd to the loft, knowing no one could trace you back to the place. And you showed up in costume?"

He shrugged. "I was on the way to your party. So was Todd. It was easy to meet up beforehand. All I had to do was tell him I'd agreed to let him in on the action. Plus, there was the added benefit that if anyone saw me"—he wiggled a finger at her—"they wouldn't know who I was."

She remembered the controversy of whether or not there had been a murder at all. And how difficult it had been to figure out how the clown had gotten in and out of the apartment. "So after you killed him, you wrapped him in a shower curtain and dragged him up the pull-down stairs to the attic?"

Never would she have suspected sweet Mr. Hamilton of being able to drag a body up to the attic. The man was in his sixties, and even though that wasn't old, it would have taken a lot of strength to move Todd Hamilton. When she thought about the biceps she'd seen on him at Buttkick, she could have smacked herself for not at least considering him as a suspect.

"It wasn't easy, but I figured it was my best bet. I knew there were going to be way too many people coming and going for the party. I couldn't really risk someone seeing me moving a body. As it turns out, that was the right call. I barely got him up there before the police arrived."

"So you *were* still there! I knew it!"

He nodded. "I was. How do you think I knew you'd seen me? I could hear everything the police were saying."

"So then you came across the street and made an appearance to scare me?"

The corner of his mouth tugged up in an eerie little smile that made her think of Norman Bates from *Psycho*. "I wanted to see your reaction. And you about fainted when you saw me. Plus, I wanted the alibi. You saw me in the clown costume, and then I rushed downstairs to take that off and put on the fireman's helmet that I had in my car—or should I say Whit's car. I made the right call driving his truck with the tinted windows and parking it behind Buttkick. I was able to run over and change, and no one was the wiser. You saw me moments later dressed as a fireman. I'm guessing you didn't make the connection that it was me, did you?"

She hadn't. Never had it crossed her mind that the clown might have changed and come back to the party. She had been so focused on Whit Hamilton and Pepper and Bree that she didn't pick up on any of the clues that might have pointed her in Mr. Hamilton's direction.

But at the mention of the truck, every muscle in her body tensed. "It *was* Whit's truck that tried to run me down. It was you."

"Whit's trying to sell it to help get money for his own place. Since it's been in my garage, I occasionally drive it. The day I saw you crossing the street was pure luck, really." He chuckled—actually chuckled—at the thought that he'd almost killed her and Adam. "You started across the street from Sliced right as I turned the corner. I wasn't planning to kill you, but it was such a perfect opportunity. It's like it was meant to be."

It was becoming harder to keep calm the more she realized just how crazy the man in front of her really was. "So what were you doing that night at my house? Did you come there to kill me? It was you who broke Kyle's arm, wasn't it?"

"Blame your sister for that one, not me."

She looked at him incredulously. "Blame my sister? How on earth do you figure that?"

"I wasn't planning to hurt anyone. I simply came to your house that night to listen. I wanted to get in and hide somewhere. I figured if I was able to hear a few of your phone calls, I could find out what you knew then sneak back out when you went to bed. When you showed up with your sister, I thought I'd hit the jackpot. Maybe she would talk about the police investigation, and I could really stay ahead of the game. But then she spotted me." He frowned. "I'm still pissed about that, by the way."

Her breath shook, and she bumped into the desk again as she tried to move farther away from him. "But I still don't understand why you had to kill Todd Lang. You said he was greedy, but how was he involved in this whole business? He's a photojournalist."

Mr. Hamilton turned and traced a finger along his desk as he walked behind it and moved his chair aside. He shook his head as he slowly opened the top right drawer. Blake shivered as he removed the dagger, turning it over and over in his hand as he thought.

Now is my chance. She bolted for the door, but Mr. Hamilton was fast. He reached the door a split second after she did. Blake only managed to open the door an inch before Mr. Hamilton's hand slammed it shut. When she noticed he still held the dagger, she backed away from him so quickly, she stumbled.

"Come now, Blake. Do you really think you're going anywhere? Besides, you asked a question. Don't you want to hear the answers?" Without waiting for her response, he continued. "Todd was in the wrong place at the wrong time. He was looking for a house after Sabrina came to her senses and got rid of him, and he had an appointment with a real estate agent the same day I was meeting with her to discuss the holding company's next purchase. You see, I didn't realize there was anyone in the office, so I thought I could speak freely. Unfortunately, Todd was early to his appointment and heard more than he should."

"You killed him because he knew you were involved with a holding company?"

"If that was all he knew, I could have dealt with it. But he wouldn't stop probing. He started to research why I was behind a holding company, and he looked into public records. That's when he saw the holding companies trying to purchase the downtown buildings." The look on his face was almost regretful. "He threatened to expose my plan. He was going to ruin everything if I didn't pay him off. I couldn't let him do that, could I?"

As he spoke, he studied the blade of the dagger, closely examining the sharp point. "I wish I could say it was difficult to kill him, but the truth is that Todd Lang got exactly what he deserved." His eyes had a hard glint as he looked at her, walking around the desk.

Blake backstepped toward the pocket door of the office.

"You, on the other hand, I'm going to miss. I sure hope someone has the recipe for those espresso brownies. Although, this could make acquiring the Mystery Cup much easier. Once you're gone, I can't imagine your family would want to continue running the café."

He started toward her, the dagger raised.

Chapter Twenty-three

Blake was vaguely aware of the doorbell ringing in the background. She faked left, trying to fool Mr. Hamilton as he closed in on her, then bolted to the right. She lunged for the pocket door, managing to slide it halfway open before Mr. Hamilton reached her, grabbing her from behind. One big arm yanked her back against his chest, and she opened her mouth to scream.

The sound died on her lips as Mr. Hamilton raised the dagger to her neck, the triple blade hovering over her jugular. "Quiet!" he hiss-whispered. "Do you really want to scare the trick-or-treaters?"

Closing her eyes, Blake swallowed, her mind racing. "You're not going to get away with this." She struggled slightly against his hold, trying to pull away from the dagger. "Rachel knows where I am. Sean knows where I am."

The doorbell rang again. If she could only get away from him, she could scream. Maybe there were parents out there with the trick-or-treaters. They would hear her and call for help.

"Maybe they do." He sounded unconcerned. "I'll just say you stopped by then left to go home, and that was the last I ever saw of you. You think anyone's going to suspect me?" A laugh rattled in his chest. "Come on, Blake. I'm an upstanding citizen. People love me around here. They'll accept my word and look elsewhere." With a sigh, his hand tightened on the dagger. "I can't really let you go singing to your detective sister, now can I? She's lucky she gets out of this with only a broken arm."

"Singing..." She didn't mean to say that out loud, but her mind was in overload.

"What?" Mr. Hamilton looked up to the half-open pocket door as the doorbell gave way to knocking. That was one persistent trick-or-treater, and Blake was thankful for the distraction as she tried to remember what Kyle had taught her.

S.I.N.G. Solar plexus, instep, nose, groin. Thank God for Kyle... and Sandra Bullock. She just needed the opportunity when the dagger wasn't two centimeters from her neck.

"Blake!" *Pound. Pound. Pound.* "Blake, are you in there?"

Sean! He had come back looking for her!

Mr. Hamilton's head jerked up, and he uttered a curse. His hand relaxed a fraction. Just enough that she could rear her elbow forward and bring it back with all her might in his upper stomach. She didn't even take the time to register the satisfying "oof" he made when she stepped to the left and brought her foot down as hard as she could on his, thanking her lucky stars that she had worn heels.

A strangled sound escaped Mr. Hamilton as the dagger clattered to the ground.

"Sean!" She screamed, fumbling with the lock on the door. "Help me!

The pounding stopped. "Blake?"

The whole door jiggled as Mr. Hamilton reached to pull her back by the hair. *Why do they always go for my hair?*

Before he could drag her back against his chest, she heaved back and up with her elbow, catching him in the nose. She didn't take time to assess the damage before bringing her fist down and punching him in the groin.

"Blake!" She was aware of the door splintering open as Mr. Hamilton jerked backward. Even though he was moaning in pain, he still had a death grip on her arm with his left hand.

When she saw Sean's face appear in the splintered hole of the door, she tried to run to him, but her heel caught on Mr. Hamilton's shoe, and she lurched forward, the older man falling on top of her.

Sean was kicking the rest of the wood away so he could get into the room as Blake fought for a way to defend herself. The dagger was an arm's length away, and she reached for it at the same time Mr. Hamilton's hand closed over it. He was fast.

But Sean was faster. Before she could blink, he was through the door, and his booted foot stomped down on Mr. Hamilton's hand. Blake could swear she heard a crunch as the man screamed. When he let go of the dagger, Sean kicked it out of the way. Then he was yanking Mr. Hamilton off of her by his hair and slamming his fist into the man's jaw. Mr. Hamilton fell backward in an unconscious heap.

Blake panted, trying to catch her breath.

"Blake, sweetheart..." Sean put his hands under her arms and hauled her up. He'd lost his hat somewhere along the way, and his mussed hair fell adorably over his forehead. His green eyes assessed her, looking for injuries. "My lord, are you okay?"

Before she could answer, he pulled her close to his chest, one arm going around her, and the other hand sliding up to cradle her head.

The scent of his cologne cascaded over her, and she closed her eyes, her muscles feeling as if they were turning to jelly as the adrenaline left her system.

"I'm okay," she said as Sean squeezed her tighter. "I'm okay now."

Chapter Twenty-four

"Are you ready?" Giselle stuck her head in the kitchen of Mystery Cup, where Blake was covering the tray of cookies with a red lace cloth. "The masses are waiting."

Rachel eyed Blake speculatively. "Blake, you don't have to do this right now. I still can't believe you freaking came in to the freaking café today. You're still shaky, for crying out loud. *Necesitas descansar!*"

"You're in trouble now," Giselle said, shaking her head. "The Spanish has started."

"I'm fine, Rach. Don't look at me like that. I'm not hurt, and I'm not going to let that... that man ruin the busiest day of the month." Blake turned her attention to Giselle. "I'm all set. Is the stepladder in place?"

Giselle smiled as she tucked a blue strand of hair behind her ear. "Yep, and Eli's guarding it like he's in the Secret Service."

"I heard that!" he called from the other side of the door.

Rachel put a hand on her back, rubbing gently. "If you were my kid, I would literally spank you and you lock you in your room."

"You literally would not," Blake said with a wink.

Rachel wrapped an arm around her shoulders. "I love you, sister. If I ever get my hands on that man for what he did to you, I'll... I'll... *Cortaré sus bolas.*"

She returned the hug, blinking at the happy tears that suddenly threatened. "I love you too. And Mr. Hamilton will only be seeing the light of day through the bars of a prison cell. So you don't have to worry about him anymore."

Giselle peeked out into the café. "Come on, you guys. They're getting restless."

Blake picked up the plate and headed for the front of the café. When she drew close, Giselle opened the door wide, and Blake's jaw dropped. She was used to a crowd gathering on the first day of every month for the reveal of the Mystery Cup ingredient, but this was the biggest crowd by far. The café was packed, and people were hanging out the door.

"Whoa, I hope everyone likes this month's ingredient."

"Uh, yeah, like the fact that you caught a killer last night has nothing to do with the crowd." Giselle shrugged. "At least we get an increase in business."

As Blake emerged from the kitchen, the crowd erupted in applause. She blushed as she handed the plate of cookies to Giselle. Public speaking topped her list of ways she did not like to start her day. When she looked around, her eyes zeroed in on the new bouquet of roses sitting atop the pastry case. Unease threaded through her. Mr. Hamilton was in jail, so it wasn't him trying to get under her skin. But she didn't have time to evaluate who the bouquet might be from at the moment. She was nervous enough as it was.

But the flutter in her stomach calmed when she saw Sean standing near the end of the counter, smiling warmly at her. She wasn't quite sure how he could make her nervous yet calm her with his presence. She would really have to evaluate that later.

"Come on! Don't keep us in suspense!" Kyle made a hurry-up motion with her good arm as she stood front and center in front of the cash register.

Blake cleared her throat, looking out over her friends and customers. She spotted Orlando standing by a couch in the corner, and he blew a kiss at Giselle, which made the barista's face turn ten shades of red. Eli's eyes never left her as a muscle worked in his jaw.

Ryan and Adam stood near the front door, pressed against the wall behind a throng of women. When she caught Adam's eye, his smile grew broad, and he winked at her. Seeing him made her insides loosen a little bit. Adam Bryant was like comfort food for the eyes, which made what she had to do all the more difficult.

She hadn't talked to him since the previous day, but he'd left several messages after hearing what had happened. She really hoped she had the chance to talk to him soon even though she had no idea how to say what she wanted to say.

Clearing her throat, she made an effort to clear her head and worry about her love life later. "Welcome, everyone! Thank you for coming to our monthly Mystery Cup reveal. We've had some great suggestions over the past month for the November ingredient. I hope you all know I take your suggestions under great consideration and work to come up with a new recipe that everyone will enjoy. So without further ado..." She climbed up the two steps of the ladder so she could reach the colorful ceramic mug in the center of the shelf above the kitchen door. "Rachel, can I get a drumroll?"

"Ooh, my favorite part!" Rachel hustled to the counter, where she rapidly drummed her hands on the wood top.

"This month's Mystery Cup ingredient is"—she reached inside and pulled out her selection—"marshmallows!"

There was a smattering of applause, but that paled in comparison to the squeal that arose from the crowd.

"That was me! That was my guess!" A little wrinkled hand shot in the air to punctuate her point.

Blake chuckled as she acknowledged the elderly lady shoving her way to the front. "Yes, Ms. Ruby Price was the first person to correctly guess marshmallows as November's Mystery Cup ingredient. And for that, Ms. Price will receive the pastry of the month for free during the month of November." She stepped down off the ladder. "And that pastry is..."

Giselle held the plate up and Blake snatched the red lace cloth off the plate, revealing artfully arranged cookies. "Chocolate-marshmallow crinkles!"

A chorus of "oohs," "mmms," and "yums" rose from the crowd in addition to a barking "Woo woo woo" from Jason, who stood off to the side, looking extremely excited about the pastries.

Blake grinned. "We will be setting out trays of cookies so everyone can sample this month's recipe, and they will be available for purchase tomorrow. "Please enjoy, everyone, and thank you for coming." She smiled and waved with both hands to the crowd, who gave her another round of applause before making their way to the cookies that Giselle, Eli, and Rachel were bringing out to set on the tables.

"SO WHIT HAMILTON REALLY had no idea that his father was a flipping psycho?" Giselle's mouth hung open as Kyle related the day's events that evening on the rooftop patio of Mystery Cup. "You really think he's telling the truth?"

"I do." Kyle's eyes rolled back in pleasure as she slid a fork down the front of her cast and apparently found the itch that had been annoying her.

Blake toed off her shoes then rested her tired feet on the seat next to her as she leaned back in her chair, thankful for the mild weather. "If you stab yourself with that thing, I'm not explaining it to your doctor."

"Oh, suck it." Kyle wiggled the fork around. "It's totally normal to have a scratching fork."

Giselle shook her head behind Kyle and mouthed, "No, it's not."

"Hang on," Giselle said. "Finish telling us about Whit."

Kyle yawned, a reminder that she had been at the police station questioning Mr. Hamilton to the wee hours of the morning. "Mr. Hamilton approached Whit with his idea of secretly purchasing the downtown buildings shortly after he moved to town. But Whit wanted nothing to do with it. He advised his dad to go talk to Bree and propose the idea to the city council. I guess he tried to get his dad to realize he needed to keep everything on the up and up. He had no idea Mr. Hamilton had gone ahead with his plan."

Blake felt like kicking herself. "I feel so guilty for thinking he was up to no good."

"Yeah, me too. He was so emotional when he was at the station today. He really had no idea his dad was capable of something like that." Kyle looked up at Blake. "He wanted to come see you today. To apologize. But I told him I didn't think it was the best time."

"Aw, you shouldn't have stopped him. I feel like the guy probably needs a friend right about now."

Kyle shook her head. "He spent an hour apologizing for what his dad did to me." She raised her broken arm. "I don't think him coming down here on your busiest day of the month would have been a good idea. Plus, I don't know that all the citizens of Wilton are as forgiving as you."

"Well, I will put together a box of cookies and pumpkin bread and take it to Crossbones." She looked across the street at Sliced, where Bree was pressed up against Micah's back with her arms wrapped around his waist as he turned the key in the front door. After he locked it, he turned and gave Bree a long kiss before they headed to her car. "I know that you can't hold somebody responsible for the actions of a family member. Whit's going to need to come to terms with that."

Giselle lifted her coffee cup and took a long sip. "And Mr. Hamilton? Do you buy his whole 'I'm doing this for the city' spiel?"

Kyle scoffed. "Considering the contracts he had drawn up detailed that he would personally be getting thirty percent of the profit? Uh, no. There is so much evidence against him. I look for him to try to get some sort of a plea deal before the week's up."

Blake lifted her arms over her head in an exaggerated stretch. "Enough with Mr. Hamilton. If I never think about him again, it will be too soon."

"Hey, where's Rachel?" Kyle looked at the stairs as if she expected their sister-in-law to appear. "We always meet up here on Sunday nights."

"Septic tank backed up again," Giselle said. "She had to go home to meet the plumber."

"Ugh. Again?" Kyle blanched. "That makes me happy I rent my house. They've spent so much on fixing their plumbing, it's not even funny."

Blake noticed that Giselle had not mentioned the one thing she most wanted to know about. "So, are we all just going to pretend that Orlando didn't show up with a mango smoothie and the biggest googly eyes I've ever seen?"

Kyle waggled her eyebrows. "I heard him say something about dinner on Friday night."

Giselle blushed. "Yeah, he finally asked me out. Like a real date, not just to come work out with him. He's taking me to some vegan place in Kansas City that's supposed to be really good."

Blake let out a whoop. "It's about time you threw that boy a bone the way he's been dancing around you."

"Oh, shush." Giselle lowered her eyes with a sly smile, and Blake decided not to ask how Eli was reacting to the Orlando-Giselle news.

"So does that mean there's really nothing between you and Eli?" Kyle asked. Apparently, she didn't have any qualms about prying.

Giselle's head snapped up. "Omigod, there is nothing going on with Eli. He doesn't even know my name."

Blake tried and failed to suppress a grin. "Oh, he totally knows your name. He knows everyone's name. The boy has a photographic memory."

Kyle's mouth popped open in surprise. "Are you serious? Then why does he get everyone's name wrong?"

"Because he's a marketing genius," Blake said. When both of them looked at her in confusion, she explained. "Most of the people think it's funny that he spells their name wrong on the cups. But even if they don't, nearly everyone takes a picture of their cup and posts it on social media. Since he's started, we've had a twenty percent increase in business."

"Wow," Kyle said on a laugh. "You're serious?"

Giselle rolled her eyes. "She's serious. There's a whole Facebook page dedicated to it and everything." She held her hands up as if to push away talk of Eli. "Okay, enough about him. Blake, it's your turn."

Kyle leaned forward expectantly. "Yes. We really need to do you."

"Me?" Blake looked from one woman to the other. "What do you mean?"

"Omigod, seriously?" Giselle laughed. "Come on. Sean saved your life last night. That has to put Team Sean in the lead, right?"

Blake groaned. "You guys really have to stop this. I like Sean, and I like Adam." She waved her arms to the sides. "Independent entities. Completely separate of each other. And I'm not going to tell you what I've decided before I've told them."

Kyle's eyes lit up as she studied her sister. "You've made a decision? You have to tell us!"

Wisps of hair blew in front of Blake's face in the evening breeze, and she reached up to yank the elastic from her ponytail, letting her hair tumble around her face. "Look, I will fill you in later. Don't worry. I haven't even talked to Adam since everything went down last night. He was in the café today long enough to grab a cookie, but I didn't get a chance to say more than just hi."

"Well, why don't we rectify that?" Adam's slight Southern drawl made Blake pop out of her chair and swing around.

The hot doctor stood at the top of the stairs, an easy smile on his face, and she was immediately caught immobile in his hypnotic blue gaze.

"Well, that's our cue." Giselle jumped up. "Come on, Kyle, I could go for a caramel-pumpkin latte before I clean the espresso machine."

Kyle just crossed her legs at the ankles and looked back and forth from Blake to Adam. "Nope, I'm good. Perfectly comfortable right here."

Blake and Adam both turned their eyes to Kyle, and Blake gave her the best big-sister glare she could muster.

With a roll of her eyes, Kyle let out an exaggerated sigh. "Fine." She dragged herself up and followed Giselle to the stairs but not before she pointed back at Blake. "But I want details!"

Adam chuckled as Kyle and Giselle's footsteps faded on the stairway. He stood there for a full minute before he stepped closer to Blake.

The wind blew Blake's hair around her face, making her wish she hadn't taken it down. "Hey." *Hey?* She mentally facepalmed.

Adam stopped about two feet from her and shoved his hands in the pockets of his khakis, shifting his feet. "Hey."

After a long moment of awkward silence, he finally asked, "Are you sure you're okay? I heard the details of what happened from Ryan."

"I'm okay." She grinned. "I think I gave Mr. Hamilton more than he bargained for."

Adam smiled back. "I'm proud of you, sugar. You caught a killer and managed to come through it all unscathed." He reached up to trail his thumb along her bruised cheek that was already turning a fun shade of yellow. "Well, almost. Although, I have to say, I hope that's the last time you're in such a dangerous situation."

"Yeah, I don't really relish that part." The mystery-solving thing was kind of fun. If she could find a way to be a volunteer in the homicide division of the Wilton PD, she would totally do it, but she was fairly certain Kyle—and especially Chief Raimy—would give that idea a big thumbs-down.

Adam dropped his hand from her face. "So, uh, we haven't had a chance to really talk since the other night at Ryan and Rachel's. I know a lot's happened since then."

She vividly remembered his quick kiss and the way it had sent sparks shooting through her body. And then she thought about how much she wanted to grab Sean and kiss him until his knees went weak.

Adam looked up at the stars and blew out a long breath, then he reached out and took her hands. "Look, I'm not going to beat around the bush. I've made it clear that I have feelings for you, Blake. I want to explore this with you. I want to see what's between us. I'm at the point in my life where I'm tired of casual dating. I want a relationship that means something... something lasting." He reached up to tuck a strand of hair behind her ear. "And I want that with you."

She shivered at his closeness but not because she was cold. "Adam..."

He gave her a tight smile. "I'm also smart enough to realize that you have more than me to think about. Sean saved your life last night. And I will forever be grateful to him for that. But talk about competition." He laughed hollowly.

Thoughts of Sean twisted her heart. She didn't want to hurt Adam. "I'm not really thinking about it like a competition. And for the record, you saved my life too."

"I know. I want you to take the time and figure out what you want, what's right for you." He shoved a hand through his hair, his frustration evident. "But the back-and-forth is getting to me. Selfishly, I hope you decide it's me that you want. I want you to be happy, and I know you would be with me. But you have to decide what's right for you, who's going to make you happy, Blake. Trust me, I wish I could make that choice for you, but I know I can't."

Blake knew what she had to do. But she wished it weren't so easy to picture her life with both men. In both versions, she was deliriously happy.

"I, um... I don't want to string anyone along." She looked into his eyes and couldn't control the tears that burned hers. "Adam, I'm sorry."

His face tightened as if a cloud had passed in front of him. "I see."

When Adam's phone beeped on his belt, he dropped his hands from her arms, running them through his hair. He let out a mild curse as he reached for the phone. "The hospital seriously has the worst timing known to man." His eyes scanned the display, and he pressed his lips together. "I have to go." He clipped the phone back to his belt. "I don't want you to... Dammit, I don't want this to be over. Maybe we can meet for lunch and talk or something."

The truth was that she truly cared for Adam. No matter what, she wanted him in her life. She smiled. "I would really like that."

"Good." He leaned forward, and she thought he was going to kiss her on the lips. But instead, he cupped her face and pressed his lips to the center of her forehead, lingering for a moment before he released her. "Goodnight, sugar."

"Goodnight," she said softly as he turned for the stairs. "Hey, Adam?"

He stopped on the top stair and turned to look at her.

"The roses downstairs. Did you send those? They didn't have a card." Just like the bouquet before didn't have a card.

"Not me. Trust me, I would have added a card. Maybe you have a third admirer." He winked at her. "You are pretty irresistible, you know."

She laughed. "Yeah, totally irresistible." Her hands squeezed into fists as her nerves ramped up. *If Adam or Sean didn't send flowers, and Mr. Hamilton didn't send them because he's in jail, then who on earth?*

With one last wave, Adam made his way down the stairs, leaving Blake alone with her thoughts. She stared off in the distance, thinking about all that had occurred over the last week. The lights in the loft above Sliced caught her attention. She knew Pepper had been cleared to move in. Blake was kind of surprised the girl didn't have any qualms about living there, given everything that had occurred, but it didn't seem to bother her.

According to the grapevine, a.k.a. Red and Ruby, she and Whit were no longer seeing each other, so she didn't have that connection to the place. The really scary part was that Pepper had quit Crossbones and had a new job working at Café Muerte. The thought almost made Blake groan. Sabrina and Pepper working at the same place would be a sight to see. Maybe Blake should start directing everyone that got on her nerves to Café Muerte for a job. If she could contain all the people she didn't like to one place, it would make them really easy to avoid. She thought about who else she would include on that list beside Sabrina and Pepper. Elaine was inching up there, the guy at the grocery store who always talked to her with his eyes focused on her chest... *Hmm... who else?*

"There you are!"

Sean's voice made her jump. She turned to see him walking to her, smiling warmly, his arms out.

"I didn't even hear you coming up." She leaned in to give him a hug. "Too lost in thought, I guess."

His strong arms went around her, cradling her to his chest, and she reveled in the comfort he seemed to instinctually give her. She closed her eyes as she felt his lips press to the top of her head. "What are you thinking about, Coffee Goddess?"

He swayed her in almost a rocking motion, and she realized how unbelievably tired she was. "Just everything that's happened over the last week." No need to tell him about her plan to give Café Muerte job applications for all the people she didn't like. Maybe she should tell him about the roses, but she knew it would only worry him more, and she just wanted one night where she could forget about all her problems.

He squeezed her tighter. "I'm really hoping that Thanksgiving and Christmas aren't as eventful as Halloween."

She chuckled. "Tell me about it. I would be happy if they were downright boring—thrilled, actually."

They stood in silence for several moments as Sean rocked her. "So I ran into Adam downstairs before I came up." His words were spoken so casually that it took a moment for her to process before she stiffened.

"Whoa, Goddess." Sean leaned back to look down at her. "You just got wicked tense. If you don't want to talk about this right now—"

"No, no, it's okay." She took a step back so she could look at his face. He didn't look angry or jealous, just... curious. *Is that a good thing?* She shook her head. "I'm sorry. I just have a lot on my mind, and that's one of them. Adam." She swallowed. "You."

He nodded slowly. "Right." He paused, waiting for her to speak, but when she didn't say anything, he asked, "Do you want to tell me what you're thinking on that particular subject?"

I'm so not good at this. "Um..." She crossed her arms over her chest. "Rachel thinks... Actually, I think I need to make a decision and move forward."

"And what do you think?" To Sean's credit, his voice was calming, lyrical, when he had every right for it to be cold and closed off.

"I know that I care about Adam, but..."

"But?" Sean stepped closer and reached up to run his fingertips along her jaw. "You know, I don't really want to talk about Adam right now. Do you?"

She shook her head. "Not really." *How does my skin spark wherever he touches me?* Surely, the man was electrically charged.

"I'm more concerned with how you feel about me... and how I feel about you."

Suddenly, her tongue felt really thick. "How you feel about me?" Even though they had talked the previous night about this very subject, they'd never had the chance to finish their conversation, what with Mr. Hamilton jumping on the crazy train and all.

His dimple winked at her as he grinned. "I like you. The more I get to know you, the more I think about you when you're not around. When I met you, I told myself I didn't know if it was a good idea to get involved with someone who worked right next door because if it didn't work out... Well, I quickly decided that was a stupid thought."

"It was?" She blew out a breath, not realizing how tense she'd felt until her insides started to loosen. That was when she realized why she had been having such a difficult time. It wasn't that she'd needed to decide. Her heart had already decided. The problem was that she was scared to put herself out there and have Sean push her away.

"It was." He moved closer as he talked, tilting his head down so mere inches separated their faces. His lips brushed her forehead.

Oh, sweet lord in heaven, please tell me I'm not just going to get another forehead kiss. Her forehead had gotten more action in the last few months than the rest of her body had gotten in, like, ever.

"I'm almost thirty-five years old, Blake. I haven't met anyone in my life who makes me feel as alive as I do when I'm with you. I would be stupid to let that go." His rich voice was nearly a whisper as he kissed the tip of her nose. "I don't want to let you go. I have tried really hard to go slow after making this big life decision. But..." He bent his head, and she let out a whimper as his lips trailed along her jaw. "I think we're way overdue."

Her whole body throbbed, and she felt as though she could barely hear her own thoughts over her racing heart. "Overdue?"

His teeth grazed her earlobe, setting her whole body on fire. "Mm-hmm. Don't you?"

"Um..." Her brain didn't seem to be firing on all cylinders anymore. "Overdue for what?"

He pulled back enough to look at her, spearing her with those intense emerald eyes. "For this," he whispered a moment before he lowered his head.

His sweet lips swept over hers, and her world froze. She had wondered if she would feel sparks when he kissed her. Sparks weren't in the same galaxy as what she felt in that moment. Never had she imagined a kiss that packed such a sizzle. Fireworks shot off inside her body, making every inch of her tingle as the blood pounded in her ears and arousal flooded her veins.

The world around her faded away until only the two of them existed. Blake barely noticed the stars overhead, which seemed to be shining brightly only for them. She barely noticed the crickets chirping or the cool fall breeze that washed over her heated skin. And she barely registered the shadow of a person standing on the sidewalk below.

A person looking up at them with sinister eyes.

A person who had plans all their own.

Mystery Cup's Chocolate-Chip-Pumpkin Bread

Mystery Cup Ingredient: Pumpkin

INGREDIENTS

1 large egg

1 cup pumpkin puree

½ cup light brown sugar, packed

¼ cup granulated sugar

¼ cup canola or vegetable oil

¼ cup sour cream

3 Tablespoons melted butter

1 Tablespoon mild or medium-flavored molasses

2 teaspoons pumpkin pie spice extract (vanilla extract may be substituted)

2 teaspoons pumpkin pie spice

2 teaspoons cinnamon

½ teaspoon ginger

½ teaspoon ground nutmeg

dash of cloves

1½ cups flour

½ teaspoon baking powder

½ teaspoon baking soda

¼ teaspoon salt

1 cup (half a bag) chocolate chips

¼ cup mini chocolate chips (optional)

Directions

- Preheat oven to 350 degrees. Spray one 9 x 5 inch loaf pan with nonstick cooking spray.
- In a large bowl, add first fourteen ingredients (through cloves) and whisk to combine.
- Add flour, baking soda, baking powder, salt, and stir until just combined; do not overmix.
- Add chocolate chips and stir to combine.
- Turn batter out into prepared pan, smoothing the top lightly with a spatula and pushing it into the corners and sides as necessary.
- Sprinkle mini chocolate chips over top if desired.
- Bake for about 50 to 55 minutes or until the top is domed and golden, the center is set, and a toothpick in the center comes out clean or with a few moist crumbs but no batter.
- Allow bread to cool in pan for about 15 minutes before turning out on a wire rack to cool completely before slicing and serving.

KEY TIP

Tent the pan with a sheet of foil loosely draped over the top at the 40-minute mark so the sides and top do not get overly brown before the center bakes through.

Chocolate-Marshmallow Crinkles

Mystery Cup Ingredient: Marshmallows

Ingredients

3 eggs, beaten

1½ cups sugar

4 ounces unsweetened baking chocolate, melted

½ cup canola oil

2 teaspoons baking powder

1 Tablespoon vanilla

2 cups all-purpose flour

About 20 large marshmallows

Powdered sugar

Directions

In large bowl, combine beaten eggs, sugar, melted chocolate, canola oil, baking powder, and vanilla. Gradually add flour to chocolate mixture, stirring until thoroughly combined. Refrigerate for about an hour.

While dough is refrigerating, slice marshmallows in half. Pinch and work each one so they're a bit more pliable then roll them between your palms so they're more in ball form.

Take a spoonful of chilled dough and flatten it. Put a marshmallow in the center of the dough then seal the dough around the marshmallow, making sure marshmallow is completely sealed in.

Roll cookies in powdered sugar and coat generously. Place cookies one inch apart on an ungreased cookie sheet. Bake at 375 degrees for 8 to 10 minutes or until cookies are set and tops are crackled.

Marshmallow will be seeping out of the tops of your cookies, and that is what we want!

Cool cookies on wire rack, and sprinkle cooled cookies with more powdered sugar if desired.

KEY TIP

I highly suggest you cover your cookie sheet with parchment paper. Otherwise, melted marshmallow will get on your cookie sheet, and you will get a serious arm workout trying to scrub it off.

Acknowledgements

Thank you to the man who has to deal with my inspirations, frustrated musings, writer's block, late nights, and long-winded rants. I love you, my dear husband, and I think my psyche would break if you weren't here to hold me together.

I am blessed that I have two children who have embraced the fact that crazy moms are indeed more fun. You two are my whole world. Thank you for listening to me, making me laugh, and offering me honest advice, whether I ask for it or not.

To Stacey, my best friend and sister. Without your support, I would not be here. Thank you for always being there for me no matter what.

A special thank you to Red Adept Publishing, especially my editors, Alyssa Hall and Kate Birdsall. You get to deal with me at my craziest when I'm determined that I don't want to change anything. Thank you for not locking me in a closet and instead remaining calm and helping me make *Cold-Brewed Murder* the best it can be.

And lastly to my readers. I am forever humbled and grateful that you have chosen to visit Mystery Cup Café and go on another twisty-turny journey with Blake and her friends. Saying thank you isn't enough, but just know that I wouldn't trade you for all the chocolate in the world.

Also by Neila Young

Coffee Cup Mysteries
Brewing Up Murder
Cold-Brewed Murder

Watch for more at https://www.neilayoungbooks.com/.

About the Author

Neila Young is a Midwestern girl and a lover of coffee, live music, and horror movies, not necessarily in that order.Writing (and reading) mysteries are Neila's passion, and she approaches each day by thinking, "everything is a story." She has been writing all her life and can't remember a time when she wanted to do anything else. She loves to take notes and spin tales about the quirky characters she meets, and she has found that she can create some great stories by asking "what if" and "suppose that..."Neila studied journalism at the University of Kansas and then spent many years suffering the trials of corporate America, writing about everything from financial risk management to software user manuals to website copy about radiators (sadly, that's not a joke). She finally decided to take the plunge and write the cozy mysteries she loves so much, complete with recipes!When Neila is not writing, she's probably hanging out at a coffee shop or fighting evil with the help of her very supportive husband, two awesome children who constantly ask to have characters named after them, and the most loveable dog in the world, Dizzy.

Read more at https://www.neilayoungbooks.com/.

About the Publisher

Dear Reader,

We hope you enjoyed this book. Please consider leaving a review on your favorite book site.

Visit https://RedAdeptPublishing.com to see our entire catalogue.

Don't forget to subscribe to our monthly newsletter to be notified of future releases and special sales.